W9-CRW-877

ALICE'S GIRLS

ALICE'S GIRLS

JULIA STONEHAM

LARGE PRINT
Oxford

First published in Great Britain 2011
by
Allison & Busby Limited

Published in Large Print 2011 by ISIS Publishing Ltd.,
7 Centremead, Osney Mead, Oxford OX2 0ES
by arrangement with
Allison & Busby Limited

British Library Cataloguing in Publication Data
Stoneham, Julia, 1933–
   Alice's girls.
   1. Women's Land Army (Great Britain) - - Fiction.
   2. World War, 1939–1945 - - Women - - England
   - - Devon - - Fiction.
   3. World War, 1939–1945 - - Social aspects - -
   England - - Devon - - Fiction.
   4. Female friendship - - Fiction.
   5. Single mothers - - Fiction.
   6. Devon (England) - - Fiction.
   7. Large type books.
   I. Title
   823.9'2–dc22

ISBN 978–0–7531–8836–1 (hb)
ISBN 978–0–7531–8837–8 (pb)

Printed and bound in Great Britain by
T. J. International Ltd., Padstow, Cornwall

Into my heart an air that kills
From yon far country blows:
What are those blue remembered hills,
What spires, what farms are those?

That is the land of lost content,
I see it shining plain,
The happy highways where I went
And cannot come again.

A.E. Houseman, *A Shropshire Lad*

CHAPTER
ONE

The weather, that Christmas, had seemed to be apologising for its earlier unpleasantness. After a bitterly cold start, when a cutting east wind, grey skies and persistent frosts had made life wretched for the workers on the Post Stone farms, December had grown milder and since the mid-winter solstice had felt almost spring-like. The trickling of moisture draining from sodden earth, the musical drippings from the eaves of the farmhouse, its barns and outbuildings, and from the twigs in the hedgerows, was soothing after the crackle of frost and the cruel silence of icicles. But although everyone enjoyed it, no one was fooled. They knew that January and February lay ahead and there would be sleet, cold winds, frosts and probably snowstorms before the days slowly lengthened and what sun there was would feel stronger and warmer.

Although there was certainty now, that the end of the war was in sight, the fighting in Europe and the Pacific continued and British civilians were still dying as a result of German rocket attacks on London.

Alice Todd, warden of a small Land Army hostel in rural Devonshire, was aware, on Boxing Day morning, that one of the pleasures of Christmas was the

1

disruption it caused to the monotony of life at the two farms known as Higher and Lower Post Stone. She crossed the yard and returned to her kitchen with two newly laid eggs in her hand. She and Edward John, her eleven-year-old son, would, this morning, have breakfast alone. She would watch him decapitate his egg, slide in his spoon and then dip fingers of toast into the rich, orange yolk. This small ceremony would confirm that the two of them were, despite everything, a family.

They were in the kitchen of the lower farmhouse in which the land girls were billeted. Today only three, who had volunteered to help with the milking, remained, while the others were enjoying a few days of leave in which to visit their families. By late morning on Christmas Eve they had clambered into the smoky compartments of crowded trains which would eventually deliver them to Leeds, London or Liverpool, while the warden did her best to prepare a traditional Christmas dinner for those few who were left in her charge.

On Boxing Day the remaining girls, having completed the morning's dairy duties, had been returned to the hostel where the day was to be theirs until the lorry arrived to fetch them back to the higher farm for the afternoon milking session. One of them, a forlorn figure, her muddy boots left in the porch, stood shivering in her socks on the slate floor of the farmhouse kitchen, filling a hot-water bottle from the kettle that had been simmering on the range.

"Are you unwell, Evie?" the warden asked her.

2

"It's just me monthlies, Mrs Todd," Evie told her, adding, smiling, "Thought I'd get back to me bed for a couple of hours' kip. Luxury!" Evie was a relative newcomer to the hostel, whose appearance the other girls considered mousey. Her unremarkable personality had made little impact on the small, isolated community.

As Alice and her son finished their eggs they were joined at the kitchen table by Gwennan Pringle who had taken advantage of the empty bathroom and now, in her dressing gown and with a towel round her wet hair, filled a teacup, and with a quick glance at the warden, plunged a spoon into the sugar bowl.

"Easy on the sugar," Alice warned her, familiar with the girl's tendency to take more than her share of the meagre ration.

Alice had completed almost two years in the role of warden and during that time had learnt a lot about the girls in her care, the majority of whom had arrived at the farmhouse when she had.

Gwennan Pringle, the oldest of the group, was, it had to be admitted, the least likeable. Her tongue was as sharp as her close-set, dark eyes, and her staccato Welsh accent added to the impact of venomous comments and self-righteous outbursts, rendering them more irritating — and even hurtful — than they would have been if delivered gently or humorously. Several factors, apart from her age, set Gwennan apart from the other girls, and as a result, for almost two years, she had lived and worked alongside rather than with them, and was well aware of their poor opinion of her. Alice had done her best to encourage Gwennan to be less intolerant of her fellows and she had been genuinely sympathetic when, six months previously, the girl's older sister had died. What she did not know was that Gwennan, by concealing symptoms of the disease that had killed her sister, and although terrified of the ordeal she was about to face, was keeping her fears to herself and depriving herself of the support and sympathy from the warden and her fellow land girls, which she could so easily have enjoyed.

The topic round the kitchen table, earlier that morning, had been further discussion of the astonishing events that had taken place on Christmas Eve. The land girls, their suitcases standing ready in the cross-passage at Lower Post Stone, had been hurrying through their morning tasks at the higher farm, when two of them, Annie Sorokova and Mabel Hodges, who had been sent up to the lambing shed with a cartload of fresh straw, arrived at a dangerous speed, back at the higher farm.

"Help!" Annie had yelled as she dragged on the reins of the heavy shire horse and brought the cart to an abrupt stand on the noisy cobbles of the yard. "It's Mabel! Two babies 'as come!"

This, to everyone's amazement, was true.

Mabel Hodges, odorous and overweight, whose history of abuse had, before she became a land girl, already resulted in the birth of one child (a little boy, who was being reared by her grandmother), had formed a relationship with Ferdie Vallance, a labourer exempted from conscription because of a farming injury that had left him lame. One thing had led to another, but Mabel's rotund appearance, shrouded by the layers of clothes and waterproofs that had protected it from the wild weather of the autumn and early winter, was hardly changed by her condition and, not for the first time, she had succeeded in concealing a pregnancy from those around her.

As month followed month, she and Ferdie had remained incapable of facing their situation. The facts, as far as they understood them, were starkly simple. If a land girl had a child she would be forced to leave the service, and Ferdie's wage was barely enough to support him, let alone a family. The two of them had fretted about this, hopelessly and helplessly, having neither the wit nor the experience to address it, while the months of the concealed pregnancy had passed.

And so it was that on Christmas Eve, when Mabel's waters broke and flowed across the mud floor of the lambing pen, and when Annie, inexperienced and horrified, had acted as midwife to the first and the second of the twins and then, with the mother and babies in the cart, driven at breakneck speed downhill to the farm, the shock to everyone concerned had been huge.

Roger Bayliss, the owner of the farm, had emerged from his office, taken in the implications of the scene, called his doctor and then dialled the number of the telephone, whose bell echoed across the yard of the lower farm and was eventually answered by Alice Todd.

"Roger!" she said, and he knew at once, from the tone of her voice, that she was smiling. "How nice to hear you!"

"Brace yourself, my dear," he warned her, "I have astonishing news!"

The relationship between Alice and her employer had, like Alice herself, undergone a slow change since the cold February morning, almost two years ago, when she had arrived at the lower farm, her marriage over, her home in London bomb-damaged.

Alice, in the opinion of the local Land Army representative, had been unsuitable for the role of hostel warden and had been hired simply because she was the only available candidate. At first almost overwhelmed by the difficulties facing her, Alice had endured the damp cold of the near derelict farmhouse, the hostility of Rose, the cowman's widow, who was to assist her, the lack of confidence of her boss and the daunting arrival of the ten girls she was to care for. Girls who, she was warned, would be demanding, rowdy, disrespectful and even defiant, and whose backgrounds were so different from her own middle-class upbringing, education and standards that she would feel isolated and even intimidated by them. But she needed this employment. She needed to earn her keep in a place, far away from the dangers of the war, where her nine-year-old son would be safe. Her only skills were domestic ones, so she had no choice but to fight her way through her difficult early days, weeks and even months at Lower Post Stone farm.

Slowly she won the respect of Rose, and in response to the warmth of her character and her natural engagement with the girls' problems, they at first tolerated and then became fond of her. Yes, she was bossy at times and she "talked posh". There were occasions when her disapproval of their behaviour embarrassed them, but she was, it was soon agreed, a good egg, worthy of their approval and their loyalty.

Roger Bayliss, too, initially doubting Alice's suitability for the work she had undertaken, soon began to respect her. As she gained confidence she occasionally defended the girls against his decisions, standing her ground and arguing her case with skill and diplomacy. A widower, whose wife had deferred to him and whose relationship with most of the women he encountered was one of master and servant, he was at first intrigued, then fascinated, and finally drawn to Alice. Long before she suspected it, he was more than half in love with her. When she did suspect it she avoided the issue. Not because she disliked Roger or found him unattractive, but because of a side to his character which confused her.

Shortly after Alice had arrived at the farms, Roger's son, a pilot in RAF Fighter Command, suffered a breakdown which spectacularly ended his flying career. Alice had been, and remained, bewildered by Roger's reaction to this. He had refused to visit Christopher during the weeks he had spent in a military psychiatric ward and had even admitted, at a much later date, that he found the boy's behaviour embarrassing, even shameful. Alice felt, on an unexplored, instinctive level, that there had to be some deep-seated reason for this. Some trait in Roger's character or some experience that had scarred him. However, her heavy workload prevented her from spending much time or energy on

7

pondering Roger's reasons for his attitude to his son. There was, for one thing, her own situation to occupy her mind, and almost always, one or another of her girls would come to her for help or advice on some complication or difficulty, and she would find herself providing a comforting shoulder or persuading someone to do, or not to do, something which would resolve the problem.

Mabel's pregnancy and the arrival of the twins took everyone, except their parents, completely by surprise. Alice had known that the good-natured, if strangely odorous and lumpen girl, was in the habit of spending her Saturday evenings in the labourer's cottage that came with Ferdie Vallance's wage, where she would cook a meal for him, consisting sometimes of the rabbits he trapped or, quite often, of the pheasants or salmon that he had poached during the course of the preceding week. She also knew of the existence of the three-year-old boy that Mabel had reluctantly admitted was hers, the identity of whose father she would never disclose. But the unexpected arrival of the twins was received by the small, close community with dropped jaws and rounded eyes.

The land girls, before setting off for their Christmas break, had insisted on climbing the narrow stairs of Ferdie's cottage to stand smiling at the babies and their proud parents of whose scandalous behaviour they were, despite themselves, slightly in awe. Of course, the erring couple would have to be married and as soon and as quietly as possible — Mr Bayliss would, for propriety's sake, insist on it. But Mabel! Funny, greedy, smelly little Mabel! A married lady now, with a home of her own, two babies and a husband — even if he was peculiar-looking and lame as a duck!

Gwennan was sitting, on that Boxing Day morning, gloomily stirring as much sugar as Alice had allowed her into her tea, when Rose arrived in the kitchen.

Rose, who when Alice had first encountered her had been stiff with disapproval at the appointment of a warden whom she regarded as unsuitable, had subsequently grown fond of Alice, and the two women, working alongside one another, had each, despite their very different backgrounds and possibly only subconsciously, been influenced by the other, their enforced association widening the experience of both of them.

Prim and middle-aged, Rose wore her widowhood like a badge of courage, her strong sense of duty focused firmly on her only child, her Dave, who was a soldier and who, although assumed to be safely in the catering corps had, in fact, been wounded in northern France shortly after D-Day.

"What about this wedding, then?" she asked Alice, challengingly, as she stooped to tie the laces of the plimsolls she always wore when doing her chores in the hostel. "Whatever we think of our Mabel she deserves a proper wedding, don't she? Even if she should of known better!"

"Mr Bayliss got 'is shotgun out, 'as he?" Gwennan smirked, sipping lukewarm tea.

"Bain't nothin' shotgun about it, Gwennan!" Rose snapped, dismissively. "They'm both keen to wed! I'll say that for Ferdie Vallance, 'e wants to do the right thing by 'er. Reckon vicar should marry 'em in church and we could have a cake after! Goodness knows who'll give her away, though!"

By the time the other land girls returned from their Christmas break the wedding plans, though modest, were well advanced.

"They have to be!" Alice explained to Margery Brewster, a competent and well-meaning woman who, as local Land Army registrar, was responsible for overseeing the hostels in the Ledburton area, of which Lower Post Stone was one. "Mr Bayliss wants everything settled as soon as possible. He wasn't in favour of anything more than a private ceremony, but I told him the girls are fond of Mabel and want her to have an occasion to remember." The registrar rolled her eyes as Alice continued, "It'll only be the girls, Margery — and Rose and you and me . . ."

"And Ferdie Vallance's sister and Mr and Mrs Jack and Mr and Mrs Fred . . . not to mention Roger himself and possibly Christopher too!" Margery was on first-name terms with the Bayliss family, whom she had known socially for as long as she could remember. "These things always escalate, Alice!" But then her flushed face had softened and she added that there was a white satin frock in what had been her daughters' dressing-up box which, shortened by about ten inches, would, with any luck, fit Mabel.

And so it was that Mabel Hodges, a week after giving birth to her twins, walked down the aisle of Ledburton church on the arm of Mr Jack, one of Roger Bayliss's two elderly yard hands, and made her promises to an almost unrecognisable Ferdie Vallance, who was wearing a suit cast off by his employer, and with Christopher Bayliss as his best man.

Afterwards everyone gathered in the recreation room at the hostel and ate slices of a sponge cake which Rose had baked using all the butter and sugar ration for an entire fortnight, filling it lavishly with clotted cream and the contents of the only remaining jar of last season's raspberry jam. Christopher Bayliss made a speech about how brave Ferdie had been when, at the age of fifteen, he had been trapped under a rolling tractor.

"Yeah," Ferdie interrupted him, "and youse crawled underneath, you did, Mr Christopher! In short trousers you was! And you brung me your dad's hip flask of brandy for to deaden me pain!" Everyone cheered and drank to the health of the bride and groom. Later, as the guests thinned, Mabel noticed damp patches on the bodice of her borrowed dress.

"Whoops!" she said. "It's me milk for me babies! I'd best go feed the little beasts 'fore I ruins me frock!"

Roger Bayliss, as soon as Mabel was back on her feet after the arrival of the twins, had called their parents into his office and told them his plan for the suddenly expanded Vallance household. He sat them down in the chill space which was known as the Farm Office, smiled what he hoped was reassuringly at their two concerned faces, cleared his throat and began to speak. "You'll have the cottage of course, and your wage, Ferdie, will be raised to three pounds. I shall put you on the farm payroll, Mabel, as you can no longer be employed by the Ministry of Agriculture, and I'm proposing to make you responsible for the running of the dairy." Mabel's eyes widened. "You will supervise the milking parlour, manage the roster and arrange cover where necessary."

"And not do no milking meself, sir?" Mabel asked, incredulously.

"No, Mabel. I'm putting you in overall charge. You'll be responsible for the hygiene, the hosing out, the scouring of the equipment, the condition of the drinking troughs and so on. You know the routine."

"Yes, sir!"

"You'll ensure that the dung doesn't accumulate in the yard and that the churns are ready at the collection point, and it will be your responsibility to inform me if the milk lorry is delayed, right?"

"Yes, sir. Thank you, sir!" Mabel practically curtsied with pride. She regarded this change of responsibility as a promotion and was as pleased by the status it involved as her employer had intended her to be. Alice Todd had been the first to draw his attention to this girl who, she had noticed, despite her lack of education and other disadvantages which could only be guessed at, showed intelligence, and in a modest and as yet undeveloped way, ambition. Ferdie, Roger understood, had no such potential. He worked as well as he could with his maimed leg and would continue to do so until he dropped. But he had no aspirations and no more will to improve his lot than his father had, or his father, whom Roger could only dimly remember, before him. He turned back to Mabel, whose bright, brown eyes had not left his. She was not a pretty girl but her two years on the land, and even the recent bearing of the twins, had had their effect on her physique, just as it had developed her personality. She looked solid, confident and robust.

"Do you think you can arrange those duties to fit in with your responsibilities for your children?" he asked her.

"Oh, yes, sir. Mrs Jack'll always keep an eye on 'em, and when they grows, Ferdie'll make 'em a nice, safe playpen!"

"I shall pay you two pounds and ten shillings per week to begin with, and when we get the milking machine . . ."

Mabel's eyes widened.

"Milking machine!" she echoed. "Will it be like the one over at Mr Lucas's place? I told Ferdie about it, didn't I, Ferdie? Lovely it is! All pipes and shiny machinery and it gets 'em milked that quick!" Roger had been impressed by Mabel's speedy grasp of the mechanics of the milking machine which his neighbour had recently demonstrated to him, proving its basic simplicity by successfully teaching Mabel how to operate it.

"Yes," he told her, "it'll be just like that one. If you can manage it, and I think you can, I shall put you in charge of it and your wage will be correspondingly increased. How does that sound? Both happy?"

They smiled and nodded. Mabel had always steadfastly believed that when it came down to it, Mrs Todd, Mr Bayliss and Mrs Brewster would, between them, somehow manage to sort out the lives of the Vallance family.

As the wedding guests left the lower farm, the girls, now wearing dungarees, heavy jackets and boots, piled into the lorry that would return them to their work at the higher farm.

Christopher Bayliss, carrying a pile of plates and teacups, followed Alice through the kitchen and into the scullery where Rose was noisily washing up. Alice was smiling as they returned to the quieter kitchen.

"You look happy, Mrs Todd," he said.

"It's one of those days, Christopher," she said, "when everything seems very positive. A wedding. Babies."

"Even if not in the correct order?"

"In quite the wrong order, in fact! But there's no harm done!"

"No harm at all!" He watched her as, with a heavy teapot in one hand, she used the other to return a handful of knives and teaspoons to a drawer which she then closed by pressing her thigh against it. She moved gracefully and was, Christopher noticed, a very charming woman. No wonder his father was so taken with her.

"And you!" she said suddenly, surprising him by cutting across his train of thought. "It's good to see you looking so well and happy!"

Christopher Bayliss was, in fact, hugely changed from the exhausted pilot she had first encountered two years previously, during his brief days of leave, and who, by then, had been perilously close to the breakdown that would see him ignominiously discharged from the RAF.

"You are unrecognisable, you know!" she told him. He was, in fact, almost fully restored to the robust and healthy young man he had been when he had reported for duty with his first squadron. His regained physical fitness was obvious and the nightmares and flashbacks that had tormented him after his breakdown now only rarely broke his sleep. "There is only one thing that bothers me," Alice said, offering him tea from the pot in her hand. He accepted, sitting down at the table and watching her as she filled his cup and added milk, his dark eyes and sensitive face reminding her, as they often did, of his father.

"So what is it, Mrs Todd?" he asked her, slightly indulgently. "This thing that bothers you?"

"It's really none of my business," Alice laughed, suddenly embarrassed. She had, she knew, developed the habit, since she had become warden, of studying the small community of which, for the time being at any rate, her world consisted. She did this, she guessed, partly as a diversion from her own problems — one of which was the enduring bruise caused by her husband's cold withdrawal from their marriage which had resulted, a few months previously, in divorce. Another was the prospect of the future as a lone mother and the effect of all this on the little boy for whom she must, somehow, properly provide. So, as she worked her way through the duties that filled her days and dealt, as best she could, with the diverse routine problems that arose in the hostel, she had pondered on the lives of the girls in her care, watched them react to the various crises they had to face and, increasingly, found her opinion sought on a whole range of subjects. Their boyfriends, their marriages, debts, illnesses, fears and grievances. When disaster struck and the war took the lives of a brother, sister, mother, father or husband, it was Alice who had helped them through their grief.

Christopher was smiling, waiting for her to continue. She sat down at the table, her own cup of tea in her hands.

"It's this estrangement," she began, her voice too low for Rose to overhear it from the scullery, "between you and your father. It's you . . . living, all this time, by yourself in the woodman's cottage." Christopher lowered his gaze. "I could understand it last year when you needed to be alone to sort of . . ." she hesitated.

"Pull myself together?"

"Yes," Alice said. "And that was, to some extent, logical. And it has done you good. The exercise. The peace and quiet after what you went through when you were flying. But there was more to your withdrawal into the forest than that, wasn't there." Her words were a statement, not a question. "I'm not prying or intruding, but the fact was that all of us — the land girls and the people here who had known you all your life — were bewildered by the way your father treated you."

"Not visiting me in the nuthouse, you mean?"

"Not only that, Christopher. He'd known for weeks that you had . . . had . . ."

"I had deserted, Mrs Todd," he said, firmly. "Don't let's beat about the bush. I had gone AWOL."

"And he never told us, Christopher! Never said a word! Kept it to himself! All that time! Then, when the military police found you and arrested you, he turned his back on you! He did! Literally. Everyone saw it and we were shocked by it. It was as if . . . as if he was ashamed of you."

"He was!"

"But why? Your record in the RAF was impeccable! You had flown more missions than anyone in your squadron! Too many more! You were exhausted! You were as much a casualty as you would have been if your plane had been blown out of the sky! So why was he ashamed?" Christopher shrugged.

"Pa just has a problem with it, I suppose," he said. "I was a big disappointment to him."

"And he was a disappointment to me — to us, I mean," she added, quickly. "To all of us here." Christopher looked baffled. "When someone you respect does something that shocks you," Alice continued, "something that seems out of character, you try to find a reason for it. Or to justify it. To excuse that person so that you can begin to respect them again. So . . . please forgive me if you feel I have no right to . . . to pursue this . . . but I found myself struggling to find a reason for his treatment of you." When Christopher made no response she went on. "I thought at first his loss of your mother might have had something to do with it."

"Could be," Christopher said, vaguely. "Pa always keeps things very much to himself. Stiff upper lip and all that."

"And now you're sounding just like him!" Alice smiled briefly and then became serious again. "But it is unusual, Chris, to allow one grief to roll on and cause another. You needed him when you were ill. He should have been there with you. He should have brought you home. Nursed you back to health!"

"He couldn't," his son said. "He just . . . couldn't."

"No!" Alice agreed, emphatically. "He couldn't. What interests me is *why* he couldn't. Why, when it should have been all about you, it seemed to be all about him!"

"I don't know, Mrs Todd," Christopher said, smiling and shrugging. "I honestly don't! And actually, right at this moment, I don't much care!" He was laughing now. Despite the warden's outburst, Roger Bayliss's son was laughing and rosy with happiness.

"You're blushing!" Alice exclaimed, peering at him. "What has happened to make you so pleased with yourself?" He got to his feet, rounded the table, and taking her by the shoulders, kissed her on each cheek.

"Can't tell you!" he said happily. "Sworn to secrecy!" He was making for the door. "Lovely talking to you, Mrs Todd! Got to go!" As he left the kitchen Rose Crocker, her hands pink from the washing-up, entered it from the scullery.

"And what was all that about?" she demanded.

18

"I don't know, Rose. I honestly don't. But whatever it is, Christopher Bayliss is happier than I've ever seen him!"

"It'll be Georgina, then." Rose announced as though it was the most obvious thing in the world, which, Alice instantly realised, it was.

Georgina Webster, when, in 1943, she had arrived at Lower Post Stone farm as one of the first intake of girls to be billeted there, had looked, her fellows had thought, very like the girl on the Ministry of Agriculture posters which were displayed that year, up and down the country, seeking volunteers for the Women's Land Army.

Georgina was sleek and healthy. The stylish cut of her dark hair suggested the Thirties rather than the Forties when most girls were favouring frizzy curls, created by "perms" and maintained by curlers. Her skin and eyes were clear. Somehow she contrived to make the much despised Land Army uniform look almost elegant.

"You've took in them breeches!" Marion had accused her.

"No I haven't! Honestly!"

"Well, you've lengthened the sleeves of that overcoat! Mine ends above me wrists!"

"I think it's just that your arms are longer than mine." Even in the dungarees, rubber boots, heavy sweaters and waterproofs which the girls wore day in and day out, Georgina Webster had a style about her that most of the other girls were always aware of and which some of them either resented or envied.

Young women who were well educated, when faced with the necessity of doing "war work", had tended to choose the more glamorous of the armed services, joining the WRENS, the WRAFS or the ATS, rather than working in munition factories or on the land. Consequently, and as a result of schooling that had been brief and often unheeded, the majority of land girls came from families regarded as working class and the Women's Land Army became patronisingly referred to as the "Cinderella Service".

Georgina's choice had not been forced on her by the level of her education, which was high, but by two other factors. The first was that as the elder of two children of a wealthy, East Devon farmer, her brother, two years her junior, could only avoid conscription if she herself volunteered for some form of war work. The second factor was that the Webster family were pacifists and the prospect of any of them being involved in combat was abhorrent to them. Georgina's farming background made the Land Army an obvious choice and she arrived at the hostel prepared for the disapproval of her fellows.

"I'm not sharing a room with no 'conchie'!" had been the uncompromising reaction of Marion and Winnie, a couple of outspoken, north-country girls, and Georgina had, at her own request, moved her monogrammed suitcases out of their room and into one of two tiny, drafty spaces above the porch, which were hardly large enough to be described as bedrooms.

The girls had smirked and nudged when it became obvious to them that Georgina was attracting the attention of Christopher Bayliss, whom they encountered when he was on leave from the RAF.

The young pilot, his nerves fraying, the breakdown he was about to experience only weeks away, approached Georgina clumsily, teased her about her pacifism and insulted her by implying that she, like most of the girls he fancied, was his for the taking. When she finally agreed to have dinner with him it was, although it was a long time before he realised it, because she sensed his underlying vulnerability and saw, beneath the gung-ho bravado, the fragile state he was in. Nevertheless it had been she, when he finally cracked, who supported him through the early months of his breakdown. This, added to several other incidents which had shocked the Post Stone community — the death of one of the girls in an air raid on Plymouth, the suicide of a Jewish refugee and now the devastation of a young man, however obnoxious Georgina may have thought him, who had, for years, been risking his life in defence of his country — began to shake and then to undermine her pacifist convictions.

Ironically, Christopher, by then slowly recovering in a military nursing home, astonished Georgina by announcing suddenly that he himself was now opposed to war. He was, unsurprisingly, dismayed when she told him of her own change of heart and that she was about to quit the Land Army and use the flying skills she had learnt as a schoolgirl to serve in the Air Transport Auxiliary, a non-combative arm of the RAF.

They had been walking in the overgrown grounds of the building to which the psychiatric hospital had been evacuated. Christopher had stopped in his tracks when she told him.

"But you can't!" he said, staring at her in astonishment. "It's against everything you believe in! Everything you've taught *me* to believe in!"

"I think I was wrong, Chris! And I think, until recently, I rather went along with what my family feels about the war instead of working it out for myself. But so many awful things have happened! Poor Chrissie getting killed! Andreis shooting himself because of what the Nazis are doing to the Jews! And you! Look what it's done to you! We have to stop them, Chris! We have to!" He began walking on, away from her, leaving her standing. After a beat she hurried after him, caught up with him and they moved on, side by side and in silence, along the mossy path.

"I'd thought you might come with me to live in the woodman's cottage," he said, eventually. It had been decided that, when discharged from the hospital, Christopher would spend some time working in his father's woodlands. There had been some discussion regarding the wisdom of this. The woodman's cottage was primitive, isolated and near derelict, but he had been determined and his father's reservations had been overruled. "I'd thought we could work together and be together and . . ."

"Just shut our eyes and ears to what is happening in this war? I can't do that anymore, Chris!"

"So you don't want to be with me?" he said flatly, and she couldn't meet his eyes because she knew that what she would see there was a side of Christopher that disturbed her. She had not cared for the brash, young man she had first encountered, but when, almost unrecognisable under three weeks' growth of beard, his hair tangled, his clothes fouled, his wrists cuffed as he was manhandled into a military police van, her temper had flared and she had shouted at his captors and tried to pull them away from him, when no one else had made any attempt to defend him.

Their relationship, in those early weeks of his breakdown, had subtly shifted. While she had become strong and supportive, he had grown needy and reliant. She had, in fact, pitied him and he, much later, had recognised this and reluctantly accepted the fact that it made him unattractive to her. They had parted, remaining curiously aware of one another, encountering each other only occasionally and unsatisfactorily. It was Alice Todd who sensed that there was something significant between the two of them, and she who remained Georgina's confidante even after the girl had left the hostel, acting as a sort of go-between, observing Christopher's recovery and Georgina's experiences in the ATA. She wisely avoided giving direct advice and had considered her words very carefully when she responded to what they told her of their lives and their feelings.

Over recent months Alice had seen little of either of them but, shortly before Christmas, on the night of Margery Brewster's party, Alice had urged Roger Bayliss to try to persuade his son to spend Christmas Day at home with him at the higher farm, rather than alone in the isolated cottage. She had insisted that they drove, on the spur of the moment and through wind and rain, up into the forest to fetch him. As they approached the cottage they had found the track blocked by a fallen tree and been surprised to discover that Christopher already had a visitor. Someone who had arrived on a motorcycle, which Alice immediately recognised as the one which Georgina often borrowed from her brother. Guessing, correctly, that Christopher and Georgina were alone together in the cottage, Alice had dissuaded Roger from interrupting his son's evening.

At Lower Post Stone, Rose, having crossed the yard to take several telephone calls from Georgina's worried father, expected and received an honest account of the night's events from Alice.

"They need to work things out between them," she told Rose, who was flushed with excitement. "We must respect their privacy. I'm sure Georgie will tell us whatever news there is when she's ready." Rose, shocked by this irregular behaviour, yet thrilled to be privy to it, had allowed Alice to swear her to secrecy.

It was several weeks before Georgina, whose Christmas leave from her base at White Waltham had been brief, visited Lower Post Stone, arriving one cold, sunny January morning, riding her brother's motorcycle and wearing borrowed leathers which she stepped out of, emerging lithe and elegant, and draped over one of the kitchen chairs. She sat, warming her cold hands, watching Alice prepare the pie the land girls would eat that evening.

"Good Christmas?" Alice asked as innocently as she could, aware that Georgina's clear, uncompromising

24

eyes were scrutinising her, and that every inflection of her voice or expression on her face which might confirm the girl's suspicions was being noted.

"It was you, wasn't it?" Georgina said, smiling. Alice was relieved by her light-heartedness. Georgina was, in fact, almost mocking her. "You and Mr Bayliss."

"Me and Mr Bayliss what?" Alice asked, blushing. Georgina was laughing now, unable to control her amusement at Alice's unconvincing attempt to conceal the obvious facts.

"You and Mr Bayliss were in the forest on the night of the storm! You got as far as the fallen tree and you recognised the bike and you fled! Right?"

Alice could not deny it. Absurdly embarrassing as it was, she remained in doubt about precisely what Georgina and Christopher had deduced or how they had interpreted what had happened.

"We thought we heard the motor of some sort of vehicle above the noise of the gale," Georgina told her. "By morning the rain had washed away most of the tyre tracks. We guessed it was the farm truck but couldn't work out why whoever it was had driven up. Then we twigged that it was someone who recognised my brother's bike."

Alice dusted flour from her hands and sat, facing Georgina across the large circle of rolled pastry.

"It was entirely my fault," she sighed. "We'd been to the Brewsters' party and you know what Margery is like where alcohol is concerned. She'd laced the punch with God knows what and we all got a bit . . . well, mellow! Roger was not as bad as I was, but . . . Anyway, I got it into my head that he should insist on Christopher coming home for Christmas and, bless his heart, he agreed to drive me up to the cottage to fetch him . . ." Georgina was staring, round-eyed. "I know, Georgie! It was madness — but actually rather fun at that stage . . . We had to use the truck, of course, and there was floodwater in the lanes and the forest track was half washed away! We got as far as the fallen tree, decided to walk the last bit and then saw the bike! I knew at once that it was Lionel's. Your scarf was hanging out of the pannier, so I was certain you were there! Poor Roger . . . I insisted that we shouldn't intrude on Christopher's privacy or some such nonsense and dragged him away! He must have thought I was insane!" Georgina was looking slightly more serious now.

"You mean . . . Mr Bayliss didn't know I was there?"

"No! And he still doesn't!" Alice hesitated. "You see, I don't know how Roger stands on moral issues. My own views have been, shall we say, broadened by some of the things you girls have got up to since I've been warden — but Roger's . . . You have to remember, Georgie, that Queen Victoria was still on the throne when he was born and if you and Christopher . . . what I mean is . . . how would he react to the fact that his prospective daughter-in-law was . . . what do they call it . . .?"

"Sleeping with his son is what they call it, Alice!" The warden had suggested to Georgina, some months previously, that she might like to use her Christian name, but the "Mrs Todd" habit, once established, had proved hard to shake and it was only now, perhaps

26

because their relationship seemed to have subtly altered, that "Alice" came easily to her. "Yes," she continued blithely, "we are sleeping together. We are lovers — and we are incredibly happy! I suppose it's odd, how we took so long to sort ourselves out, but he was rather horrid when I first met him, you know."

"He was ill, Georgie!"

"Yes, he was ill. But then he got all fragile and clingy and I was such a brute to him!"

"My dear girl, you were never a brute! You couldn't have been expected to know what was going on in his poor head! He didn't even know himself!"

"But then there was Fitzie!" Georgina murmured, guiltily. "What was all that about?"

"Squadron Leader Fitzsimmonds was an attractive man who offered you a light-hearted flirtation at a time when that was exactly what you needed."

"It went a little further than that, Alice!"

"But . . . not . . . ?"

"No. Not!" Georgina confirmed. Then she was laughing again.

"What's funny?" Alice demanded, half seriously.

"You are! One moment you're all 'modern woman' condoning fornication! Oh, yes you were! And the next you're sighing with relief because I didn't misbehave with poor Fitzie . . . who just got married, by the way! To my flying friend Lucinda! So now they're off somewhere, looping the loop together. So sweet!"

"Good heavens, Georgie! The way people talk these days! The things they do!"

"It's the war," Georgina said, suddenly serious. "It's driven us all out of our minds."

They sat for a while in silence, Georgina picturing the handsome Canadian flier with whom she had come close to having a serious affair, and how she had understood, quite suddenly, one morning when she was ferrying a Mosquito cross-country, from the RAF storage unit at Little Rissington to the airfield at Filton, that it was Christopher Bayliss who mattered most to her, and not only most, but hugely.

It had been a short flight and the visibility was good. A blustery wind had moderated considerably since she had taken off and she was relaxed and enjoying the unusually stress-free assignment when the image of Neil Fitzsimmonds came into her head. There he was, self-confident and handsome, enviably at ease with the way he was moving through what he described, almost affectionately, as his war. When they had met, nine months previously, and he had been a senior member of her group of fliers and she a new recruit, they had been mutually attracted to one another. He had sought her out, and despite their heavy workloads and constant movement between the various airfields and repair workshops, they had contrived to see a lot of each other. When their feelings had deepened they had planned what Georgina regarded as a voyage of discovery — a week of leave, which was to be spent alone together, in a borrowed cottage on the North Devon coast. However, on that morning flight, as she glimpsed, through broken cloud, the southern Cotswolds and the meanderings of the River Avon, the image of

Neil Fitzsimmonds became replaced in her mind by Christopher Bayliss, and she understood suddenly, and without doubt, his overwhelming importance to her.

"Fitzie took it very well," Georgina explained to Alice, "and quite soon afterwards discovered Lucinda. So all was well. Except that Chris had changed. When I first arrived at the cottage I thought it was going to be a disaster."

"Well of course he had changed, Georgie! Six months had passed and he had recovered."

"I know, and I was stupid not to have expected him to be different. It was a bit embarrassing at first, getting to grips with how our relationship had altered . . . But he was so adorable, Alice!" She remembered the scene, only weeks previously, when she and Christopher, having found their way through the confusion and near tragedy of the previous year, had comprehended each other and understood what the result of that comprehension was going to be.

Rose's footfalls, as she moved about the bedrooms on the floor above them, and the squabbling of the farm jackdaws at the top of the kitchen chimney stack, were the only sounds.

"We're very happy, Alice," Georgina said solemnly, and Alice told her she had always believed they would be and asked whether they had got as far as making any plans for the future.

"Chris has a plan, and of course, I'm included in it now. I can tell *you* but we are not going to make any announcements to our parents until —"

"Announcements?" Alice queried. "That sounds a bit, well, formal!"

"It's just until . . . until things are more definite. Dates and things. Dates of sailings, Alice. Of ships." She was watching Alice's face.

"Ships?" Alice echoed.

"Yes. To New Zealand."

Alice was speechless. Then Georgina was explaining that Christopher, always fascinated by trees, had been studying arboriculture intensively over the past year. "He's completed all the practical stuff and got some sort of diploma which he needed in order to qualify for a job he's applied for with the New Zealand Forestry Commission." She paused, watching Alice's astonishment. "He's working on his final thesis now and it's almost finished . . . We don't want to tell anyone until everything's settled . . ."

"And . . ." Alice was hesitant, "you're going with him?"

"Of course I am! I can't just walk out on the ATA, of course. But as soon as I can, we'll just . . . get married and go!"

"Have you thought . . . *really* thought, about leaving everything — everyone — behind? Your parents, Georgie? Christopher's father?" She paused, watching Georgina's face. "Oh, dear! That's what's at the bottom of all this, isn't it! This wretched problem between father and son." Georgina sighed. After a moment's silence she admitted that it was true that Christopher now found his relationship with his father impossible and felt the only solution was to get away from it.

"He's always been a bit weird, apparently, but since Chris was chucked out of the RAF his father can't even look him in the eye, Alice! You saw what he was like when it happened. It's no better now. Chris has had enough of being treated as though he was a coward when he was *not* a coward! Of feeling a failure when he never failed! It's just . . . intolerable! His father has virtually driven him away, Alice! Chris loves this place! Post Stone valley is his home! He would probably have taken on the farms when his father wanted him to. But now he says he simply cannot bear to spend the rest of his life facing that look! The accusation, Alice! The reproach! So he's going. And I'm going with him. Only you must promise not to breathe a word just yet."

It was at this point that Rose, having finished sweeping the bedrooms, entered the kitchen.

"All right, Georgina?" she enquired, curtly.

"Yes, thanks, Mrs Crocker."

"Well that's good then, isn't it?" Rose continued, making an irritable clatter with dustpan and brush as she returned them to their cupboard. Whether Rose disapproved of Georgina's recent behaviour, or whether she was miffed because she felt excluded from the latest developments in the story, Alice was unsure. "Only, your father was very worried about you, the night of the storm when no one knew where you was," Rose continued, shooting a sharp glance at Alice who contrived to avoid it. "Very worried indeed, he was, poor gentleman."

"The track was blocked," Georgina said, truthfully, if lamely, "by a fallen tree . . ." She floundered on, unsure of precisely what Alice had told Rose about the deception of that night.

"A fallen tree, was there?" Rose muttered, sourly. "Well, that's as maybe, I daresay." She had replaced her plimsolls with the rubber boots she wore in the yard and was moving towards the kitchen door. "I'd best go see if them 'ens 'as got round to layin' again. Proper tardy they be, lately . . ." Her voice trailed into silence and she closed the yard door, more firmly than was necessary, behind her.

CHAPTER
TWO

It was a Friday night. Edward John Todd normally left his weekly boarding school early enough to catch the four o'clock bus from Exeter to Ledburton village where, although it meant making a slight detour, Mr Jack, his lorry laden with tired, muddy land girls, would pick him up and deliver him to his mother, where he would spend the weekend with her at the farm. Today there had been a telephone call from the school matron. Several of the small boys who shared a dormitory with Edward John had developed chickenpox. Although he was not one of them, the matron, who knew about the girls in Alice's care, suggested that until it was certain that Edward John was not infected it might be sensible for him to remain at the school. Alice had agreed.

"Has anyone ever had chickenpox?" she asked her girls as they devoured the steak and kidney pie — which, because the butcher had been able to supply only a very small piece of stringy meat and one kidney, consisted mainly of onion, swede and carrot.

"I have," Gwennan murmured with her mouth full. "You gets spots."

"And you itch," Winnie told them. "I'ad it when I was a nipper. You did too, Marion." The two of them had known each other for as long as they could remember, living next-door-but-one in the same grimy street.

"I never!"

"You did too! And your brother Herbert."

"That were mumps!"

"Mumps too! We all 'ad everything, we did! Mumps, measles, croup and the chickenpox!"

At ten o'clock Alice, assuming that all of the girls who had gone out that evening had returned together, was surprised, when she went to lock the outer door, to find a latecomer hurrying up the path.

"You only just made it, Evie!" she laughed. "I thought you came in with the others!" Evie seemed disconcerted and apologised, stammering out some complicated explanation for her separation from the other land girls until Alice interrupted her, assuring her, as she turned the lock in the door, that there was no harm done. She had called goodnight as the girl went quickly up the stairs, after which she thought no more about it, made herself a cup of cocoa and carried it through the quiet recreation room and into the bed-sitting room which, when he was home from boarding school, she shared with her son. Alice's room was on the ground floor of the farmhouse and ran the width of the squat, old building. There was a window at each end of it and a small fireplace broke one wall, its breast intruding into the oddly shaped space and suggesting two areas. A pair of threadbare armchairs faced the fireplace and there were divan beds, disguised with rugs and cushions, under each of the windows. Usually, at this time on a Friday night, Edward John would be in his bed, often still reading, sometimes already asleep. Alice had grown to accept his absence from Sunday evenings until late Friday afternoons, but treasured the two nights in each seven when he was with her. Tonight his absence depressed her.

Although the room was still warm, her fire was almost out. It would have rekindled easily enough if she had thrown a handful of twigs onto the embers, but she did not and sat, sipping the cocoa. She wondered why she was missing Edward John so keenly and realised suddenly that this was not what was lowering her spirits. The ramifications of the news Georgina had confided were, she realised, more serious and more complex than she had at first thought and, worryingly, indirectly involved Alice herself.

It was not simply that Georgina had sworn her to secrecy but that Christopher's plan to emigrate was the direct result of his father's treatment of him, which, although the father might not realise it, was about to drive the son from his home as surely as if he had been banished from it. It was possible, too, that Georgina's assumption of the basic qualities of care and sympathy which Roger Bayliss had failed to deliver at the time of his son's breakdown, had made Christopher more aware of that failure than he might otherwise have been. His girl had provided concern and support when his father had failed to do so. As a result, Christopher had cast Georgina in a role that had been at odds with a more conventional boy-girl relationship. This had proved too challenging for her and she had, for a while at least, withdrawn from it. Eventually, with Christopher recovered and Georgina recognising the strength of her feelings for him, they had rediscovered each other. Alice's concern now was for Roger Bayliss who, if he could not be persuaded to address the difficulty between himself and his son, was going to lose him, possibly for ever. Yet Alice's promise to Georgina made it impossible for her to warn Roger of Christopher's decision or to disclose the reason for it.

As she sat, her cup of cocoa growing cold between her palms, turning the problem over and over in her mind and finding no solution to it, the rain began. There was no wind behind it. It fell in a steady and increasingly noisy torrent. Its impact on the farmhouse itself was muffled by the thatch, but it hammered, deafeningly, on the iron roof of the lean-to where logs for the fires were stored. Downpipes spluttered and water barrels overflowed, flooding the patch of sodden grass between the porch and the low wall which separated it from the lane.

As dawn broke behind a leaden sky, and the girls, whose waterproofs would be no match for this downpour, ran, heads bowed, out to the truck that would take them up to the higher farm, Alice could see that the whole of the floor of Post Stone valley, barely visible through the solid wall of rain, was already inundated by a sheen of shallow water.

Rose, stumbling under her warped umbrella, crossed the flooded yard, the puddles almost overtopping her rubber boots, and announced that she'd never seen such rain.

"And it'll not stop, Alice, not with cloud like that it won't! And no wind to shift it! You mark my words!" And she was right.

Mostly, the Post Stone girls laboured as a team, working in uneven lines, hoeing their way down the long rows of brassicas, lifting the potato crop, filling hessian bags with sprouts, turning the hay, or stooking the barley and the oats at harvest time. Sometimes, when the work required it, the girls would be split up into smaller groups of four, three or even two. When it was two, Marion and Winnie usually contrived to work together on whatever task was assigned to them, and so it was, that on the first day of the flooding, the pair of them were in one of the lower meadows where the ewes were huddled miserably, their fleeces, despite their resistance to water, already heavy with it.

Marion and Winnie had been instructed to open the small gate that gave onto a field where the land rose steeply towards the area of the Post Stone farms known as "The Tops" — where the sheep would be safe from the rising water levels in the lower meadows — to drive them through the gate and fasten it behind them.

The girls, rain running off their waterproof coats and dripping from the wide brims of felt hats — which, dusty, warped and dating from the First World War, they had bought for sixpence each from an army surplus store in Exeter — could barely see through the

downpour. Their rubber-booted feet slithered dangerously on the muddy riverbank.

"Watch out, Win!" Marion shouted above the roar of
the flooded stream as Winnie struggled to keep her
balance. "Don't think I'm comin' after you if you fall
in!" In fact, if either Winnie or Marion ever did need
rescuing, then Marion or Winnie would instantly have
volunteered. Closer than many sisters, the two girls had
grown up together, walking to school along the bleak
streets of the north-country suburb in which they, like
their parents, had been born and bred and where, had
it not been for the outbreak of World War Two, they
would probably have seen out their days: working in a
nearby factory, marrying a local likely — or possibly
unlikely — lad and raising a clutch of undernourished
and undereducated kids whose fate would have been
similar to their own. But these two small girls had soon
grown to be different from their peers. Whether it was
the effect of one upon the other, or whether each
possessed similar characteristics which would have
emerged independently, no one would ever know, but
the fact was that these children both began, at an early
age, to develop a strong sense of ambition. They had
aspirations. There were things for which, even when
they were very young, they longed.

Marion, always a plain child, understood, when she
first viewed her reflection in her mother's dressing table
mirror, that to look the way she wanted to look was
going to be a challenge.

By their early teens the girls were in love with the
cinema and the glamorous creatures they stared at,

round-eyed with admiration, whenever they could raise the ninepence each which it cost them to gain entry to their local picture palace. They would sit through the cartoons, tolerate the Pathé News and squirm with impatience while the organist, posed in front of silky curtains and bathed in a familiar sequence of changing lights, worked his way through a repertoire which seemed, to the two impatient children, interminable. Then, at last, bolt upright in their velvet seats, Marion and Winnie would revel in the feature films.

By their mid teens Marion was determined to look like Jean Harlow. As soon as she was allowed to she would reach for the bleach bottle, pluck her untidy brows and pencil in provocative replacements. Winnie, the prettier of the two, took Jane Russell as her role model and planned to perm her dark hair until it stood out in the same stiff frizz as her heroine. By sixteen, both girls, still restrained by their strict, working-class parents, were labouring in a factory which manufactured small metal objects — the purpose of which they neither knew nor cared to know — and were obliged to contribute, to their respective parents, half of their weekly wage towards their keep. It was at that time that they identified their ambition and focused on a lifestyle which they decided they would enjoy and which, with luck and hard work, they believed they might be able to achieve.

"You want to run a pub? What, *you* two?" had been the astonished reaction of Marion's uncle Ted when, because he seemed to them to be a man of the world, they unveiled their plan.

"Why not?" Marion had challenged. "There's lots of women running pubs!"

"Mostly they're just hired to manage 'em," Ted told her, suppressing a persistent cough as he drew cigarette smoke into lungs already damaged by mustard gas in the trenches of the First World War. "They're not your actual landlord."

"Maybe not, but that's what we're gonna be, Uncle Ted. Actual landlords. Lady landlords."

"With our own licence!" Winnie had added, firmly.

"You'll be wanting to buy a lease, you mean?"

"Yeah!" Marion told him, although she was unsure what a lease was, where you got one or how much whatever it was would cost.

"Blimey! And what are you gonna use for money, eh?" Ted asked them, watching their expressions cloud.

"We'll save up," Marion announced. "We're both earning. We'll put money away. A bit every week til —"

"'Til doomsday!" Ted told her, laughing wheezily. "You're talking big money for a lease on an even half-decent pub!"

"What d'you call 'big money'?" Winnie enquired, nervously.

"Five hundred quid, I reckon. Minimum. Then youse gotta get licensed and that's not easy. They're choosy who they give a licence to, specially where women's concerned. And two young girls . . . I dunno . . . What d'you want a pub for, anyhow? Funny thing for a couple a kids like you to want!"

But it was what they wanted and what they continued to want over the years which led the country up to and into the Second World War. By then Marion and Winnie had opened a joint post office savings account. On the day war was declared it contained seventy-five pounds, three shillings and sixpence and the girls were in their early twenties.

Hopes of joining the WRENS, the WRAF or the ATS were soon dashed. Both Marion and Winnie had left the elementary school — where they had sat carving boys' initials into their desktops, dreaming of freedom and paying very little attention to their teachers — as soon as the law allowed. They could read, write, add up, take away and divide, but that was all. The smartly uniformed women at the military recruitment centre had been unimpressed, not only by this lack of education but by the slightly confrontational manner both girls exhibited when they were interviewed.

"What are we supposed to do, then?" Marion demanded when first one and then another of the armed services rejected them.

"You'll have to choose between a munition factory and the Women's Land Army," they had been dismissively informed.

They had opted for the Land Army because, as Marion announced to her astounded family, "We feel like a bit of a change!" This was partly true. The prospect of employment at the munition factory, a gloomy establishment only a few miles from their homes, seemed to offer a life unacceptably similar to their existing one. The countryside would provide not only a change of scenery but an escape from the parental discipline which, despite the fact that they were by now grown women, continued to restrict the way they dressed and behaved.

"We seen your girl down the pub," a neighbour had whispered to Winnie's mother. "Singin', she was, round the piano with a load of soldiers, and that Marion were sittin' on one of 'em's knee!"

They had been issued with uniforms and a railway pass and had sat, all day, in a crowded train which rattled interminably southwards. In a howling gale, it lurched to a stop at Ledburton Halt, where they stepped down onto a rain-swept platform and were met by a man in a truck that reeked of something which would soon become all too familiar to them. Dung.

"Phoar!" Marion exclaimed. "What's that pong?" The man, whom they later came to know as Mr Jack, shrugged and turned his attention to the twisting lane which was narrower, steeper and muddier than any roadway either Marion or Winnie had ever seen before.

Working conditions on the Post Stone farms came as a shock to both girls, who had been allocated to Roger Bayliss a year before he had decided to use the lower farmhouse as a billet. During that year, while they struggled with the hard physical labour and had survived their first wet, cold, Devonian winter, they had been housed in an attic room in Ledburton's only pub. Here, not only were conditions more comfortable than the homes they had left, but the saloon bar was immediately beneath their bedroom floorboards, together with the social life that came with it. Here they met the few local men who had, for one reason or another, escaped conscription, and better still, the increasing numbers of American servicemen, the GIs, who were undergoing training in preparation for the Allies' inevitable invasion of northern France.

"Loaded, they are, Win!" Marion had sighed, relishing the generosity, in the form of chocolate, silk stockings, cigarettes, perfume and packets of chewing gum, that she had experienced that evening at a local hop. "And their uniforms is gorgeous!"

Frequently their escorts would borrow army staff cars and drive them into Exeter to the dance halls, cinemas and hotels. There would be nights at the various military training establishments, when regimental bands would provide the music for quickstepping, jiving and jitterbugging. Often the lads would organise "a whip-round so the girls can go buy themselves something cute for the hop", and Marion and Winnie would add five and sometimes even ten pounds to the pittance they saved from their weekly Land Army wage.

By February 1943, when the lower farmhouse was opened as a hostel and Marion and Winnie were forced to move into it, together with the other eight girls for whom Alice Todd was to be responsible, the money in their post office account had risen significantly, and the prospect of acquiring a lease on a pub of their own was solidifying satisfactorily.

Two setbacks followed. The first was that Winnie, too liberal with her favours, conceived a child which had to be dislodged. While Gwennan Pringle and Rose Crocker guessed the real reason for Winnie's indisposition, caused, she claimed, by straining to lift heavy bags of swedes, Alice took a different view of it. If the truth of the situation had been revealed to Roger Bayliss and thence, via the Land Army Registrar, to the Ministry of Agriculture, Winnie would have been dismissed from the service and Marion would have gone with her into who knew what sort of future. So Alice Todd, in whom the two girls had confided their ambitions to run a public house and the means by which they hoped to obtain it, and who was also aware of the genuine distress which the induced miscarriage had caused both of them, contrived to gain a second chance for them, despite being uneasy about the considerable amount of money the girls had already accumulated.

"The thing is, Mrs Todd," Winnie had endeavoured to explain, "that the GIs is always givin' us stuff! Far more chocolate than we could ever eat and enough pairs of stockin's to last a lifetime! So what we do is, we sell 'em on to the rest of the girls! And not just the Post Stone girls but other land girls billeted round 'ere. The word soon went around and now we've got an order book, see? Half a dozen pairs of stockin's 'ere, some chocolate there, a bottle of Evenin' In Paris an' a carton of ciggies somewhere else!"

"It's not illegal, Mrs Todd!" Marion added, aware of Alice's concern. "Them things is gifts! It's up to us what we does with 'em!"

Alice had been forced to concede this point and avoided enquiring precisely what it was the two girls had done to deserve such generosity. She had become, largely through her dealings with the land girls, worldly-wise enough to know that, had they been dismissed, Marion and Winnie would probably have taken lodgings near one of the military training bases in the area and from there the slide into prostitution would have been difficult to avoid. So she turned a blind eye to the facts, demanded and got assurances from both girls that they would behave more responsibly in future, and on a possibly more practical level, contrived, with the help of the free-thinking matron of Edward John's boarding school, to procure contraceptives for them.

The second setback in Marion and Winnie's quest for funding happened as a result of the D-Day landings, when all available troops took part, first in the invasion of Normandy, and then the liberation of France and the huge push on into Germany itself. But even with most of the men gone there remained a steady flow of personnel, on leave, recovering from minor wounds or in training, and Marion and Winnie found that their irregular income did not suffer as badly as had at first seemed likely.

Having urged the sheep through the gate and onto the rising ground, the two girls, heads lowered against the driving rain, returned to the lane to begin the half-mile trudge back to the higher farm. It was past midday and they were hungry. Their packed lunches and thermos flasks filled with milky tea were waiting for them in what had been the saddle room at Higher Post Stone.

Rounding a corner, they reached the point where a footpath, a short cut to the farm, left the lane and ran steeply uphill. Here they came upon a scene of activity that had not been there an hour previously. Roger Bayliss, his sharp eyes checking on the level of the floodwater in his valley, had noticed that a tree stump, dislodged further upstream, had come to rest against the supports of a timber footbridge. The log was jammed sideways, obstructing the flow of the water, while debris steadily accumulated against it, adding to the pressure on the flimsy structure and threatening to carry it away. Roger had left his truck, and unable to shift the log without help, had flagged down a lorry transporting half a dozen of the local contingent of Italian prisoners of war. Their driver had agreed to allow his charges to help Roger move the log and would return to collect them after he had picked up another group who were working a mile off.

The Italians, an amiable mob, who seemed to enjoy the diversion, had quickly got a rope round the stump, hauled it aside and tethered it to a substantial willow where, when the floodwater eventually receded, it would be left high and dry. While they waited for the lorry, which would return them to their internment camp, Roger had suggested they took shelter from the continuing downpour in his open-sided barn which stood, disused and beyond repair, part of its thatched roof already collapsed, beside the lane.

The men huddled in the limited shelter, drawing enthusiastically on the cigarettes which Roger, unable to thank them for their help in any other way, had handed round. They had responded to his kindness, nodding, smiling, murmuring *"grazie, signor!"* and watching the approach of two figures, their faces sharpening with interest when they realised that the heavy waterproofs, wide-brimmed hats and muddy boots concealed not men, as they had at first thought, but girls.

Slightly inhibited by Roger's presence and not eager to be seen so unglamorously attired, Marion and Winnie continued, past the barn, towards the short cut which would take them up, through the wood, back to the higher farm.

It was then that they heard, above the roar of the river and the softer fall of the rain, a faint but increasing rumble. The trees on the hillside which rose steeply behind the barn seemed to be reverberating strangely, quaking and juddering, while the rumbling sound intensified and was joined by the crack of splitting timber. Then, as the girls stopped and stood transfixed, a wedge of the woodland began to slip downhill, gathering momentum as it approached, and then struck, the rear of the barn.

The landslip, it was established afterwards, had originated near the top of the hill in a hollow formed by a disused slate quarry which the relentless rain had filled with thirty feet or so of floodwater. This had placed a huge pressure on the unstable downhill side of the quarry which, collapsing, had released the accumulated water, taking with it a section of the hillside and all the timber that had been growing on it and sliding, with increasing force, down the incline.

The solid walls of the barn took the full impact of the landslide and halted its progress into the lane, but not before what was left of a roof, already weakened by years of neglect, was driven forward, collapsing and burying the Italian prisoners under piles of rotting thatch and the timber beams that had supported it.

The men clambered out, checking first to see if they were themselves unscathed and then assuring themselves that all their companions were accounted for.

"*Allesandro!*"

"*Si, bene!*"

"*Stai bene, Luca . . .?*"

"*Giorgio? Vai bene?*"

"*Si . . . Luigi?*"

Then it was discovered that all that was visible of Luigi was a booted foot protruding from a heap of mouldering thatch. But the thatch, they discovered, as they tried to extricate him, concealed an oak beam which had trapped his left forearm against a granite lintel that had once supported the entrance to the barn.

Having cleared the beam of thatch the men heaved at it, straining every sinew in their strong backs, shoulders and thighs. It was the length of the beam that was the problem. Two thirds of it was embedded in a pile of collapsed stonework.

The trapped Italian was howling with pain as his fellows swarmed over the heaped masonry, heaving the limestone slabs aside and frantically scooping away the loosened debris with their bare hands.

Winnie, who had pushed forward in an attempt to reach the injured man, succeeded in freeing his head and shoulders from the damp reeds, and while she tried to support him more comfortably, Marion examined his trapped arm. The beam had caught him just below the elbow. What was visible of his lower forearm was already contused. She turned to Roger Bayliss.

"You haven't got a rug or nothin' in your truck, 'ave you, sir? Only it's the shock, see. You're s'posed to keep 'em warm." When Roger did not respond, Marion became aware that he was standing, stock-still, his face gaunt and stark white, even in the half-light of the barn. His eyes were on Luigi's shattered arm and he was breathing strangely.

"It was like Mr Bayliss never even 'eard me!" Marion told Alice, later that day. "Like 'e'd seen a ghost or some' at! Shakin' like a leaf 'e was! So I went out to the truck to see if I could find anything to wrap round the fellow what was 'urt and I found a horse blanket. As I ran back into the barn Mr Bayliss went past me and got into the cab of his truck. 'E looked that strange, Mrs Todd! 'E just sat there, shakin' and breathin' funny. Then he puts his head down on the steerin' wheel and he starts cryin'! Honest! Sobbin' 'e was. It were awful to see! A man like Mr Bayliss, cryin' 'is eyes out! I put the rug round the Eyetie fellow. By that time they'd dug away the stones so they could shift the bit of timber off of his arm. You should of 'eard 'im 'olla! Then the other lorry come back and they took 'im off to 'ospital. It were touch and go with 'is arm, though, it bein' that badly broke."

"And what about Roger — I mean, Mr Bayliss?" Alice had asked. Winnie took up the story.

"'E were still sittin' in his truck . . ." she said. "'E wasn't cryin' no more and 'e told the pair of us to get in and 'e drove us back up to Higher Post Stone. 'E didn't say nothin' to us. Just drove, starin' ahead."

"We was an hour late for our sandwiches, Mrs Todd!" Marion added. "Starvin' 'ungry we was!"

Alice was concerned by the girls' account of Roger's reaction to what was, after all, a natural disaster caused by the extreme weather. But the old building was his and its poor condition could be said to be his responsibility. Did he, she wondered, feel guilty about what had happened?

She crossed the yard to the barn which housed the farm telephone and dialled his number.

"Are you all right, Roger?" she asked him.

"Bit damp!" he said, sounding relaxed, and as far as she could tell, normal. "You? Lower Post Stone's not under water yet, I trust?" Was he, she wondered, a little too jovial, considering what had happened that day? She reassured him that apart from the lower farmhouse being filled with damp clothing, all was well with her and her girls.

"It must have been a bit of a shock, the mudslide, I mean. And the Italian soldier getting hurt like that. Poor chap. From what they tell me he could easily have —"

He interrupted her. "Lost his arm. Yes, it was a pretty close call apparently. Bones can usually be fixed but if the circulation to the lower arm had been cut off for much longer . . . gangrene, you know . . ." He paused and then excused himself, saying that Eileen, his housekeeper, was about to serve him his evening meal.

50

"We 'eard this rumble," Marion was telling her fellows, not for the first time, at supper that night, "and down come 'alf the wood! Trees crashin' right and left they was! Great boulders and mud all roarin' downhill like one of those avalanche things they get in Switzerland — only not snow!"

"Right through the back wall of the barn, it come!" Winnie cut in, matching her friend's excitement. "And the roof fell in! Down came the rafters and all the thatch! Right across the lane it went! And those Eyeties was all buried underneath!"

"You should of seen the state of 'em!" Marion continued, when Winnie stopped to draw breath. "Covered in mud they was! And cut! And bruised! Could of been worse. Only one of 'em was hurt bad. You should of seen 'is arm! Ughh! It didn't 'alf upset Mr Bayliss!" she added, thoughtfully, picturing their boss huddled over the steering wheel, racked with sobs.

"What was 'e called?" Evie asked suddenly.

"What was who called?"

"The one what was hurt? What was 'is name?"

"'Ow should I know?" Winnie asked her. "No one said."

"Not Giorgio?" Evie asked, casually.

"Why would it be Giorgio?" Gwennan asked, eyeing Evie, her curiosity aroused.

"I dunno," Evie said, shrugging. "I just wondered. Lots of Eyeties is called Giorgio, aren't they . . .? Can I 'ave another cup of tea, Mrs Todd?"

"Well, all's well that ends well," the warden said, rather too brightly, as she drained the pot into Evie's cup. She caught Rose's quizzical glance and added, "What I mean is that whoever he is he'll be in good hands by now and will most probably be repatriated as soon as he's well enough!"

"What's 'repatriated', Mrs Todd?" someone asked.

"Sent home," Alice explained. "To his home in Italy." This brought smiles to some of the girls' faces and had the effect, as Alice began stacking the pudding plates, of changing the topic of conversation. The girls drifted off to sprawl in the recreation room or go, early, to their beds.

Alice's concern for Roger persisted for some days after the collapse of the barn. Why, she wondered, had he been so upset by it?

The injured POW was discharged from hospital, and with his arm heavily plastered, repatriated to his native Calabria, months before his fellow prisoners would be released. The barn, with the assistance of a larger group of Italians from the same detention centre, was razed to the ground and the slate quarry made permanently safe with a wide drain that would prevent rainwater from accumulating in it.

Alice knew better than to question Roger about the accident and was left to speculate on the strange effect it had had on him. Gwennan Pringle told Alice that she had read in the paper that some men who had been injured in the war "came over funny", like Mr Bayliss had.

"It's to do with that shell shock the Tommies got after the Great War, it said in the paper," she continued, watching Alice ironing one of Edward John's school shirts. "But Mr Bayliss has never fought in no war — so it couldn't be that, could it!" Alice slid the iron across the white cotton and it seemed to Gwennan that the warden was paying very little attention to what she was telling her. "Anyhow," she concluded, "that's what it said in the paper." If Mrs Todd took no notice of her or even of what it said in the paper, what was the good of talking to her at all? "I'll go to my bed now," she sighed. "I'm that tired . . . Goodnight Mrs Todd."

"Oh . . ." Alice said, suddenly aware that Gwennan was speaking to her. "Sorry, Gwennan, I was —"

"Miles away. Yes, you was, wasn't you? 'Night, Mrs Todd."

"Goodnight, Gwennan."

"Mrs Todd . . . could I have a word?" This phrase, or something very much like it, was a familiar one to Alice, and after almost two years as warden of the Post Stone hostel, there was hardly a girl who had not, at one time or another, made the request.

Today it was Hannah Maria Sorokova — whom everyone at the farm called Annie — who had tapped on the door marked "Warden" and was waiting, respectfully, to be invited into Alice's bed-sitting room.

"I'm of Polish extraction," Annie had solemnly informed the other land girls on the day they had all arrived at Lower Post Stone.

"Extraction?" Marion had bellowed. "You make yourself sound like a tooth!" And she and Winnie had howled with such ribald laughter that Rose Crocker, spooning out mashed potato, that first supper time, had pursed her lips in disapproval.

Apart from her name, her classic Jewish looks and the nationality of her antecedents, Annie was an East Ender, born, if not bred, in Duckett Street and — when she had arrived at the farm — had spoken with a broad, cockney accent. This, Alice noticed, had, over the past few months, become moderated. Possibly due to her friendship with the well-educated Georgina, or because of her association with Alice herself, Annie no longer dropped her aitches and now said "singing" instead of "singin", "I came home" instead of "I come 'ome", and "how d'you do" rather than "pleased to meet you". If she wanted to attract the attention of a waitress she did not attempt to summon one by calling her "miss".

Winnie and Marion accused her of putting on airs.

"First off she sets 'er cap at Georgina's toffee-nosed brother and now she's after this Hector fellow!"

While it was true that Annie's intense but brief affair with Lionel Webster ended badly, it had, for both parties, been an innocent and mainly happy interlude. When Lionel had succumbed to the pressures of his middle-class upbringing and ended the relationship, Georgina had been ashamed of her brother's snobbishness. Annie, however, accepted the situation, consigning it easily enough to the past, possibly because Lionel, although handsome and passionate, was hardly more than a schoolboy in her eyes and no match for her lively mind and more mature temperament. Hector Conway, on the other hand, and rather to her surprise, suited her well.

54

The two of them had met when Hector, in his capacity as a researcher with the War Artists Scheme, had visited the farm to inspect the huge mural which a Jewish refugee had painted on a pair of barn doors shortly before taking his life. Hector's interest in the painting, which represented the persecution of the Jewish community in Amsterdam at the time of the Nazi invasion, was genuine enough, but it was the mutual attraction between him and Annie Sorokova that had drawn him back to the farm on several occasions and had resulted in him being introduced to Annie's Polish family during her brief Christmas leave.

"It's about Hector," Annie told Alice, who was unsurprised to hear it.

"How is he?" she asked, lightly. "You saw him at Christmas, didn't you?" Annie nodded.

"He came to tea," she said. "He met my family. Everyone liked him, Mrs Todd, and he talked to Grandfather for ages about Polish art, and he'd heard of my uncle who was a well-known engraver. He wants me to visit his family in Oxford and stay overnight so he can show me the colleges . . ." Annie paused, watching Alice, who was very aware of the importance of her reaction to this news.

"That sounds lovely, Annie. When d'you hope to go? You'll need a couple of days' leave, I expect? We'll have to sort it out with Mr Bayliss and he is a bit short-handed at the moment, what with Mabel only working part-time because of the twins . . . But we'll manage something . . ." She watched Annie's delicate face cloud, the perfectly shaped lids were lowered over her expressive eyes. Alice asked if there was anything wrong.

"Not exactly *wrong*, Mrs Todd, but . . . well . . . Hector's father is a don, you see."

"Yes. I remember you telling me. But how does that affect . . .?"

"They're what's called academics, Mrs Todd. All his family are. With letters after their names. Hector's father, his brothers and even this Aunt Sybilla person who lives with them. They're all scholars and that. His mother died, you see, when the boys were quite young and there's a housekeeper and everything . . . I just think they might reckon I'm, you know, not . . ."

"Not what, Annie?"

"Not . . . not educated enough, Mrs Todd! And that I don't speak like they do or think what they think or know about the things they know about. That I'm not . . . well . . . not good enough for them." Annie's voice faltered into a doleful silence and Alice sighed.

"Oh Annie! It's this class thing, isn't it?" she said. Annie nodded and they sat without speaking for a moment or two. "We've talked about this before, haven't we?"

"Yes, we have. And you said it's all nonsense and that what with the First World War and then the suffragettes and now this war, society is changing and it's not where you went to school or your accent or whether you say 'serviette' or 'napkin' that matters, it's who you are and what you do!" Although Annie had precisely remembered Alice's comments, she repeated them without much conviction. Alice nodded and waited, guessing that

Annie's next word would be "but". "But . . ." she began, exactly on cue, adding, embarrassed, "You're laughing at me, Mrs Todd! Am I being stupid?"

"No. Not a bit stupid. A little predictable perhaps, but not stupid. The thing is, Annie, that most of the people who worry about what is correct or incorrect, and who look down their noses at people whose accents are different from theirs, and who either don't know or don't care about the so-called 'rules', do so because they're insecure."

"Insecure? Are they?"

"Conforming to the rules is a sort of protection."

"Is it?"

"They feel safe and even smug, hiding behind all these meaningless conventions. You're a clever girl, Annie! You got excellent marks in your Ministry of Agriculture exams! You've read all the books on that list Georgina left with you. You're sensitive and you're courteous and you're very, very beautiful. Hector's a lucky fellow! He is also, from what I've seen of him, a very nice one. What's more," Alice added, laughing, "Rose approves of him!"

"Does she?" Annie was smiling now. "Well that's good news, then!" she laughed. "There can't be nothing . . . I mean anything . . . wrong with Hector if he passes muster with our Mrs Crocker!"

"Go and visit him, Annie! He'll look after you! He loves you! His family will probably surprise you. They won't be like anyone you've ever met before, but nor was I when you and I first met, and we get on together pretty well, don't we?"

The attraction between Annie and Hector had surprised everyone. Gawky and tall, his poor eyesight exempting him from conscription, the kindest description of Hector would be that he looked "bookish". His forehead was high and his long hair flopped, except when he drove at speed about the countryside in the course of his work, the canvas hood of his bull-nosed Morris folded down. Then, with his hair whipping in the slipstream and his chin slightly lifted, Annie had seen a different Hector. A man of sensitivity and determination. A man who knew things. Who shared his knowledge with her and who encouraged her curiosity without patronising her. Who made her laugh and found her funny. A man who for a long time had done nothing more than hold her hand, but whose first kiss had expressed his feelings more eloquently than any words could have done.

Alice seldom gave her girls direct advice, suggesting, instead, various ways of approaching whatever problem was worrying them. Having been more specific on this occasion, she was concerned that her optimism where Annie was concerned might backfire. That Hector's family could, possibly unwittingly, make her feel inferior and destroy her growing confidence. Nevertheless she encouraged Roger Bayliss to allow the girl the three days leave she requested, and when Mr Jack came to collect her and deliver her to Ledburton Halt, Alice was waving goodbye to her from the farmhouse gate.

"It is one of those tall, thin houses, with a basement and then, on the floor above, a kitchen and a dining room and then, above that, on the next floor, an enormous room with windows in the front and at the back and then, further on upstairs there were bedrooms that the boys and Mr Conway and Miss Sybilla Conway use as their studies as well as to sleep in. Miss Conway said I was to call her Sib, like everyone else does!"

Annie, straight off the train and with her overnight bag beside her, had found Alice in the hostel kitchen, checking the boxes of groceries that had just arrived, and was keen to lay the details of her visit to Oxford before the warden, rather as a labrador delivers a pheasant to its master's feet.

"You were right about them being different, Mrs Todd, but they were lovely and not at all stuck-up! There was always someone laughing about something, and if I wasn't sure what was funny, Hector explained! The Mrs Potter person, who looks after them, is a very good cook and they eat round the kitchen table — almost like we do here. One of Hector's brothers — Howard, he's called — had the books he's studying propped open on the table beside his plate because he has to have his thesis finished by Tuesday. He apologised for his terrible manners, but I thought it was nice that he felt I was sort of part of things and would understand, although Mrs Potter — Pottie, they call her — said he should be ashamed! Hector showed me round the colleges and we went into some of them! He explained about their history. They are so beautiful, Mrs Todd! We went to the Ashmolean Museum and there were things from Knossos and Troy! Then we walked along the river where they go punting, but it was too cold for that so we had cinnamon toast and a pot of tea in a café instead! Mr Conway asked me about the Land Army and the Blitz and about my family arriving from Poland in the Twenties and everything, and I asked him about Oxford and him being a don and he told me about his work and his students and the papers he's had published. I enjoyed myself, Mrs Todd! I really did. It's made me think about what I want to do when the war's over. I don't reckon I want to work on the land, even as a farm manager. And I don't want to go back to our factory in London."

"But what about your family?" Alice asked, encouraging Annie to face the decisions she was soon going to have to make. The Sorokova family were modestly successful and hard-working garment manufacturers in London's East End and Annie, who had already proved herself to be useful, was expected to please her father and grandfather by working her way up through the ranks of first and second cousins into a responsible position. "Aren't they expecting you to return to the family business?"

CHAPTER
THREE

By mid February the weather had turned milder and Georgina, arriving at the farmhouse early one Saturday afternoon, had needed only a thick sweater and a woollen scarf to keep her warm when she rode over to Lower Post Stone on her brother's motorbike.

The land girls, still sitting over their lunch and, except for those on weekend dairy duty, enjoying the prospect of freedom from work until Monday morning, were relaxed and planning trips to Exeter or, after a lazy afternoon, to the pub in Ledburton. Evie, as she often did, was planning a walk through the woods and up onto The Tops.

"I like it up there," she would reply when the girls teased her about her long, solitary excursions into the surrounding countryside. "You can see for miles and miles."

"What's up, Georgie?" Marion asked when Georgina arrived in the kitchen. "Face like a cracked pisspot, you got!" Georgina looked from one smiling face to another, sat down at the table and slowly unwound her thick scarf.

"You haven't heard about Dresden, then?" she asked. For a moment everyone looked blank. Then Alice, who was struggling with the lid of the last jar of bottled plums, which she and Rose had preserved the previous summer and would use in a pie that evening, finally loosened it.

"You mean the bombing?" she asked, licking plum juice from her thumb.

"Yes. The bombing," Georgina repeated, heavily.

"What about it?" Gwennan snapped back, her Welsh accent crisp, her tone self-righteous. "So Dresden got bombed. So what!"

"It wasn't just bombed, Taff. It was obliterated!" Winnie wasn't sure what obliterated meant so Georgina told her, adding emphatically, "The whole city, Winnie! Acres of it. Hundreds of buildings gutted! Roofs gone! Just the walls standing! Thousands of people . . . Thousands! Incinerated in the fires!"

"Like Liverpool!" Gwennan announced, firmly. "Like Southampton and Bristol!"

"And the London docks," Annie added and, thinking of Chrissie, "and Plymouth."

"That was different," Georgina countered. "They were military targets!"

"Not all!" Marion said. "Bath wasn't!"

"Nor was Exeter." Rose, sitting knitting, beside the range, remembered the night when the thuds of exploding bombs had been audible from the Post Stone farms, six miles away from the shuddering city.

"Or Coventry!" Evie added. She had gone with her mother to see the smouldering ruins that were all that remained of the cathedral, and had stood beside the pile of rubble in a nearby side street where her Auntie

Gladys and two of her cousins had died. "Eight hours that blitz lasted!" she said, her eyes narrowed and fixed accusingly on Georgina's. "Wave after wave of bombers come over. You never saw so many planes. Incendiaries, they dropped! Then high explosives to spread the fires! On an' on it went! People was lyin' dead in the streets and by mornin' there wasn't nothin' left but rubble as far as you could see!" She paused, breathless, the other girls shocked and silent. "So 'ow come you're so steamed up about this Dresden place, Georgina?"

"Because it was the worst!" Georgina said, quietly. She had been shown aerial photographs of the bomb damage inflicted on most of the cities the girls had listed but the air attack on Dresden was more extreme than any she had seen — worse, at that time, than any bomb damage that anyone had ever seen.

Reconnaissance photographs taken by the RAF, during and after the Dresden raid, had been passed around the mess at White Waltham where Georgina was based. Even here, there had been disagreement about the justification of the level of destruction wrought on the city. Georgina had sat with the pictures in her hands until Fitzie and Lucinda had removed them and passed them on to a group of fliers who were waiting to examine them, and whose reaction to what they saw was one of such unrestrained jubilation that Georgina, followed by Fitzie and Lucinda, had left the mess in tears.

"They had it coming," Fitzie had said, gently. The three of them had wandered past the deserted hangars and out onto the grass strip beside the runway. The air was cold. Frost crackled under their feet. The sky was clear and starry.

For Georgina, the bombing of Dresden was to prove to be another turning point in her confused convictions about war. Before arriving at the farm that day she had called at the woodman's cottage, expecting to be able to unburden herself to Christopher, knowing that he would understand and share her feelings. But all she found at the cottage was the note he had left for her in case she arrived unexpectedly. He was away on a week's course with the Forestry Commission. She had ridden back down the track and then turned right, into Post Stone valley, vaguely hoping for tea and sympathy from Alice Todd. Now, with the eyes of everyone upon her, she got to her feet and began winding her scarf round her neck.

"I'd better go," she said, tightly. "Sorry. I might have known how you'd all feel." Before Alice could dissuade her, she left them. They heard the bike engine, loudly breaking the afternoon silence. Then, in the kitchen, the ticking of the clock and the click of Rose's knitting needles were the only sounds.

"See?" Gwennan sighed, as though strangely satisfied by what had happened. "Once a conchie, always a conchie, I reckon!" She turned and stared at Alice. "Don't you think so, Mrs Todd?" she demanded, her hard eyes delivering a challenge which the warden chose to ignore.

Georgina's journey, from pacifism to ferry pilot for the RAF and now, it seemed, back to her earlier convictions, did not surprise Alice. Nor was she disposed to comment on it or debate it with Gwennan Pringle. Instead she turned to Rose and examined the small, white garment she was knitting.

"Is that for one of Mabel's twins?" she asked, expecting an affirmative answer.

"No it bain't!" Rose said, sharply. "Mabel's twins 'as got more'n enough woollies to last the pair o'em till kingdom come! Mrs Fred and Mrs Jack 'as been knittin' fit to bust since the minute they was born!"

"Who's it for, then, Mrs Crocker?" Annie asked.

"'Tis for Thurza, that's who!" Rose was slightly flushed and her needles were flying so fast there was a danger of dropped stitches.

"Thurza? Who's Thurza?" Winnie queried, turning to Marion, who shrugged.

"Thurza be Hester's child, that's who!" Rose announced firmly and everyone froze.

"Hester's child?" Gwennan repeated incredulously. "You're knittin' clothes for Hester's child?"

When Hester Tucker had climbed down from the lorry that had brought her from the bus stop in Ledburton, she stood out from the rest of the first intake of girls to arrive at the hostel that day. Unlike them, she was not wearing the Land Army uniform with which she had been issued at the recruitment centre and which remained, still in its cardboard box, at her feet and beside the carpet bag which contained the rest of her belongings. She stood, shivering, either from the cold February air or from the nervousness that overwhelmed her, and waited, miserably, to be told where to go and what to do. The other girls were sporting their dowdy uniforms with as much flair as was possible — hats on the backs of curly heads, belts tightly buckled round bulky jodhpurs, lips darkened with ruby-red lipstick and, in some cases, lashes stiff with mascara, while Hester's pale and anxious face was bereft of make-up, her skin scrubbed and almost transparent over delicate bones, her mass of fine, golden-blond hair drawn tightly back into a bun. Her shapeless clothes were in shades of brown and grey, her thick, woollen stockings and laced-up shoes, black.

Befriended by Annie, with whom she shared a bedroom, Hester slowly grew to trust the girls into whose company the war had thrust her. As the weeks and then months passed, the facts of her upbringing emerged.

She was the daughter of a religious zealot. A man who exerted an unhealthy dominance over his family and anyone who fell under his influence. The sect, in whose name he preached each Sabbath to a series of small, intimidated congregations who met in barns, deserted chapels and sometimes on the open cliff tops of the North Devon coast, had split, when Hester and her brother Zeke were still young children, from a less fanatical faith which was based in Plymouth.

Jonas Tucker spent most of his waking hours in prayer, working his smallholding only enough to provide a meagre living for his submissive wife and obedient children. He had been reluctant to deliver his elder child into the hands of the authorities when she turned eighteen and was required to do some form of war service, and had seen to it that she enrolled in the Women's Land Army, considering it to be a better option than exposing Zeke to the risk of conscription when, in a year's time, he would reach that age. A bit of farm work wouldn't hurt her, Jonas reckoned, and it would be one less mouth for him to feed. He was, at that time, ignorant of the reputation Land Army girls were acquiring.

Hester, brought up to fear her maker, had left home for the hostel with her father's harsh voice ringing in her ears, reminding her of his rules on modest apparel, no paint, and hair which must never be cut and should always be coiled out of sight. She knew better than to consort with strangers, would say grace before she ate, and go down on her knees night and morning. On Sundays, her father told her, members of the Brethren would collect her from Post Stone farm and convey her to their nearest meeting place for prayer and supplication.

As the weeks passed, Alice had witnessed a change in Hester. When she had first arrived she had flinched at the language she heard at the supper table and at the raucous laughter that greeted jokes which she didn't initially understand. But soon she began to respond to the warmth and good humour of her companions. Eventually she yielded to the temptation to try on the clothes they offered to lend her, and sometimes, when the girls were out dancing with soldiers or drinking with them in pubs, she experimented with the make-up which cluttered their dressing tables. Then, one Saturday afternoon she went into Exeter with

Georgina, visited a hairdresser for the first time in her life and had returned to the hostel, transformed and almost unrecognisable, with her hair floating around her head like Lizzie Siddal's in a painting by Dante Gabriel Rossetti.

"You wouldn't credit how that girl's come on since'er got yer!" Rose exclaimed to Alice on the first occasion when, after a lot of persuasion, Hester finally agreed to go with the land girls to a local hop.

It was a Saturday evening and Edward John was sitting at the kitchen table dipping fingers of bread into the yolk of the boiled egg that was his favourite supper. Rose had brought Alice a snapshot she had just received in which her son Dave was the centre of a group of khaki-clad conscripts who were peeling their way through a mound of potatoes.

"I'm that glad he's in the caterin' corps! Be worried sick if they'd given 'im a gun! It's his feet, see, too flat for the marchin' they said!" Rose paused, sliding the snapshot back into its already dog-eared envelope and comforted by the thought of Dave's comparative safety. "You reckon young Hester'll be all right, do you? Gaddin' about with our lot?"

Alice was well aware of the influences that were affecting Hester but she had confidence in the common sense of most of the other girls who, she rightly believed, would make sure the youngest and least experienced of the group came to no harm. They would keep an eye on her much as they would have protected a younger sister from unwelcome advances.

Over the preceding months, on the evenings when Hester had refused to go out and about with the other girls, she had begun to confide in the warden. Often confused, and even occasionally shocked, by the land girls' behaviour, she had confessed that her father, given the chance, would have consigned them all to the everlasting flames. But Hester soon came to understand that her fellows were, despite their sometimes brash manners, both good and kind, and that they were innocent of most of the evils her father had warned her of. She began to question his rules. Why was cutting her hair and wearing coloured frocks a sin? Whether or not her frock was blue and her hair floated prettily around her head, she knew right from wrong and would behave herself accordingly. When she asked Alice if she should go to the hop with the girls, Alice, knowing that both Georgina and Annie would be with her, had encouraged her to. She left, having been astonished and slightly disconcerted by her reflection, in a dress borrowed from Annie and shoes borrowed from Evie. She had even been persuaded to wear a trace of lipstick.

Then, at a cricket match — a light-hearted fraternisation between Alice's girls and a group of infantrymen training at a nearby army base — Hester had met Reuben Westerfeldt, an American GI who was as young and inexperienced as she. It had been love at first sight for both of them and had possessed all the overwhelming passion of a first infatuation, heightened by the war and the threat of looming separation. Rose's Dave, who, during a brief leave, had encountered

Hester, carried the image of her back to his barracks and found himself unable to think of anyone else, had stood little chance against Reuben Westerfeldt who proposed to Hester, was accepted and, despite her father's refusal to approve the engagement or attend the wedding ceremony, married her.

Rose, observing her son, had from the beginning been aware of the intensity of his feelings for Hester Tucker and had warned him that she was already spoken for. Nevertheless she felt then, as she was increasingly to feel, that fate had somehow failed not only her boy but the girl he wanted so much. The two of them were, Rose felt, suited. More than suited. They were destined. Both were Devonian born and bred. Both spoke with the same soft accent and, before the advent of Reuben, there had been, Rose was certain, an attraction between the two of them at their first, brief meeting.

"But you can't 'ave 'er, son!" she told Dave, when, on leave shortly after the wedding, he slouched aimlessly about her cottage and refused to socialise with his village friends. "She'm a married lady now and that's that!" Dave sat, looking, his mother noticed, and despite his low spirits, a picture of health and strength. His robust frame, the shock of thick, chestnut hair and lustrous, dark eyes still reminded her of the chubby baby she had suckled. But sometime between his sixteenth and seventeenth birthdays, and following the unexpected death of his father, Dave had become a man, and now, at almost twenty and despite his flat feet, was approaching his prime. "'Tis no good you

70

sulkin' like a spoilt brat, Dave! I know's you spotted 'er afore Reuben come on the scene but 'twas Reuben she wanted and Reuben she got and there's an end to it!" Her words, she knew, were falling on deaf ears, yet she persisted. "Eileen says as 'er niece Albertine were askin' after you las' week. 'Er works as barmaid over to The Anchor at Lower Bowden these days. Ever such a nice girl she be. Alus liked you, Albertine did. You should go see her, Dave. Better nor broodin' about the place sighin' after some girl you can't 'ave!"

But Dave was remembering Boxing Day when, Reuben having returned to his barracks, he had taken Hester tobogganing. He had settled her between his thighs and kept her safe while they flew downhill and she shrieked with the thrill of it, the cold air making her cheeks glow, snow crystals catching in her pale lashes, and he had loved her so much it seemed impossible that she couldn't feel it. And perhaps she did feel it. And perhaps it had disturbed her. But Reuben had slipped his grandma's ruby ring onto her finger only twelve hours previously and there it was, like a drop of blood, the tiny diamonds surrounding the central stone, glittering in the winter sunlight, reminding her of Reuben's whispered promises. And the next day Dave too was gone, back to his unit with the catering corps.

By May, Hester, three months married, was pregnant. With Reuben soon to be deployed in the Allied invasion of northern France, the American military authorities decided to ship Hester, along with a few hundred other GI brides, out to the States as soon as was feasible. Her pregnancy meant that she could no longer be employed as a land girl and her parents had disowned her, so light domestic work had been found for her at the two farmhouses while she awaited embarkation.

Three weeks after the D-Day landings, news of Reuben's death reached Hester and she had withdrawn into a private world of grief, into which her father had briefly and cruelly intruded, telling her that because she had defied him she was cursed and that her sins would bring the wrath of God down onto the heads of all whose lives touched hers.

While Alice was shocked by the effect Jonas Tucker's visit had on his daughter, and concerned by the distress it caused her, Rose wrestled with more complicated concerns. Hester's widowhood made it likely that, after a while, Dave would approach her. Rose's feelings about this were confused. While she was fond of Hester and, in other circumstances, would have welcomed her as a daughter-in-law, and although Reuben had been a fine, upstanding lad, she was not entirely happy with the prospect of her son raising another man's child, having, understandably enough, expected her grandchildren to have been sired by her own son, rather than by someone else's. This, however, was not her main concern, which lay with Hester's mental state. Her subservience to her father and to his fanatical religious beliefs seemed, to Rose, to have affected her sanity.

Rose had watched, from her cottage window, when Dave, on a twenty-four-hour pass, approached Hester in the cider apple orchard. She guessed, correctly, that he was asking her to be his wife and promising to raise

Reuben's child as his own, and she knew, by the droop of his shoulders as Hester left him, that she had refused him.

"I don't know what to think an' that's a fact!" she confided miserably to Alice. "It bain't so much the babe, 'cos Reuben were a nice enough lad an' died for his country an' all."

"And for ours, Rose," Alice added, quietly.

"Yes, and for ours. I knows that, Alice . . . But you can see what I mean, I'm sure. A woman would rather have her own son's flesh and blood for a grandchild . . . But, no. It bain't just that, see, 'tis Hester herself, poor child! She's . . . well . . . a bit . . . odd, bain't she, Alice? Which be understandable, what with losing poor Reuben and the way her father do go on! I never heard of a religion so full of evil! 'Ow would my Dave cope with all that? I don't reckon 'twas Reuben's death as drove Hester half out of'er mind, neither! T'was more likely her father and what he said to 'er that day he come 'ere! You 'eard 'im! Wicked it were! Poor child. I don't know . . . And now she's sayin' she don't want to go to Reuben's folks over in America! When that would surely be the best thing all round!" Rose paused, hoping for Alice's approval of this solution to Hester's problems. "Don't you reckon it would be?" Alice kept to herself her honest opinion, which was that for Rose, Hester's immediate departure for Bismarck, North Dakota, might have been the "best thing", but for Hester herself, for her unborn child and possibly for Dave, too, it might not be. The warden's silence on the subject did not escape Rose.

The land girls, who were keenly following every twist and turn of Hester's story, were more outspoken.

"I reckon you'd be 'appy to see the back of her, Mrs Crocker," was Gwennan's opinion. "Pack her off with the other GI brides, eh? Then p'raps your Dave would settle for some nice local girl with a dad who's not a ravin' loony like that Jonas Tucker!"

"I just want what's best for Hester," Rose declared emphatically, but the other girls were clearly sceptical and the discussion would have continued had Alice not put a stop to it.

Two days later Hester vanished. Although officially, having left the Land Army, her welfare was no longer its responsibility, Margery Brewster, as local village registrar, assuming that Hester had returned to her parents' smallholding in north Devon, had persuaded the Ministry of Agriculture to allocate to her enough petrol for her to drive over the moor to confirm Hester's safe arrival there.

While Margery's description of what she found — the near derelict cottage, Hester tremulous and silent under the sharp eyes of her hostile parents — had depressed everyone at the hostel, it was Rose who was most lastingly affected by it. She knew that Dave's feelings for Hester were unlikely to change and was unsurprised when, months later, when the time had passed when the baby's birth was due, Dave rode his bicycle north-westwards, over the moor.

The baby girl, he told his mother when he arrived home, soaked to the skin by icy, November rain, was to be called Thurza. Hester seemed well enough, although her father was now bedridden, cursed, Hester insisted, by the same evil that her sins had brought down on all her family.

"First Reuben," she had told Dave, "then my father, getting the fallin' down sickness, and if I don't repent, t'will soon be my baby! Stay away from me, Dave, or it could be you who's next to suffer for my sins!"

"So she be just the same, then?" Rose asked Dave while he sat, his clothes steaming, sipping hot tea by her fire. "About the religion and that?"

"Yeah," he said, dully, "she be just the same. But I can't let go of her, Mum. I won't never let go of Hester."

Rose bought a rag doll for Thurza's first Christmas and Dave wrote a message to go with it and posted it in mid December at Ledburton post office. They did not hear from Hester and did not know that her mother, on her father's instructions, had burnt the doll in the grate on the day it arrived. Hester had read Dave's message before her mother threw it, too, into the flames. In it he promised to fetch her whenever she would come to him and told her he would love her for ever.

With her son now serving in northern France, Rose found herself consumed with anxiety not only for him but, because he loved her, for Hester herself and for the child whom she had begun, almost without realising it, to regard as her granddaughter. "Matinee jackets is all very well, Thurza," she murmured to herself, knitting needles clicking as she cast on the required number of stitches, "but what a little girl needs this time of year is leggin's! Nice, warm, woolly leggin's!" So she knitted leggings and the land girls, asking who the baby clothes were for, were amazed when she told them.

"How on earth did you get there, Rose?" Alice asked, one late afternoon a few weeks later, when Rose arrived back from her trek across the moor to the Tucker smallholding.

"Got the early bus from Exeter to Bideford and started walkin'," she said. "Then a fellow in a milk truck give me a lift! Right to the Tuckers' gate! And 'e said as 'e'd give a toot on his horn on his way back!"

"And did you see Hester?"

"I did," said Rose, crisply. "She come out the cottage and we stood in the yard with her ma peepin' through the curtains at us! I give her the leggin's and she were that pleased! She said to tell Dave she got his message at Christmas and thanked him for the doll, but when I asked her if Thurza liked it she looked away. She said her father can't walk no more and Zeke was called up some time ago. Down the mines, they've sent 'im. In Wales. Bevin Boys, they're called . . . I don't know how they Tuckers live, Alice! Their place be that run-down! Then Hester said she must go back inside, but she come to the window with Thurza in her arms, so I could 'ave a look at 'er. She's a bonny child. Golden curls, she's got, just like her mother's. And the same blue eyes! But she shouldn't be there, Alice. Not in that house. Not with that man. Neither of 'em should be."

With the twins thriving, their parents respectably married, Mabel now in charge of the dairy and the proud mistress of the newly installed milking machine, all should have been well in the Vallance household. But it was not so. Despite the fact that Germany was facing inevitable defeat, the V2 rocket assaults on the south-east of England continued, as, in consequence, did Mabel's concern for her firstborn who, since his inappropriate birth, when she had been barely sixteen, had been virtually adopted by Mabel's grandmother, a woman now in her early eighties and in declining health. Encouraged by the news that her granddaughter was now a married woman with not only a husband and a home of her own but also now with twin babies, Ada Hodges had written, in her laboured, cursive hand, to ask when she might expect to be relieved of the responsibility of raising her great-grandchild.

Ferdie's assumed ignorance of Arthur's true parentage overlooked the fact that although his mind might work in the same lurching, uncertain and hesitant way as his damaged leg, he nevertheless possessed the practical, slow-burning shrewdness common to Devonians. Without descending into artful cunning, Ferdie was astute and observant enough to have come to the conclusion that Mabel's feelings for little Arthur were stronger than is usual between a girl and her baby brother. Where Arthur was concerned Mabel was not merely fond and affectionate, she was defensive, protective and passionate. More, in fact, like a mother than a big sister. Perhaps, possibly without being conscious of it, Ferdie may have absorbed a half-heard piece of gossip, or caught the expressions on the faces of his wife's fellow land girls when, on visits to the farm, they had observed the relationship between the plump and motherly girl and the little boy who so closely resembled her. Whichever way it had happened, Ferdie, possibly by a process of osmosis, found himself in possession of the fact that Arthur was Mabel's child. Concerning a decision about how this fact should be addressed, Ferdie had made little or no progress and had failed to respond satisfactorily to Mabel's increasingly frequent references to it.

"Me Gran's poorly," she told him one day, after carefully rereading the old lady's most recent letter. "She reckons Arthur'd be better off here with me now I'm married. So what d'you reckon, Ferdie?" She watched her husband consider this while he forked his way through a plate of baked beans which, with a solitary sausage and a pile of mashed swede, was all Mabel had managed to produce for his supper that evening. "Gran says that three kids is no more work than two."

"Do she now!" he mumbled, with his mouth full. "An what about the dairy? The boss be payin' you to run 'is milkin' machine, Mabel, not to play sadie sadie, married lady!"

"Mrs Jack and Mrs Fred'll keep an eye on Arthur, you knows that. And the twins is good as gold — so long as me milk holds out. And by the look of me," she said glancing down confidently at her impressive breasts, "these'll keep 'em quiet for a good few months yet!"

But Ferdie would not commit himself, and tension grew in the tiny cottage which always seemed to smell of something. Washing. Tom cats. Dirty nappies. Ferdie's pipe. Mabel's milk . . .

Until, one morning, Margery Brewster, driving between hostels on her usual rounds, saw, ahead of her in the lane, a familiar figure. She was surprised to recognise Mabel Hodges or rather Mrs Ferdinand Vallance as Mabel had recently become. Mabel, striding strongly towards the railway station, had, tucked under each of her arms, a baby.

The village registrar slowed her car to walking pace beside Mabel, wound down her window and asked her what on earth she thought she was doing. Mabel kept walking.

"If he won't 'ave all of us, 'e's not 'avin' none of us!" she announced with breathless emphasis.

Margery Brewster knew the facts of Mabel's irregular history and that the small boy whom she had at first insisted was her brother was, in fact, her son, but it took her some time to understand that Mabel, exasperated by her husband's prevarication, had decided to deprive him of her presence and that of their twins until he agreed to absorb little Arthur into his family. "It's no good your sayin' nothin', Mrs Brewster! I've been that patient with Ferdie you wouldn't believe! Now me mind's made up!" Mabel had stopped walking and was standing, breathing heavily. The weight of her two robust babies was considerable, and tired of being jolted along and clutched too tightly, both were now writhing noisily. "I'm off to me gran's," Mabel announced, shouting above the clamour of the twins. "If he wants us he'll have to come and get us! And if I stands 'ere talkin' I'm gonna miss me flippin' train!" She strode on, staggering slightly, under the weight of her wailing babies.

Margery hesitated briefly and then, almost as much to her own surprise as to Mabel's, moved alongside her.

"Get in the car, Mabel!" she said. "Quickly!"

After depositing Mabel on the station platform, Margery drove back to the farm to find Ferdie standing in the centre of the yard, a look of total devastation on his usually placid face.

"It's me Mabel!" he told her. "Me Mabel's gone! And she's took me twins wiv 'er!"

Three hours later, after a long and serious discussion with Margery Brewster, which was followed by a shorter one, involving Roger Bayliss and Alice Todd, and which focused on the needs of the farm as opposed to the drama within the Vallance household, Ferdie capitulated. He wanted his twins and his wife back, and having been encouraged to regard little Arthur as his stepson, promised to be a proper father to him. Ferdie put on his wedding suit, and with Mabel's London address on a piece of paper in his breast pocket, boarded the next London train.

"But how on earth will he find her?" Alice wondered, as she and Roger stood on the platform at Ledburton Halt and waved goodbye to Ferdie whose face, as he was borne away, wore the look of a man delivered neck and crop to the will of God. "He's never been to London before!"

Ferdie found a seat in the smoky compartment in which four dishevelled soldiers were already sprawled, two asleep and two playing cards for matchsticks.

"Got wounded, did yer?" one asked, having noticed Ferdie's limp as he lurched into the carriage.

"In a manner of speakin'," Ferdie told him, "but not in the war. A rollin' tractor did for me. I works on the land, see." The soldier inhaled the last fumes from his roll-up and narrowed his eyes against the smoke.

"So where're you off to now, then?" he asked, and Ferdie paused before replying that he was going to London to fetch home his wife and kids who were visiting her family. He produced the scrap of paper on which the warden had printed the address of Mabel's grandmother.

"Over to some place called Deptford, she be," he added, vaguely. The soldier ground his fag end into the littered floor.

"That's where our Charlie's headin', innit, mate!" he said, nudging his companion's shin with the toe of his boot.

This chance encounter with Corporal Charlie Arnold proved to be a blessing to Ferdie, who otherwise might never have found his way out of Paddington station, let alone across London to the distant neighbourhood where Mabel had arrived some hours previously. He limped after Charlie as they crossed the city on an underground train, rode on one bus and then on another. Then, with Charlie's instructions ringing in his confused ears, Ferdie had negotiated a final maze of grimy streets, checked the address against the scrap of paper Alice Todd had given him and knocked on a door which had been opened by Mabel. His Mabel.

Within three hours, his wife trotting beside him and towing Arthur by the hand, Ferdie Vallance, with a twin under each of his arms, had recrossed London and installed himself and his family in the overcrowded carriage of a train that was due to arrive at Ledburton Halt late that evening.

Ferdie was never quite the same after that. What he had undertaken and what he had achieved amazed him. He had followed Charlie down tunnels, ridden in strange trains that turned day into night, climbed on and off buses that had seats upstairs as well as down, the like of which he had seen only in cinema newsreels. He had made his way along streets where the brickwork was as black as the inside of a country chimney. He had found Mabel and his twins and fetched them home. It was true that he had been made to agree to give young Arthur his name and raise him as his own but that, he assured himself, had always been his intention. He just hadn't got round to it as fast as Mabel had expected, that was all. He was a family man now. A man with responsibilities. He had even been to London. The thin, limping man, who, when Mabel first arrived at the Post Stone farms, had been living in a filthy hovel, his clothes unwashed and his cupboard, more often than not, bare, was now a husband and a father of three, with food in his pantry and a fire warming his kitchen.

Three weeks later and with Roger Bayliss's solicitor handling the legal side of Arthur's adoption, the little boy was christened, together with his infant half-brother and -sister. From that day on he became known as Arthur George (after the King) Vallance.

"Lunnon?" Ferdie would brag at every opportunity. "Bin to Lunnon? 'Course I 'as! Wouldn't give 'e tuppence for it, though! Bain't no place for my family! Fetched 'em home quick smart, I did!"

A mild, moist spring, followed in mid-April by warm sunshine, meant that an early crop of hay was almost ready for mowing by the first week in May, by which time the war in Europe was dragging through its final days. Although the news had not yet been made public, Adolf Hitler had already perished in his bunker. The land girls had pored over newspapers displaying gruesome and grainy photographs of Mussolini, his bullet-riddled body swinging by his heels above a crowd of jeering Italians.

"I s'pose they'll be sendin' the Eyetie POWs 'ome now, won't they, Mrs Todd?" Evie asked, and Alice said yes, she supposed they would be.

The world seemed to hold its breath until, at one minute after midnight on Tuesday May the eighth, the end of the war with Germany was officially declared.

That day church bells rang. Special prayers were said in schools from which the children poured, allowed home early, to celebrate. The horns of vehicles blared through towns and villages. Trains roared across the countryside, the drivers sounding their whistles in a continuous, triumphant screech and waving out of their cabs at everyone — and everyone waved back.

At the higher farm, Roger Bayliss, defying regulations, had a pig slaughtered and set to roast above a fire supervised by Ferdie Vallance, Mr Jack and Mr Fred, whose wives, together with Eileen, Mabel and Rose, set about turning any food they could lay their hands on into buns and puddings and pies. Land girls from some of the other, smaller hostels in the neighbourhood were to join the Post Stone girls and bring with them their own contributions to the festivities, and by six o'clock, having rushed through their evening ablutions in record time, curled their hair, applied their make-up and put on their prettiest frocks, Alice's girls had arrived at the higher farm, where they were joined by Margery Brewster and her groups of land girls from nearby hostels and where they had all been greeted by the intoxicating smell of pork, perfectly roasted over a fire which was now reduced to a shimmering pile of powdery, white-hot ashes, and were clustering round the barrel from which Mr Jack was filling glass after glass with cider.

Trestle tables covered in white sheets ran the length of the yard and would be lit, as the light faded, by a row of oil lamps and candles placed down the centre of each. Every chair, bench, milking stool and garden seat at Higher Post Stone and from the labourers' cottages had been commandeered. Roger Bayliss presided at one end of the table, with Alice on his right and Margery Brewster on his left, Gordon, her beaming husband, beside her. Then came the farm workers and their wives and then the Post Stone land girls and their visitors.

Two hours later, when everyone had eaten all the food, drunk all the cider and sung all the songs, Roger Bayliss got to his feet, and followed by Margery Brewster, spoke solemnly about the ending of the war with Germany and of the land girls' contribution to the victory. Then they all charged their glasses, rose to their feet and drank two toasts, one to the King and one to Winston Churchill.

"'Ere's to Winnie!" the girls roared. "Good ol' Winnie!" This was followed by "For He's a Jolly Good Fellow" and the national anthem.

Edward John, who had been fetched home from boarding school, was given the honour of putting a taper to the towering bonfire which had been assembled that afternoon and stood in an adjacent field, safely downwind of the farmhouse. He could only dimly remember the pre-war firework parties, the last of which he had been taken to at the age of six. He stood back from the growing heat of the fire, watching, round-eyed, as the flames took hold, curling towards a pale sky. The bells in Ledburton church tower were ringing again but their sound was soon drowned by the roar of the bonfire and the shouts of laughter as everyone joined hands, and with glowing faces and shining eyes, moved round it in a wide, noisy circle.

That day Christopher had caught, borne on the wind and from various distances, the sound of church bells pealing in the belfries of the steeples scattered across the valley his woodland overlooked. For five years the ringing of bells would have announced an invasion by the German army, something which, during the early years of the war, had seemed inevitable. Today, with that army routed and its leaders captured or dead, the bells confirmed that the news everyone had been waiting for had finally broken. Hoping that Georgina might have snatched a few hours leave in order to join her parents to celebrate it, Christopher drove the truck, cross-country, to their farm.

"She telephoned," her mother told him and was touched by the disappointment in his face. "But there was some official celebration at the base at White Waltham which she had to attend. She hopes to be home in a day or so and I'm sure she'll come and see you then. I believe she has some news for you," she added, smiling. "Don't ask me what. I'm sure she wants to tell you herself."

Christopher was struck, forcefully but not for the first time, by how closely Isabel Webster resembled her daughter. She was regarding him now with the same direct eyes and the same quizzical expression that Georgina often wore. She caught his look.

"What?" she asked, smiling.

"Nothing! I mean . . . I hadn't noticed before how incredibly alike you and Georgie are."

"That is because," Georgina's father said, his pipe clenched between his teeth, "when my daughter is here your eyes are on her and not on her mother! Which is, of course, just as it should be!"

Two days later the sound of Lionel's motorbike broke the silence of the woodland and Georgina was dismounting, unwinding her scarf and welcoming Christopher's kiss.

"You are looking at a person who has just resigned their commission!" she announced, stepping back from him and executing a neat RAF salute. "In four weeks' time I'll be in Civvy Street!"

He led her through a stand of beech trees where new foliage, which would darken as the summer proceeded, was still a fragile lettuce green above drifts of bluebells. They lay down together on a rustling pile of last year's fallen leaves. Their lovemaking had become a sequence of enchanting encounters. They treasured the privacy of the woodman's cottage but once, on her father's land, a thunderstorm had driven them into a barn where a pile of hay had proved irresistible. On another rainy occasion, on the way back from a farm sale where Christopher had bought some equipment, they had been suddenly so overcome that Christopher had driven the truck up a green lane and they had made love with the rain drumming on the cab roof. Days became weeks and then a month had passed and they had not told either her parents or his father their plans.

Since the day, many months previously, when Gwennan, self-diagnosed with the cancer that would surely kill her, had spitefully deprived Marion of a letter intended for her from her GI admirer, she had frequently experienced a frisson of shame. But, she persuaded herself, what was done was done. How could she undo it, even if she wanted to? The letter lay where it had fallen when she had deliberately let it slip from the shelf of the kitchen dresser where the land girls' mail was always propped, ready for them to claim when they arrived back from work. It had lain now for many months, undetected amongst the dusty cobwebs caught between the massive piece of furniture and the wall against which it stood. What possible reason was there to pull the dresser away from the wall? How, otherwise, would the letter ever be discovered? After six months or so had passed, Gwennan had half-hoped that Rose, while spring cleaning the kitchen, might have found it but, probably because of the weight of the dresser, she obviously had not attempted to sweep behind it.

Then, on a thundery evening, not long after the VE Day celebrations, when the girls were polishing off their rice pudding, Evie screamed shrilly and pointed at something that was crawling clumsily across the kitchen floor.

"It's only a bat!" Annie said. "Shut up, Evie, or you'll scare it!" Whether it was Evie's scream or Annie's approach, the little creature took fright, scurried across the slate floor and inserted itself into the tiny space between the dresser and the wall.

"Best leave 'im," Rose said. "'E'll come out when he sees fit."

"But 'e might get stuck!"

"'E could die be'ind there!"

"And then 'e'll stink!"

Gwennan watched as four of the girls heaved at the dresser and, struggling with its weight, managed to ease one end of it a few inches away from the wall. They craned forward, peering into the dark space.

"Ooooh, there it is! Yuck!"

"It's horrible!"

"Don't go near it!" Winnie shrieked. "It's a vampire! They suck your blood, they do! And then you die! I saw it at the pictures!"

The bat had crawled as far as it could from the looming, shouting faces and had wedged itself tightly into the sharp angle where the dresser touched the wainscot.

"Out the way!" Rose ordered. She'd show them how a true country woman deals with such things. With one firm stroke of her besom she drew the little creature towards her, lifted it off the floor in the folds of her apron and shook it out of the kitchen window where it flickered away into the twilight. "Don't go moving the dresser back," she said, "'til I fetch me dustpan and brush and sweep be'ind it." The girls watched as Rose lowered herself onto her knees, reached forward and began to raise the dust, muttering virtuously about making a proper job of it whilst she was at it. "There be a comb behind 'ere," she announced, her voice muffled in the confined space. "And a pencil . . ." She emerged, crawling breathlessly backwards and sat on her heels, a spider's web caught in her greying hair, the comb and the pencil safely in her dustpan. "And there's this!" she said, brandishing a letter.

The letter was thick with dust. Something had nibbled at one corner and the ink of the address was smudged.

For one unguarded moment Gwennan's eyes were locked onto the envelope. Then she gathered herself.

"Who's it for, then?" she asked, as casually as she could. Rose peered at the scrawled address.

"Can't see without me specs," she said, handing the letter to Winnie.

"Marion!" Winnie read. "Miss Marion Grice!" Her face was alight with excitement as she turned the letter over. The name and rank of the sender were printed on the reverse side. "Oh, Marion! It's from the little sergeant! He didn't die after all! And he's wrote to you! I just knew he would! Oh, Marion! He's wrote to you!"

"Give it here, then!" Marion said abruptly, and with her eyes lowered, took the letter and left the kitchen. They heard the creak of the stairs. The faces of the other girls were alive with curiosity and speculation. They remembered the stocky GI sergeant who had taken a shine to Marion and then vanished, as so many men had, lost, more often than not permanently, in the chaos of the war.

"Fancy that!" Gwennan said, experiencing a strange sensation of relief that her long deception had ended and even feeling that now the letter had at last reached its destination, she was perhaps, after all, innocent of causing its disappearance. Whatever the sensation was, it somehow reduced her defensiveness. "Stuck behind there!" she exclaimed. "All that time!"

"All what time?" Winnie asked sharply. But Gwennan was ready for her, her latent shrewdness instantly back in place.

"How should I know?" she answered easily, shrugging her thin shoulders. "Long enough to get covered in cobwebs and chewed by a mouse, I s'pose." She turned to Alice, and with an expression which came as close to innocence as she ever achieved, asked for an aspirin. "'Cos I feel like I might be comin' down with something, Mrs Todd."

CHAPTER
FOUR

Dear Marion, the sergeant's letter began,
I should have wrote you soon as I got your photo which I have carried with me next to my heart ever since. I would have done but a training exercise went wrong and I was the only guy in my section to survive. It was hushed up because of D-Day being only weeks away but it was a rough time for me and I felt like my luck had run out and what was the point of worrying you when I most likely would not come marching home like it says in the songs. But I never stopped thinking about you babe and after I came through the Normandy landings I started to feel lucky, so here I am, writing to my girl. It would be just great to hear from you but I guess that things might have moved on for you after all these months. Anyhow, like the man says here's lookin' at you kid.

From your devoted and loving Marvin J. Kinski. Sergeant.

"I dunno what to do, Mrs Todd!" Marion sat in Alice's room, her fingers pulling at the scrap of lace on the corner of her damp handkerchief. "I mean, I'm ever so glad to hear from 'im and that he's alive and not wounded or nowt but I can't let our Win down over the pub, can I? We swore an oath that we'd go it alone, Win and me! We didn't want no men interfering with our plan, and we've been saving up our money and everything was in order . . . Then along comes Marvin!" Alice looked at Marion's anguished face, which today appeared somehow softened by her confused feelings. The crudely bleached hair had always contrasted too strongly with her hard, dark eyes and absurdly plucked brows. The thick mascara on her lashes, and the beetroot-red lipstick she wore when dressed for going out, had given her face the harsh, bandbox veneer of the film stars whose appearance she tried so hard to match. But today, in the diffused light of Alice's room, her face devoid of make-up and her hair slightly tousled, the brown eyes soft and expressive, she looked, the warden realised, almost vulnerable. Alice had assumed that, being an American, what had attracted Sergeant Kinski to this flashy, north-country land girl was her boldness, the brash, shiny, "come hither" quality of the style in which she presented herself. The face confronting Alice would never be a beautiful one, the nose was too long and the jaw too strong. But there was, Alice saw that day, an underlying sensitivity, almost a delicacy about the basic structure of it. Was it possible that Kinski, as well as enjoying her glamour, had seen through the veneer and identified in Marion other qualities that he valued?

"What does Winnie think about all this?" Alice asked.

"Dunno," Marion replied, thoughtfully. "She likes Marvin. Always calls him 'the little sergeant', on account of he's not that tall." Alice asked whether the two friends had ever discussed the possibility that one or the other of them might, for whatever reason, want to withdraw from their shared ambition to run a pub together. Marion considered this for a while. "Not really. We'd sort of got into the habit of it. Like it was fixed." She pointed into the air in front and slightly above her eyeline. "Like a star you follows. Like the three kings in the Bible." Then she caught Alice's slightly baffled expression and laughed briefly. "We thought we might have to give up because of not 'avin' enough money, but never because one of us might not want to do it no more. We never, ever, thought of that. P'raps we should 'ave . . . And anyhow it's not like the sergeant's asked me or anything, Mrs Todd. It's months since he wrote that letter, and what with it getting lost . . . He most prob'ly thinks I'm not bothered."

"But you are bothered, aren't you?" Alice asked her. Marion sat in silence for a moment or two, considering this.

"Yeah. I reckon I am," she said.

"Then perhaps you should write to him."

"But what about Winnie?"

"One thing at a time, Marion. It might help to start by sorting out how things stand between you and your sergeant, mmm?"

"Yeah. I should of thought of that meself, Mrs Todd."

"You would have done, Marion."

"Yes, I 'spect I would of done, on'y I was a bit took by surprise."

"Quite understandably."

"I feel like a marriage broker," Alice said, after explaining the situation to Roger Bayliss who, over the next days, used some military contacts to discover the whereabouts of Sergeant Marvin Kinski.

"I've managed to get a US army address Marion can write to, but apart from the fact that Kinski was involved in the invasion of Okinawa in April they can't, or won't, give any more information than that."

"Okinawa!" Alice exclaimed. "Our lovers could hardly be further apart, then!" She gave this news, together with the address, to Marion.

"Okinawa!" she echoed, her face falling. "That's in China or somewhere, isn't it?"

"Japan, actually," Alice told her.

"Well it might as well be China, mighten it?" Marion muttered, depressed and then brightening slightly when Alice pointed out that at least this information confirmed that Marvin was alive and well.

"He don't half get around, your little sergeant!" Winnie said, when Marion shared her news. Alice was uncertain whether or not the two friends were ready to address the problem of what was to become of their long-standing plans should the sergeant's feelings for Marion have survived the intervening months.

"He might 'ave gone off of her, after all this time," was Gwennan's contribution to one of the land girls' speculative discussions on the subject. She continued to experience a sense of relief that her own involvement in the situation was over, and resisted a desire to share her true opinion, which was that in view of Marion's shady reputation, Sergeant Kinski would be better off without her.

Over the next few evenings Marion wrote and rewrote her letter.

Dear Marvin,

In the kitchen there is a dresser where our letters get put ready for us when we come back from work of an evening. Only your letter must of slipped down the back because the other day a bat crawled behind it. We had to move it to get the bat out and there was your letter that you wrote to me last summer. It was in a bit of a mess and something had chewed off a corner but I knew straight off it was from you, dearest Marvin and I was that glad to hear you are OK and I'm pleased you like the snap of me in the river but it wasn't me as sent it, see. It was my friend Winnie. I will explain why some time but it is complicated. Anyhow I didn't know she had sent it til months later. Harvest time it was when she told me and I never got your answer because it were down behind the dresser by then and god knows where you was. We thought you must be dead because of so many GIs getting killed on D-Day. Poor Hester's Reuben did. I never stopped thinking about you Marvin and lately I have been thinking about you more and more but now you are in blooming China. [She crossed out China and replaced it with Japan.] I hope you will get this letter, not like the one you sent to me. It says on the wireless that the Japs will give in soon so take care and come home safe to your ever loving Marion who is waiting for you because there is nobody like you, Marvin nor ever was.

From M. Grice XXX.

With the war in Europe over, everyone at the Post Stone farms was conscious of approaching change. For years it had been possible to accept the status quo, and the phrase "for the duration" had been an easy way to avoid serious thought about a post-war future. The demobilisation of the armed forces would be a slow process, so there was no immediate threat to the survival of the hostel, but Roger Bayliss was aware that, with an increasing dependence on mechanisation and the eventual return to the farm of Rose Crocker's Dave and of Mr and Mrs Jack's son, Archie, an able seaman on minesweepers — both of whom had applied for early release on the grounds that their labour was needed on his farms — a time would come when the number of land girls whose labour he required would be too few to justify the use of the lower farmhouse as a hostel. What began to disturb Roger was not the prospect of losing the girls but of losing Alice. Although the warmth, even the intimacy of their friendship, was slowly increasing, he had not yet disclosed to her the depth of his feelings for her or his overwhelming desire to cease to be simply her affectionate friend and become her passionate lover and husband — though not necessarily in that order. When she spoke with enthusiasm of the likelihood of a future involving consultancy work in the catering industry, Roger was obliged to take a polite and even encouraging interest, although the tension this produced gave Alice the impression of a detachment on his part which was in direct contrast with his feelings. The fact that Alice was privy to Georgina and Christopher's plans, not only to marry but to emigrate, on which subjects she was sworn to secrecy, made her guard her tongue in case she unwittingly revealed something which might rouse Roger's suspicions.

Weeks passed in which the farmer and his warden continued to see each other socially as well as professionally. She, wearing a sleek, black velvet dress that almost stopped Roger's breath, partnered him at a Farmers' Union celebration during the victory celebrations. As they danced, the closeness of Roger's embrace had pleased both of them, but although their eye contact had expressed an unashamed intimacy, their conversation had failed to match it.

Margery Brewster took it upon herself to counsel the land girls about their post-war plans and prospects, interviewing them, one at a time, on a Sunday morning in the recreation room at Lower Post Stone.

She was an observant woman where the girls in her charge were concerned and it had not escaped her that Gwennan Pringle was looking thinner and more gaunt than usual.

"And how are you, Miss Pringle?" she asked her. The registrar always referred to the Welsh girl as "Miss Pringle" rather than as Gwennan, or Taffy, which was how the other land girls addressed her. Gwennan enjoyed the distinction but was uncertain of the registrar's motives. Was she "Miss Pringle" because she was the senior girl at the hostel and as such deserved respect? Or was it some sort of joke? Despite the possibility of it being a joke, Gwennan liked Margery Brewster. She had been sympathetic when Gwennan's sister had died and, occasionally, when the other girls' behaviour threatened to bring the Land Army into disrepute, Mrs Brewster's disapproval matched Gwennan's, bolstering her sense of self-righteousness.

"I'm quite all right, thank you, Mrs Brewster," she lied. When asked if she had made any plans for the peacetime life which Mrs Brewster assumed lay ahead of her, Gwennan had replied, coolly, that she had a sister in Vancouver and had thought of settling there. In fact, she had no intention of emigrating, being convinced that her illness, if nothing else, would prevent her. Margery, clearly excluded from the details of Gwennan's plans and feeling put down by her lack of response to what was, after all, a kindly interest, wished her well and hoped she would be happy in Canada.

Margery had assumed that Annie Sorokova, having done so well in her Ministry of Agriculture exams, was likely to apply for a job as a farm manager and was surprised to hear that this was not the case.

"I want to be a librarian," Annie told her, and went on to expand on her plan, which was to return to

London, enrol in evening classes and work as an assistant librarian until she was fully qualified. "It's all arranged," she told the registrar. "My friend Hector helped me with the application forms, and his father, who is a don at Oxford, wrote me a reference. You look ever so surprised, Mrs Brewster!" Margery had known of Georgina's interest in Annie's education, but not that Roger Bayliss had given her access to his modest library, where she had diligently made her way through the books on Georgina's list of required reading, and which had introduced her not only to Dickens and Thackeray but to Thomas Hardy, Scott Fitzgerald and H.G. Wells.

"Well done, Hannah Maria," Margery said, reverting to the name on Annie's enrolment form and recalling the young Jewess who had arrived at Lower Post Stone farm with no experience of the countryside and a background confined to the East End garment factory owned by her family, where, had it not been for the war, she would probably have spent her life. "Very well done indeed, my dear!"

While Margery quizzed first one and then another of the land girls about their plans, some of which were as simple as a desire to "go 'ome and stay 'ome, thanks very much!", Margery herself faced the unappealing prospect of resuming her own pre-war existence. She would explore the possibility of making herself available to various local charities, but she knew that none of them would offer the responsibility, the status or the sense of achievement that being a village registrar in Lady Denham's Women's Land Army had brought her.

She would miss the contact not only with Alice but with several of the other hostel wardens in the Ledburton area, and the satisfaction of being useful and sometimes important amongst her colleagues and to the young women in her charge. There were girls she had been able to help with personal problems when they had turned to her for advice. On several occasions she had been instrumental in averting disasters and, as she had once revealed to Alice, she was ashamed of the fact that she actually dreaded the end of the war and her inevitable return to the humdrum existence she had endured before it.

After her interviews, Margery joined Alice in her bed-sitting room and eagerly accepted the glass or two of sherry which Alice felt almost obliged to offer her. As she sipped, Margery ran through her findings, closing her file of notes on the Post Stone girls with a heavy sigh.

"And what will *you* do?" Alice asked her, hoping that Margery might have discovered a post-war occupation which would appeal to her and utilise the skills that the war years had developed. But the registrar shrugged and turned the question back to Alice.

"I have no idea," she began. "And you? What about you?" Before Alice could make a reply she was surprised when Margery, emboldened by the sherry, gathered up her notes, rose, slightly unsteadily, to her feet and announced that it was obvious what Alice should do.

"Is it?" Alice queried. "What?"

"Marry Roger, of course!" Margery continued, cheerfully. "Put the poor soul out of his misery! He obviously adores you! Whoops! Have I spoken out of turn?" Alice, still seated, was staring up at the registrar's florid face, a slow blush colouring her own.

Mabel, with all three of her children safely under her roof and with Ferdie proving to be a contented, industrious and obedient husband, happily set about refurbishing the Vallance cottage. Ferdie whitewashed the walls, repaired the doors and windows, and because his wife knew best, used several pieces of his late mother's redundant furniture for firewood. The Vallances ate well, supplementing their rations with Ferdie's various poachings and pilferings. Mabel, as her employer had accurately forecast, was developing impressive organisational skills and running her home, caring for her children and carrying out her duties in the Bayliss dairy in one streamlined flow of work. She loved to cook, and now that she had her own kitchen to cook in, her own husband and children to cook for and — from one source or another — a plentiful supply of raw materials, the aroma of her stews, her roasted meats, her fish pies, when Ferdie had been lucky with a salmon, and her pasties, drifted tantalisingly round the yard of the higher farm.

"Yours be better nor mine," Rose admitted, biting into a pasty that was hot from Mabel's oven. Mabel repaid the compliment by bicycling down to the lower farm one Saturday lunchtime and, with Rose's assistance, baking pasties for all the Post Stone girls, creating, under Mabel's instruction, a culinary production line that resulted in a Saturday lunch which, for days, was the talk of the hostel and had, although no one recognised it at the time, more significance than anyone realised.

Rose had never forgotten the success of the Devonshire cream teas she had produced for the staff and patients in the ward of the military hospital where, twelve months previously, Dave had been treated for a shrapnel wound in his leg. Nurses, orderlies and wounded men alike had enthused about the freshly baked scones piled with strawberry jam and crowned with dollops of clotted cream, and had declared their intention, when the war was over, to visit Devon for their holidays, find themselves a nice little café and sit down to a real "Demshure cream tea like what Corporal Crocker's mum makes".

As the months passed, a thought which had taken root in Rose's imagination became a private dream and then hardened into an identifiable project.

There was only one labourer's cottage at the lower farm. To this, as a bride, Rose had been brought by Dave's father. During the early, childless years of the marriage she had pined for the village life and the people with whom she had grown up and who were now a thirty-minute walk away, but, after a difficult confinement, which deprived the couple of the possibility of further children, Dave had been born, and apart from helping out with the farm work during the various harvest times, his mother had devoted herself to raising the little boy whose labour, as soon he was done with school, was incorporated into Roger Bayliss's workforce. Dave was eighteen years old when, on a wet winter's day, his father dropped dead and the lease of the Crocker cottage, as was the custom, was put into his name. On his marriage it would be his wife who would be mistress of the cottage and his children who would be raised there.

Since her widowhood, Rose's attention had been more than ever focused on her son. The feelings of panic when his call-up papers had arrived might have destroyed her had it not been for Roger Bayliss's decision to use the lower farm as a billet for his land girls. Suddenly there was work for Rose to do. There were scandals and gossip to amuse her, and a small but welcome income to augment the tiny pension which was all she received after her husband's early death. But more important to Rose than the money had been the increasing sense of achievement and involvement which her work at the hostel brought her.

Her familiarity with the farmhouse, its plumbing, its temperamental and inefficient boiler, its leaks, its overflowings, rattlings, creakings, howlings and gurglings, had given Rose an early advantage over the newly appointed warden, the interloper who, to begin with, seemed to Rose to be both unsuitable and incapable of the work she had undertaken. Initially hostile, Rose soon, if reluctantly, had come to admire Alice Todd's fumbling attempts to master her task, and before long these two women, whose experience of life came from hugely contrasted backgrounds, had not only developed a strong, working relationship but had become friends, forming a united front in their dealings not only with the vagaries of the farmhouse, but with the uncompromising and sometimes difficult Roger Bayliss, as well as the forthright and often rebellious land girls themselves. As the war progressed and its conclusion loomed, Rose, like everyone else at the two farms, had begun to speculate on what the future held. Gradually her half-formed ambitions had solidified and, unsurprisingly, it was to the warden that she first confided them.

"I've already found me premises," she announced one afternoon, when she and Alice were preparing the land girls' evening meal. Edward John, on a corner of the kitchen table, was assembling a piece of a model Hurricane from his latest kit and listening, as he always did, to the grownups' conversation. "'Tis the old bakery in the village square," Rose continued, smoothing sprinkled flour across the pastry board. Alice said she didn't know there was a bakery in Ledburton. "'Tis closed down now 'cos the local stores gets their loaves from that big new place in Exeter these days. But years ago all our bread come from that little shop and the smell of the bakin' used to waft round the square, makin' your mouth water! Lovely it were! Drove us kids mad with hunger! There's still a counter and shelves in the front bit of the shop, and that's where I'll put me tables and me chairs. Six there'll be, with gingham clothes on 'em and yellow crockery! Then comes a kitchen space where the dough used to be got ready for the ovens, and be'ind that there's a yard with a gate to an alleyway. Upstairs be three good rooms where the baker's family allus lived. Just a pot of tea, I'll do, and a plate of freshly baked scones, buttered and still warm from the ovens and served with plenty of jam and bowls of Demshure cream! One and six per person, I'll charge, and I'll be open for business for the trippers, see! All summer, from two o'clock until six o'clock every afternoon! In the winter, I'll just do Sat'days and Sundays. I've done me sums, Alice, an' I knows what me costs are, not counting me rent, though, 'cos I doesn't know how much that'll be 'til I asks Mr Bayliss."

"Mr Bayliss?" Alice queried.

"Yes, cos 'e owns the old bakery, see. Part of the Post Stone estate it be. Reckon I'll 'ave to fill in some forms for to get permission for it to be a café, but Mr Bayliss'll know about all that better nor I do. So . . . What d'you reckon?" she concluded. Alice had stopped, knife in hand, and was staring at Rose, her face expressing a mix of astonishment and respect.

"I think it's a brilliant plan, Rose. I just hope . . . I mean . . ."

"You mean am I up to it?"

"No! I'm sure you are . . . but . . ."

"There are a few things that'll need sorting, I knows that . . . One thing is the walk from here into the village and back. It's a good mile and a bit each way. I'm not bothered about the walk. I'm used to that. But it's the time, see. 'Alf an hour each way it takes, easy, and that's an hour a day . . . I could live over the shop, o'course. I'd like that! But my Dave'll be demobbed before long now, and with 'im still fixed on that Hester, it don't look like 'e'll marry any time soon! So I'll 'ave to stay on at the cottage to look after 'im, won't I!" She smiled firmly at Alice and then continued. "And there's another thing," she said, thumping the lump of dough for the piecrust down onto the board. "With the shop on'y bein' open in the summer afternoons and at weekends in the winter, I'll be payin' out rent for a lot of hours when there's no money goin' in me till!"

Alice had considered this problem for a while as she sliced into cubes the rather tough piece of stewing steak which would form a small but vital part of tonight's pie. Edward John looked up from the balsa wood shape he was carefully sanding. He remembered watching Mabel assembling the batch of pasties she had recently baked for the land girls' lunch and how economically and speedily the pasties had been prepared and cooked. "It don't half make the meat go a long way, a good pasty do!" Mabel had announced that morning, happily dicing her way through the pile of vegetables which would form the main ingredient of her creation.

"Mrs Crocker," Edward John began, coolly, "I've just had an idea." Rose was concentrating on rolling out the pastry.

"What's that, then, Edward John?" she asked him in the tone of voice she used when indulging small boys.

"What about serving Mabel's hot pasties in the mornings . . . and your cream teas in the afternoons?"

Mid afternoon on a hot day and the farmhouse, except for one person, was deserted. Rose, her arm through the handle of a large punnet, had strolled along the lane to the field where strawberries were ripe and ready for use for tonight's pudding. Alice, as quite often happened these days, had been collected by Roger Bayliss and driven off for what he called a "spot of lunch". Which left Gwennan, who, feverish following a bilious attack, was lying, half asleep in her bed.

Hearing an unfamiliar vehicle draw up in the lane outside the farmhouse, followed by the rattle of the catch on the gate and heavy footsteps on the cobbles approaching the front door, Gwennan left her bed and peered out of her window.

The vehicle at the gate was a jeep and someone, their identity concealed by the porch, was rapping their knuckles on the front door.

"What d'you want?" Gwennan called sharply. A figure in an American army uniform stepped back-wards, out from under the porch, tilted his head, saluted crisply and smiled up at her.

"Hi there!" he said, squinting into the sunlight. "Which one of the gorgeous Post Stone babes are you?" It was Sergeant Marvin Kinsky. He was smiling, his white teeth gleaming, his five o'clock shadow just beginning to darken his jawline.

"It's Gwennan Pringle," Gwennan told him, crisply, disconcerted by his arrival and attempting to conceal this reaction in a show of irritation.

"Aha!" he grinned, "the Welsh one! The one they call Taffy, right? I recognise the accent! I was stationed in Wales just before D-Day, ma'am, indeed to goodness I was!"

"I s'pose you've come about Marion," she said. Kinski laughed, dropped his head and walked round in a small circle before looking, almost shyly, back up at her, his jaw working on a lump of peppermint gum.

"That's a quaint way of putting it!" he said. "But yeah, I guess I have. So . . . Where can I find her, ma'am?" For a moment Gwennan hesitated, then she told him to wait and said she would come down. She pulled on her dressing gown and tied it firmly, slid her feet into her carpet slippers, went down the narrow staircase into the cross-passage, opened the front door, led Kinsky into the recreation room and told him he had better sit down. He sat, holding his cap loosely in his hands and watching her as she perched herself neatly on an upright chair. He was still smiling.

"This is where I first met her," he said, glancing round the quiet room. "Christmas Day. Forty-three. Reckon I was smitten straight off!" There was a silence. "You OK, lady?" he asked her, his face suddenly serious. "Only you look real peaky."

"I was ill in the night," Gwennan told him. "I'm s'posed to rest in my bed today." He was on his feet.

"Jeez! I'm sorry I disturbed you! You get off back to bed and I'll . . . I'll . . ."

"Don't you want to know where Marion is?" she asked him.

"Sure I do, but . . ."

"If you go up to the higher farm someone there will know," she said. He thanked her and was apologising again for disturbing her when she suddenly interrupted him.

"But if I was you I wouldn't bother with her." He turned to face her, gaping in surprise. "You seem a nice fellow," she said, her voice, even in her ears, sounding harsh in the quiet room. "You deserve better than Marion Grice!"

"Better?" he echoed, astonished. "Better than Marion?"

"You don't know how she goes on, do you? With blokes, I mean. With soldiers and airmen and GIs!" Her voice had thinned into an unattractive whine. "'Specially with GIs! They gives her presents! Loads of presents! Frocks and smokes and silk stockings and undies! And you don't get nothing for nothing in this world, do you!" He was gazing at her, his jaw frozen, his chewing gum forgotten. "What do you want with a girl like her?" she finished and was aware, as the silence closed on her final words, of the sergeant's eyes, searching her face. Sharp, dark and unreadable, his gaze held hers. After a moment, she lowered her head and stared at the floor. "You don't know nothing about her, do you?" she concluded lamely, her voice wavering.

He stood for a moment, still looking at her, taking in the stony features which had been distorted by an outburst that had remained for so long locked into her head, waiting for this moment. Now that it was over, the words out and the air still vibrating with their intensity, an emptiness washed over her face as she raised her eyes and stared at him, blank and blinking, uncertain what to expect from him. There was a considerable pause.

"Maybe I don't," he said quietly. "And maybe she don't know much about me, neither. No more'n you do, ma'am. I'm no angel, see. I bin around. I done things I'm not proud of and I guess she might have, too. Haven't we all? But with Marion things was different, see. Right from the start. For me and for her too, I reckon. We just . . . clicked," he finished, unable to find a better phrase. "Just clicked," he repeated, his voice stronger and increasingly confident. He squared his sturdy shoulders and lifted his chin. "You say I don't know her . . . But do *you*, ma'am? Do *you* really know her?"

"I've seen her rowdy!" Gwennan retaliated, defensively, feeling her heart beating against her ribs. "I've seen her flaunting herself!"

"Sure! Me too! And she's got a sharp tongue and a quick temper when she feels like it! I seen that too. But it's a tough old world out there, Taff, and Marion's had to fight her way through it. Don't reckon things have been that easy for her, one way and another." He paused. "But is she unkind?" he persisted. "Is she dishonest? Have you ever known her hurt anyone?" He paused again and fumbled for something in his breast pocket. "Mind if I smoke?" he said. She shook her head and watched him light the stub of a cigar and in the silence she heard, in her head, the faint thud of the envelope containing his letter to Marion, dropping down behind the dresser, almost twelve months ago, and she felt her own unkindness and her own dishonesty break over her like a wave. He was observing her keenly, screwing up his eyes against his cigar smoke. "Reckon you should get back to your bed," he said, almost gently. "Reckon you're real sick." There was, he saw now, a sort of desperation about her. He got to his feet. "I guess what you said just now was kindly meant, ma'am. Your intentions were good, and I sure'preciate your concern, I really do. It was kind of you to worry on my account, even if I don't deserve it, and I thank you for that. I reckon you're a good person, you know that? Now, you get upstairs and I hope you get well real soon, OK?"

Gwennan nodded dumbly and stood stock-still in the recreation room while the little sergeant clicked his heels and inclined his head in a gesture suggesting respect. Then he left her, his boots loud on the slates of the cross-passage, through the porch, along the cobbled path and out through the gate. She heard the jeep's engine rattle into life and then fade to silence, the sound quickly absorbed by the dense foliage of the lane. She realised suddenly that tears were sliding down her face.

"But I'm not!" she whimpered. "I'm not kind and I'm not a good person." And then she thought, "But perhaps I am, though." She stood in the empty room, considering the circumstances. Perhaps it had been the shock of discovering her illness that had made her hide the sergeant's letter all those months ago. Not unkindness at all. And not dishonesty. It had been the fear of being ill and dying unloved that had made her commit a stupid, jealous, spiteful act. And warning the sergeant that Marion's no good . . . Perhaps he was right and she did mean that for the best. She began to feel slightly light-headed and almost virtuous. Perhaps that was all it had been, after all. A silly, thoughtless act and an attempt, however well meant, to interfere between two people who were best left to make their own decisions. And now it was over and done with. Kinsky, after all this time, had found his way back to Marion. He might even marry her. Which meant that she, Gwennan Iris Pringle, was innocent! She might even be, as Sergeant Kinsky had suggested, "a good person" with worthy motives, not cruel, vengeful ones. She climbed the stairs to her room and lay, comforted, dozing in her narrow bed.

After a while Rose returned from the strawberry field. Later, Gwennan heard her boss's car deliver the warden back to the farmhouse. She heard the chickens in the yard and the geese and the ducks on the pond and the house martins under the eaves. She may be going to die, painfully and slowly like her sister Olwyn had and her Aunt Rhiannon before her, but she would bear it bravely. She knew the other land girls disliked her, and that neither the warden or the village registrar had much time for her, but Sergeant Kinski understood her. He had valued her intentions and believed in her goodness. There was a tap on her bedroom door. The warden had brought her a cup of tea. She flushed with pleasure, raised herself on one elbow, smiled as she took the cup and said "much better, thanks" when Alice asked her how she was feeling.

"Reckon I'll get up now," she added. "Grab the bathroom before the others get home, right?" Alice smiled. It was typical of Gwennan to take advantage of

113

her indisposition to snatch a hot bath from under the noses of the rest of the girls, who had been working all day.

Dear Georgina, Alice wrote and then sat, tapping her fountain pen against her teeth, trying to decide how to say what she needed to say.

It has been a long time since we had any news of you, although I have heard, in a roundabout way — from Jack, actually, who tells me that, when delivering supplies to Christopher, he often sees you at the woodman's cottage and that you are no longer with the ATA.

When you swore me to secrecy about your plans to marry Christopher and go out to New Zealand with him, I had no notion that it would be not even weeks but months before you discussed all this with your parents and, in Christopher's case, with his father. Have you any idea how embarrassing this is for me, in view of my association with Christopher's father? I mean with my professional association with him, as his hostel warden, as well as in terms of my acquaintance with him on a personal level?

Alice thought this sounded very formal and slightly pompous but she was finding Georgina's behaviour increasingly irritating, and after some thought she wrote on in the same vein.

I do understand that it is a complicated decision for you both to make and that it will be difficult for Christopher to explain to his father his reasons for emigrating. I wish, believe me, that I did not know anything at all about this but, since you did confide in me and, in doing so, involved me in it, making me, in effect complicit, I feel you should consider my position. Frankly, I am surprised you have not had the courtesy to come and see me in order to discuss things. Perhaps you have not realised quite how long it has been but now that I have drawn your attention to it I hope to hear from you very soon. I'm sorry if I sound cross, my dear, but I am rather.

Yours, Alice

She gave her letter to Jack who, the next morning, took it with him, up into the forest where he found Christopher and Georgina working in a plantation of young hardwoods.

In the afternoon of that day the pair of them arrived at Lower Post Stone, contrite and apologetic. Alice made a pot of tea and led them through to her room.

"Alice, we're so sorry!" Georgina began. "We should have thought! Well, we did think, but mostly about ourselves!" Christopher, carrying the tray of tea things, followed the two women and set the tray down on Alice's low table. "At first we had to wait until Chris's appointment was confirmed," Georgina explained, "then we didn't know exactly when they want him to start work for them, and then there was all the emigration palaver . . . And we still hadn't told my folks . . . and . . ."

"And have you told them now?"

"Well, most of it."

"Most of it?" Alice echoed, starting to pour the tea. "And which bits haven't you told them?"

"We haven't told them exactly why we're going," Christopher said. "I mean the part about my problem with my father." Alice passed his cup of tea to him and indicated that he should help himself to milk and sugar if he wanted them.

"They must find it hard to understand why you would even think of turning your back on the Post Stone farms, Christopher. On your inheritance, in fact. Everything your father and all the generations of the Bayliss family before him have built up and cherished. And to a great extent, on Georgina's future too. And that of any children you may have."

"They do," Christopher told her. "They find it incomprehensible." He was trying, unsuccessfully, to make it sound like a joke. "They think their daughter is marrying a lunatic!" He glanced at Alice, who was clearly not amused.

"Would they understand if you told them the real reason?" she asked him.

"They would," Georgina said. She had accepted her tea from Alice, carried it to the window and was standing, staring out across the lane and into the cider apple orchard. "They would understand but Chris won't tell them because he hasn't told his father yet. He says it would be unfair on his father, for them to know while his father still didn't." There was a pause before Alice spoke and when she did it surprised both Georgina and Christopher.

"I think you're absolutely right, Christopher," she said. "It would be outrageous." She resisted going on to emphasise that he owed it to his father to tell him what his plans for the future were and why he had decided on them. That he needed to be courageous enough to face his father with the way he had made him feel about his breakdown and that he needed to do it soon. Instead she controlled the temptation to give direct advice and confined herself to asking, rather sharply, what he intended to do. "Are you proposing to simply tell your father that you and Georgina are getting married, Christopher? And then add, 'Oh and by the way, we're emigrating to New Zealand so I won't be around anymore and no, I don't give a damn what happens to you or the Post Stone farms, now or ever'?"

Georgina stared at Alice and was slightly affronted that the warden seemed to be viewing the situation more from Roger Bayliss's perspective than from Christopher's, who appeared to consider what Alice had said, but after a moment, shook his head and sat down heavily on the window seat.

"I don't think that telling Pa the main reason for wanting to go would work, Mrs Todd," he said. "He's always been impossible to talk to on those sorts of subjects. Personal stuff . . . you know . . . it's hopeless. Believe me, I have tried. If I told him I found his obvious disappointment in me intolerable, that I simply can't face his obvious contempt on a daily basis for the rest of my life, he'd think I was behaving like a sulky kid. He wouldn't say so, of course, but that's what he'd think."

This, Alice realised, was almost what she herself was thinking and the realisation made her aware of how defensive of Roger she had become. She stared at her teacup and let the silence lengthen. A moment later the sonorous mechanism of the clock in the recreation room began to wheeze its way towards the striking of five o'clock. Alice got to her feet.

"I have things to do in the kitchen," she said, quietly. "Bring the tray through when you've finished your tea, will you, Georgie . . .?" They were both regarding her, their expressions like admonished children. She sighed. "I can't advise you, my dears," she said. "You're grown-up people now and you have to make your own decisions. But do try not to lose sight of the effect those decisions have on other people." From the doorway she turned to face them, put the tips of the fingers of both her hands to her lips and blew two kisses across the room to them.

Dave Crocker's demobilisation happened sooner than anyone anticipated and he arrived back at the Crocker cottage wearing the "civvies" with which he had been issued by the Ministry of Defence. The trousers fitted reasonably well, but the jacket was tight across his robust chest and its sleeves were too short by at least an inch, exposing thick wrists and strong hands, confirming, if confirmation was needed, that here was a man designed more for corduroy, for overalls, oilskin waterproofs and rubber boots than for the double-breasted suits, lace-up brogues and trilby hats of Civvy Street. He transferred his gratuity to his post office account and was reabsorbed into the Bayliss workforce, relieving the ageing Jack and Fred of the excess workload they had been shouldering during his absence. Plans for several projects, shelved by the war years, were put into action. The dairy herd was to be increased, a larger poultry house would be constructed, the pigsties refurbished and a new breeding programme instigated. Dave shouldered these new challenges with an assurance he had not possessed when, an immature boy, he had left the farm three years previously. Now he confidently undertook his new responsibilities and was paid accordingly.

With Dave's wage coming into the Crocker home and the number of land girls at the hostel now reduced, Rose was free to develop her plan to open a café in the village. She had reached what she called "an accommodation" with Roger Bayliss, who proposed leasing the old bakery, rent-free, to her, on the understanding that she, with her son's help, would undertake the interior decoration necessary to convert it. Planning permission for the café was sought and granted and if, after twelve months, the project was viable, a modest rent would be agreed upon.

Rose purchased a bolt of blue and white checked gingham at a fire sale and, using her treadle sewing machine, soon had a pile of tablecloths hemmed and folded ready for use. Yellow crockery proved to be

119

much more expensive than the plain white she settled for, and to begin with she would have to make do with two small tables and two long trestles. Six chairs, cast-offs from a local hotel, were hers, free of charge, provided she arranged collection, and she purchased two benches at an auction in Exeter for half a crown each. She used the remains of the gingham to make cushions for the benches and curtains for the windows.

There was already a trickle of holidaymakers in the area, tentatively returning to pre-war habits, wandering round the village, buying postcards, their kids playing with bats and balls on the green or sailing their boats on the pond while the parents enjoyed a quiet pint at the Maltster's. Yet Rose hesitated before officially opening her café for business. She still had her obligations to Alice, while Dave, returning home, famished, each evening, needed a proper dinner.

"What are you waiting for, Mrs Crocker?" Annie asked her.

"It looks smashing, your little caff!" Winnie added.

"Tell you what," Marion announced firmly, "you open up Sat'dy afternoon and us girls'll all come down for a cream tea! We will, won't we?" The girls agreed enthusiastically. "And we'll pay! One and six each! Right?"

Rose, glowing with pleasure, was touched by their support.

"Ah . . ." she said, regarding them with more affection than was usual. "But I couldn't take your money off of you . . . Tell you what . . . a bob each for as much as you can eat! How does that sound?"

On the following Saturday, dressed in their "going out" clothes, the girls, Edward John and Alice arrived at the café, took their places at one of the trestle tables, spread the strawberry jam on the warm scones, topped them with cream and bit into them, sighing with pleasure and, with their mouths full, assuring Rose of their total approval. More scones appeared, more bowls of cream and more cups of tea were poured. Suddenly a silence fell, the girls stopped spreading and chewing and sipping and stared. A group of people had come in through the open door of the tea shop. Two women, a man and a little girl. Strangers. Holidaymakers. Trippers. Customers! Rose stood transfixed. The land girls continued to stare. It was Edward John who spoke.

"Good afternoon," he said, and smiling, got to his feet and approached the strangers.

"The cream teas are very good here! Please sit down!" He led them to one of the small tables, and by the time they were seated, Rose had risen to the occasion and was delivering plates of warm scones together with jam, cream and a large pot of tea to their table while Alice encouraged her girls to indulge in small talk and behave like regular customers.

"And what about that Edward John!" Evie exclaimed when, later, the events of the afternoon were being discussed. "Proper little gent he was! Showin' 'em to their table! Sittin' 'em down!"

"That's boarding school for you," Gwennan announced. "They get taught 'ow to conduct theirselves proper. It's like that thing they say about the playing fields of Eton." The girls looked blankly at her.

"You don't half talk a lot of baloney, Taff!" someone murmured.

"It's not baloney! It's to do with the Battle of Trafalgar!" Gwennan protested. "But what would you lot know about it! Dead ignorant, that's your trouble." Then, being slightly unsure of her facts, Gwennan opted for silence.

With the tea shop now up and running, Rose contrived to bake her scones and serve her cream teas every afternoon and, having met her costs, was encouraged by the small amounts of money she was regularly able to deposit into her savings account. Being a practical woman her concerns soon turned to the future of her son.

"'Course, if you was to wed, Dave, I'd go and live over me tea shop. Ever so convenient, it'd be, and I'd like being back in the village. But I 'as to live 'ere for now, on account of'avin' to cook your dinner of a night, whereas if you was to wed, you'd 'ave your wife to cook for you." Dave agreed, without paying much attention to his mother, that this was so. But he was, after all, her baby boy. Her son and heir. So of course she would cook his meals, darn his socks and wash his clothes. If he had a wife it would be different. But he hadn't. So it wasn't. He took his chop bone in his fingers, and with his teeth, stripped it of its remaining meat.

"So what about your Hester?" his mother asked suddenly — Hester not having been much mentioned since Dave's last attempt to fetch her from her home to his.

"What about 'er?" he mumbled.

122

"Well, do you want her or don't you, Dave? And if you do, what are you going to do about it, eh?"

"Reckon there's nothing more I *can* do about it, Ma. 'Er knows how I feels about 'er. I've told 'er more'n once as I'll fetch 'er any time she wants me to. She on'y 'as to say the word. But *she* 'as to say it, Ma. It 'as to come from 'er now. I bain't goin' creepin' over to 'er place no more, beggin' 'er."

"So you'm gonna let pride stand in the way of 'appiness, is that it?"

"It wouldn't be 'appiness, Ma! And it bain't pride. More like a bit of self-respect, is all." She watched him lick the grease from the lamb off his fingers.

CHAPTER
FIVE

Christopher dropped Georgina at the farmhouse gate, reversed the truck and drove away.

"We've told my parents," she said when she found Alice in the linhay, folding the sheets and towels she had just brought in from the washing line.

Apart from Alice the hostel was empty. Rose was at her tea room and the land girls were lifting the carrot crop on the far side of the higher farm.

"Including the bit about you emigrating?" Alice asked.

"Yes." Georgina said. "Including that bit. And Chris is on his way to see his father."

Roger assumed, when his son tapped on the farm office door, that he had come to discuss arrangements regarding the harvesting of a plantation of softwoods which, when felled, would be delivered to a local sawmill and cut into lengths for use as pit props.

"I can let you have Dave Crocker for a week," Roger told him. "Jack can do the driving and I might be able to borrow a couple of Lucas's POWs if you think you'd need them." He glanced at his son, sensing that something other than the woodland was the subject of his visit. "Something on your mind, Chris?" he asked, offering a cigarette, and when Christopher declined, lighting his own and inhaling deeply, almost, Christopher thought, as though bracing himself for whatever was to come.

"Thing is, Pa, I have some rather big news." His father sat, his eyes on his son's face, and listened as Christopher told him how his increasing interest in arboriculture had led him to study the subject, how he had successfully completed various required courses and reached a level that had resulted in the offer of a lucrative overseas contract as a forestry manager. He went on to give the details of what was involved and precisely where he would be working.

"New Zealand?" Roger repeated, understanding at once, from his son's expression, that he had either already accepted the offer or that he intended to.

"Yes," Christopher said. "Georgina and I are going to be married and then we're . . ." He was searching his father's face. Trying to read him. Was he angry? Shocked? Or merely astonished? Whatever it was, the news had obviously taken him off guard. "Sorry, Pa. I realise this is a bit of a bolt from the blue . . ." Roger was shaking his head, incredulously. "But everything started to move rather fast and it seemed pointless to tell anyone until we — Georgina and I — knew the details and had thought things over." Roger, his face blank, drew heavily on his cigarette.

"And when is all this going to happen?" he asked. "The wedding. The emigration. And what about the Brewster girl's parents? How do they feel about it?"

"I believe they rather think it's up to her, Pa. I mean
. . . they don't want to lose her but they've brought her
up to know her own mind and make her own decisions.
They're delightful people. I'm sure you'll like them.
They're very keen to meet you."

Half an hour later Christopher was back at the lower
farm where he sat down heavily at the kitchen table and
thanked Alice for the cup of tea she put in front of him.
She caught in his face a hint of the same tension that
had dominated it when she had first encountered him,
two years previously and only a few weeks before his
breakdown. He looked as though he felt trapped in an
impossible situation. But he caught her eye and smiled
wryly.

"Well . . . that went well!" he said, carefully sipping
the hot tea. He looked from Georgina to Alice. Then,
setting down his cup, searched in his pockets for
cigarettes and lighter. "D'you mind, Alice?" She shook
her head. He inhaled smoke and sat for a moment,
staring ahead.

"Well — are you going to tell us what happened, or
what?" Georgina asked him, with, Alice thought, a hint
of impatience in her voice.

"Not much to tell," he said, blowing smoke and
relaxing slightly. "You know Pa. I would say he reacted
exactly as you would expect him to. Just sat there for a
while. Staring me down. Like he used to when I was
a kid and broke his rules or displeased him in some
way. Not exactly angry. Just . . . disappointed!" Georgina
raised both her hands in a gesture of exasperation.

"That wretched word again!" she exclaimed.

"Then he asked me if I understood exactly what would be involved if I was to turn my back on what he described as 'all of this'. He meant the farms and the land of course. I told him I did understand and that it wasn't a decision I had made lightly or on an impulse, that I'd thought long and hard about it and that you had too, Georgie, and we both felt it would be the right thing to do, in the circumstances. I thought he might ask what I thought the circumstances were."

"And he didn't?" Georgina queried.

"No. He just sat there." Christopher ashed his cigarette.

"And you didn't tell him?" Georgina was obviously irritated by Chris's restraint. "You didn't tell him how impossible he is? And how he makes you feel? And how hurtful it is and how insulting? And how you can't and won't put up with it anymore? Didn't you tell him all that, Chris?"

Alice, observing the pair of them, was aware of how difficult their relationship might become if Roger continued to feature in it.

"I started to," Christopher told her. "I said I didn't feel that he and I were temperamentally suited to working together. That he obviously considered that I always fell short of his expectations and that I was sick of being made to feel second-rate."

"Hey!" Georgina said, mollified. "Well said, Christo! And what happened then?"

"Then he did a thing he used to do when I was a kid and he considered that my behaviour was out of order."

"And what was that?" Georgina asked.

"He got up," Christopher said, "went to the window and stood with his back to me, staring out. And he said, very calmly, very coolly, 'I think that's enough of that, Christopher.' In those days I was expected to leave the room at that point and not speak to him again until I was ready to apologise for my unacceptable behaviour." Christopher smiled at Alice and Georgina, and at their astonished faces. He drew on his cigarette and was still smiling as he exhaled. "Well . . . perhaps it's more civilised than having a blazing row. I don't know."

"That's it, then, is it?" Georgina asked him. "No attempt to persuade you to stay?"

"Do we want to stay?" he asked her. There was a pause while their eyes met and held. Then she smiled. It was what Alice had come to think of as a real Georgina smile. Her chin was lifted, her eyes met Christopher's, fixing him with a straight, strong, positive gaze, her lips were parted and she was laughing.

"Well, *I* don't," she said. "I want to go! It'll be such an adventure. Just think! Across Biscay, past Gibraltar, through the Med, down the Suez Canal. Aden, India, Ceylon, Perth, Sydney. Then across the Tasman to Wellington!"

"And then it'll be back to reality, Georgie. What happens if we don't like it there?" Christopher asked, watching her face.

"We *will* like it! And anyway . . . if we don't, we'll come back! It's not the end of the world!"

"It's as near as damn it!" he said, laughing at her. "And I shall be committed for a minimum of two years, remember!"

"I know! I know! And I can't wait, Chris!" She rounded the table, and standing behind him, lent over him and noisily kissed his cheek. Then she went to Alice, put her arms round her, hugged her tightly and kissed her, too. She was, Alice realised, totally, blissfully happy. Georgina felt Alice stiffen and released her. "What?" she asked her. "What's up, Alice?"

"I was just thinking," Alice said, "about Roger." She looked at them and watched their smiles fade. "Sorry," she said. "Didn't mean to spoil things."

Alice was uncertain whether to contact Roger and admit that she knew of Christopher's plan. This, it seemed to her, would put her into the possibly difficult position of confessing to having known of it for some time. Would Roger have expected her to pass the news on to him as soon as she received it? Would her failure to do so be perceived as an alliance with the son at the expense of the father? She had waited, hoping that some hostel business or other might result in a meeting between the two of them, but when several days had passed she telephoned the higher farm.

"Mr Bayliss is gone to Winchester for a memorial service," Eileen told Alice. "He'll be back Friday. He said to give you the phone number of his hotel if there was an emergency. There isn't an emergency, is there, Mrs Todd?" Alice told her that no, there was no emergency.

"Don't get involved, Alice," had been Georgina's advice.

"But what if he asks me how long I've known about all this? I mean, the two of you being engaged to marry, as well as the New Zealand thing? Do I lie?" Georgina was apologetic.

"We shouldn't have involved you, Alice. I'm so sorry. I reckon Roger will guess you knew. But he'll also know that whatever you did was in accordance with your good judgement and he trusts your judgement and he trusts you. More than that, I think he really, seriously loves you!"

"Oh . . . why is he so difficult?" Alice sighed, almost to herself. "It's as though he is on one side of a six-foot wall and all the rest of us are on the other!"

Roger made no contact with Alice until late on the Sunday afternoon when he arrived, as usual, to drive Edward John to Ledburton to catch the bus back to his weekly boarding school. With the boy in the back seat there was no opportunity for Roger, or indeed Alice, to broach the subject of Christopher's plans.

Gwennan and Annie were, at that moment, returning to the higher farm after driving the milking herd back to their pasture. They paused, breathless after the steep climb, to lean on a gate and look out, across Post Stone valley. The water meadows were already in shade and the shallow river meandered through stands of shadowy willow and alder to the point, almost vertically below the girls, where the lane, carried by a narrow, humpbacked bridge, crossed it, and having descended

130

sharply from the west, began to climb, equally steeply, to the east. From their vantage point the two girls gazed down at the solid contours of the granite structure, watching idly for a flash of colour from the plumage of the pair of kingfishers often seen on that stretch of the river.

"C'mon, Annie," Gwennan said, slapping at the skin on her bony forearm, "the midges is biting!" At that moment the girls heard the sound of a car's engine descending the opposite hill and invisible in the deep lane as it rapidly approached the bridge. Annie suggested that the car was probably their boss's.

"Mr Bayliss usually drives Edward John into Ledburton about this time on Sunday evenings, to catch the Exeter bus," she murmured.

"Where 'e gets the petrol from I dunno!" Gwennan sighed, piously. But the car was not Roger Bayliss's.

"It's Mrs Brewster!" Gwennan murmured, shading her eyes against the low sunlight, as the car came suddenly into view.

"And she's going way too fast!" Annie said, her fingers tightening on the top rung of the gate.

The angle of the lane's approach to the bridge was a familiar hazard to those who used it. Jack, driving the truck in which he ferried the land girls to and fro between the farms, always slowed, almost to walking pace, before negotiating it, and Roger Bayliss took a pride in precisely positioning his Riley before making the tight left- and then right-hand turns necessary to cross it safely. But, as Gwennan and Annie watched, Margery Brewster barely slackened her speed as she hurtled down the last section of the descent, seeming to sense, too late, that a collision with the bridge was inevitable. Perhaps there was time, even then, to slam on the brakes but, to the horrified girls, Margery appeared not to and her car struck the solid granite with enormous force, buckling and slewing violently sideways against the parapet. The passenger door was wrenched off by the impact and Margery Brewster herself was flung out of her seat and slammed against the stonework on the far side of the bridge.

Instinctively both the girls began to run down the steep lane towards the wreckage. Then Annie pulled at Gwennan's arm.

"No," she said. "One of us had best run to the farm and call for help! I'm faster than you, Taffy!" She turned and began striding up the steep incline towards the cluster of grey slated roofs of the higher farm.

When Gwennan reached the bridge she was conscious of a stillness and an eerie silence in which one wheel of the stricken car continued to spin while the rest of the crumpled metal tilted precariously above the river. Margery Brewster's handbag lay where it had been flung into the narrow roadway, while she herself sprawled, unmoving, against the parapet of the bridge. She lay on her side, blood pooling from under her head and spreading slowly across the gravelly surface of the lane.

"Mrs Brewster?" Gwennan said in a voice that was barely more than a whisper. After waiting for a response she went closer, knelt beside the injured woman and put her hand on an inert shoulder. Her touch was light but it was enough to redistribute Mrs Brewster's weight, and she rolled, like a rag doll, onto her back. Her open eyes were blank and unfocused. A thread of liquid trickled from one corner of her mouth. As Gwennan leant over her, searching for some sign of life, she became aware of the strong, unmistakeable reek of alcohol. Released from Margery Brewster's hand as she rolled over, a bottle of Gordon's gin lay, unbroken and half empty, it's screw top in place.

Gwennan had many failings but stupidity was not one of them. It was obvious to her that the reason the village registrar had crashed her car was because, and not for the first time, she had been too drunk to drive it safely.

Initially a sense of superiority swept over Gwennan. Here was a woman who had been in authority over her. By whom she had, on one or two occasions, been reprimanded. Whose dominance she had frequently resented. But, as she looked at the spreadeagled body and the blood which was ceasing to flow from whatever appalling wound lay under the smashed skull, Gwennan thought suddenly of the registrar's support when she had requested leave to visit her dying sister. And of the concern she had shown when, after Olwyn's death, she had listened while Gwennan tried to explain why, having lost her faith, she would not go home to Wales for the funeral. Yes, she was posh and a bit bossy but she was, at heart, a good woman, and neither she nor her family deserved the spiteful gossip that would sweep the Ledburton area, provoking nods and winks for years on end if the cause of her death was revealed as too much of the gin in the bottle which lay, intact, beside her corpse. Gwennan could almost hear the tongues wagging. "Always one for a drop, was Mrs Brewster! Many's the time I seen 'er tipsy! Standin' on a chair singin' 'Nellie Dean' she were, at 'er Christmas party! Young Albertine had to help get 'er to bed after!" Then she pictured the registrar's husband, the benign Gordon Brewster. Nothing could spare him the grief he was about to suffer but she, Gwennan Pringle, had it in her power to protect him from the scandal and the shame which would follow any suggestion that it was his wife's weakness for the bottle that had caused the accident that had killed her.

As Annie had correctly guessed, Roger Bayliss had, that evening, driven Edward John into Ledburton where Alice had seen him onto the bus and waved goodbye to him as it pulled out of the village square. Roger put his car into gear and turned into the lane that led back to Post Stone valley. For a while they drove in silence.

"This news of Christopher's," Roger began, his eyes on the lane ahead. "I imagine you knew a little of what was going on?"

"Georgina confides in me so, yes, for a while I probably did know a bit more about their plans than you did. They told me they would tell her parents and you, of course, as soon as things were settled and they had decided what to do." She was unable to read Roger's silence. After a moment she added, "Whatever any of us feel about their plans, Roger, it's their decision, not ours, don't you think?" They were at the top of the long, steep descent into the valley.

"Did he tell you why he wants to go? Why he feels strongly enough to sever all connections with the farms and with me? Because that is what this amounts to, Alice."

Here the lane was at its steepest, winding down towards the bridge that was out of sight a hundred yards ahead and almost as many feet below them. Roger engaged first gear and descended with his usual caution, positioning his car precisely in the narrow lane.

At that moment Gwennan heard the approach of a second car, nosing its way down the lane towards the bridge. Closing her mind against further thought, she reached for the gin bottle, unscrewed the cap and emptied its contents over Margery Brewster, watching the liquid splash onto her skin and darken the silk of her blouse. Then she replaced the cap, raised the empty bottle and flung it, hard, against the stonework beside the registrar's gory head, where it exploded into a thousand shining, emerald-green pieces.

By the time Roger Bayliss had reacted to the sight of Margery Brewster's mangled car, brought his own to a halt and, followed closely by Alice, was running towards the two figures on the bridge, Gwennan was kneeling beside Mrs Brewster, anxiously chafing one of the dead woman's limp hands.

"It's too late," she announced, genuinely tearful. "She's gone to her maker, poor lady."

It was slightly later, after Mrs Brewster's inert body had been lifted onto a stretcher, into an ambulance and driven away, and Constable Twentyman had inscribed all the details of what he called "the incident" into his notebook, that Gwennan asked Alice what was wrong with Mr Bayliss.

"Only he's gone that white, Mrs Todd, and he seems to be breathing funny."

Roger had crossed the bridge and was leaning on the parapet. His face was turned away from the place in the roadway where the bright green shards of the broken gin bottle glittered so oddly through the crimson gloss of Margery Brewster's coagulating blood.

"Roger?" Alice enquired, going to him and asking tentatively, "are you all right, my dear?" He seemed not to hear her, and although his eyes appeared to focus on hers, he showed no sign of recognition. Then he suddenly turned, spread his hands on the granite parapet, leant out over the river and retched. He stood swaying for a moment before slumping against the stonework of the bridge, drawing into himself great gulps of air while perspiration ran from his blanched face.

"It's the shock," Constable Twentyman announced staunchly. He himself had turned pale when Margery Brewster had been lifted onto a stretcher and the extent of her head injury had been apparent. "Best get him home, madam," he advised Alice. "My superior will be needing a statement, of course. From the witnesses. You two and the young lady," he said, meaning Gwennan. "And now I must go and break this sad news to poor Mr Brewster. It's the worst part of my job, I can tell you . . ." With his mind already occupied by his next, unpleasant duty, Twentyman heaved his leg over the bar of his bicycle and peddled off. Because of the steepness of the incline he was soon forced to dismount and push the machine up the hill.

Gwennan stood open-mouthed, staring at Roger Bayliss. "How are the mighty fallen" was the phrase that came suddenly into her strange mind. For here, in the space of half an hour, both the powerful village registrar and Mr Bayliss, her formidable employer, had been struck down by the same tragic incident. An incident in which she herself had played a significant part. She stood, slightly flushed, her own personal disaster forgotten, wondering what on earth was the matter with her boss. Yes, it had all been a terrible shock and some men went funny when confronted by blood, but Mr Bayliss? An experienced farmer and man, presumably, of the world? Reacting like a green girl in a fainting fit? Alice's voice cut across her train of thought.

"Mr Bayliss is unwell, Gwennan. I need you to go up to the higher farm and tell Eileen to call his doctor. I'll drive him up as soon as he's well enough." Her tone, together with another glance at her semi-conscious boss, was enough to persuade Gwennan to do as she was told.

Usually, when required to obey an order, Gwennan felt obliged to make some comment on it. Was the instruction justified? Or was it not? What, in the circumstances, would a better course of action be? What would she have done or said or even thought, if consulted? But on this occasion, because she herself had just done something of significance, she was almost grateful for Alice's instruction which meant that she could leave the scene of the accident, and as she walked, as fast as she could, up the steep hill towards the higher farm, consider the implications of her action at the scene of the crash.

The broken bottle, with its cap in place and the liquid it had contained spilt, would, Gwennan correctly believed, account for the reek of gin that would have been discovered to be emanating from Mrs Brewster's person and the clothes which had become saturated with it. The accident would be blamed on the narrowness of the lane and the dangerous angle of its approach to the bridge, and with the fact that the driver, familiar as she was with the route, had been seen to be taking the corner just a little too fast.

"Because of me . . ." Gwennan whispered breathlessly to herself as she climbed the hill. "Because of me, Gwennan Iris Pringle, Mr Brewster and his daughters will be spared the humiliation and the gossip. Their memories of the dear one they have lost will be unsullied by scandal." Gwennan's language, when it came to serious matters, took on the weight and tone of Wilkie Collins, or Galsworthy, or Dickens, whose words had made an impression on her when she had read them aloud to her dying sister. What Gwennan did not, at that time, recognise, was the fact that the decision she had made on the bridge that evening, which would have the effect of protecting the Brewster family from so much unhappiness, was almost certainly the first truly generous action she had ever taken in her life.

138

She glanced back from time to time at the scene on the bridge and saw that the warden was still on her knees beside Roger Bayliss.

Later, after she had done as she had been told and instructed Eileen to telephone for Mr Bayliss's doctor, Gwennan bicycled down to the lower farm where Rose Crocker was ladling out vegetable soup which, with slices of bread spread with margarine, and followed by cold rice pudding, was Sunday supper. Here Gwennan gave a detailed account of the evening's events to the group of girls sobered by the tragic news.

"Poor Mrs B," said Annie, who, as she had run to raise the alarm, had hoped that the registrar had somehow survived. "And poor Mr B, too."

"You should of seen our boss, though!" Gwennan continued. "Pale as a ghost 'e went and started shakin' and throwin' up!"

"Throwin' up?" Rose asked sharply, the tea pot poised over a cup. "Why would he be throwin' up?"

"I dunno, do I!" Gwennan countered. "The policeman said it were most likely the shock. And maybe the blood. There was ever such a lot of blood, see." Several of the girls flinched.

"Mr Bayliss 'as seen plenty of blood in 'is time," Rose protested. "'E be a farmer for goodness sake!" Gwennan ignored this interruption to her flow of information. "It were like that time the Eyetie POW got his arm smashed when the barn fell in on 'im. You remember? Mr Bayliss went funny then, too! Took himself off and sat in his truck, he did! Pass the marge, Annie . . . And could I have a drop more soup, Mrs

Crocker? Ta . . . Anyhow, Mrs Todd said to say she'd be back as soon as she could. Eileen was to phone for the doctor to come and see to Mr Bayliss, he were that bad!"

Alice had knelt down in the roadway in front of Roger and had taken his clammy, shaking hands in both of hers. She had tried to engage his eyes and attract his attention to words which she hoped might soothe and reassure him. But although his gaze seemed to be fixed on her he was obviously not seeing her or hearing her. It seemed to Alice as though he was, in some curious way, under attack. He flinched, almost cowering, from an unseen onslaught and his grip on her hands was crushing her bones. When she tried to withdraw them, his fingers tightened and he seemed not to hear her when she cried out in pain. She moved closer to him, the stones of the roadway biting into her knees, her hands in his, which, when she stopped pulling away from him, lessened their grip. And so they remained for some time while the twilight thickened around them, and the only sound was the shallow water moving over the stones below the bridge.

After a while Alice sensed that Roger's tension was lessening. Slowly she slid her hands from his and got to her feet, drew him up beside her and walked him to his car, put him into the passenger's seat and took the wheel. She was unfamiliar with the car, and the space between the parapet of the bridge and the wreckage of Margery Brewster's car was restricted. Roger did not speak as she took the car carefully through the gap and then, still in first gear, slowly on, up the hill. She could not locate the switch for the headlamps and was grateful for the luminous light of the evening as she reached and entered the yard where the doctor, having approached from the opposite end of the valley, had already arrived.

Robert Talbot was of the same generation as Roger. He had opened his practice when both men were in their late thirties. His surgery and his family home were in a nearby village. It had been he who had diagnosed the disease that had killed Roger's wife, seen Christopher through the usual childhood illnesses and been the first medic on the scene of the accident that had maimed Ferdie Vallance. In all those years he had not attended Roger who, apart from the odd bout of influenza, had never been unwell enough to call on his services.

Eileen, who, when Annie's news of the accident had reached her, had been about to leave for her home in the village in time for evensong, had remained at the farmhouse until her employer was safely returned to it.

Eileen had already shown the doctor into the drawing room and provided him with a cup of tea by the time Roger had joined him. Alice, not wishing to intrude on the consultation, remained in the hallway, sitting on an upright chair and holding the cup of tea that Eileen had brought her.

"I'll be off home now, Mrs Todd," Eileen had said, in a lowered voice, "if that's all right? Only they'll be wondering where I'm to, see, on account of I'd said I'd be at church for evensong. If the master needs anything

I reckon you'll see to him, won't you?" Alice had nodded and was soon alone with the noisy ticking of the grandfather clock, which was more immediate than the muted voices which reached her from the drawing room. She sat sipping the tea, the doctor and his patient visible through the glazed doors.

Talbot had pulled up a low chair and was sitting in front of Roger. His fingers were on Roger's wrist, examining, Alice assumed, his pulse. The two men were talking quietly. Alice could not hear their words. From time to time the doctor nodded his head.

Alice, although she did not realise it, was herself in a mild state of shock. The upsetting details of the registrar's death lingered in her mind's eye, and the light cardigan she had thrown round her shoulders when she left the lower farm with her son to make the short journey into Ledburton in Roger's car was not warm enough for the cool summer evening. She shivered slightly as she swallowed the lukewarm tea. Then Talbot was approaching her.

"How is he?" she asked him, getting to her feet, the cup and saucer noisy in her hands. Talbot looked puzzled.

"Physically all seems well," he said, almost to himself. "Pulse slightly raised — but his colour has improved and his breathing is normal now." He paused and had almost forgotten that this was not a wife with whom he was discussing his patient's symptoms, but a woman who was, in fact, his employee. He had encountered Alice Todd on several occasions when one or other of the land girls in her charge had been unwell

142

and knew her to be a sensible woman. He smiled and cleared his throat before continuing. "I've given him something for the shock, which should relax him, and advised him not to take any alcohol tonight. The incident has clearly upset him . . ." He paused again and Alice, understanding his reticence, told him that although she understood that he could not breach his Hippocratic oath by revealing any conclusions he might have reached as a result of his examination of his patient, she needed to know how to care for the man whom circumstances had placed in her charge. Talbot was impressed, both by her sensitivity and her accurate grasp of the situation. "A hot drink, a quiet evening and an early night would be the best thing for him," he told her.

"His housekeeper doesn't arrive until seven-thirty in the mornings. Will he need someone in the house with him overnight?" Alice asked, and while the doctor considered this she explored the possibility of sending for Christopher.

"I'll leave that to you, Mrs Todd," Talbot said, possibly sensing that Alice was more than capable of handling the situation, while he himself was eager to drive home and, if the light was strong enough, to resume the game of tennis which Eileen's telephone call had interrupted.

As he took his car smoothly along the familiar lanes that ran between his patient's home and his, Talbot pondered on his analysis of Roger's symptoms. The unpleasantness on the bridge, which involved the sudden and horrendous death of a woman he had known most of his adult life, had undoubtedly shocked him. But it seemed, to his doctor, to have set off a more severe reaction than one would normally expect. Talbot's medical experience, centred as it was on general practice, had polished his skills in the treatment of minor illnesses and developed in him a keen eye for symptoms of the more serious ones. As a student he had been fascinated by psychology and had considered specialising in that area of medicine until he was made aware of the fact that the prospect of being a country doctor's wife and raising a family in rural England had strongly appealed to the girl he was in love with. He had now been happily married for the past twenty-five years, during which he had satisfied his earlier interest by studying any papers on psychology which were published in *The Lancet* and other medical journals. He was, of course, familiar with the effects of trauma and understood how symptoms of extreme anxiety could be triggered by events similar to those which had caused the initial damage. As a young man he had read extensively on the effect of what was then referred to as "shell shock", a condition suffered with varying degrees of severity by soldiers who had endured the atrocities of the First World War. Less severe after-effects of this damage were recurring nightmares and a tendency for the victim's nervous system to break down under pressure, rather as Roger Bayliss appeared to have done that evening. The same symptoms, Talbot knew, were being experienced by survivors of the worst disasters of the recent hostilities. Dunkirk had produced its own crop of psychologically wounded men. Survivors of torpedoed ships experienced problems, as did RAF pilots who had been shot down or put under constant and extreme pressure. All these men had to some extent broken down and many were still suffering the effects of their various traumas. Present-day casualties were, Talbot knew, being better cared for — now that the condition was recognised and understood — than their First World War counterparts had been, many of whom, accused of desertion, had been executed by firing squad. But, Talbot reflected, as he turned his car onto the long driveway that approached his house, Roger Bayliss was too young to have been damaged by the first war, nor had he been personally involved in the second.

The doctor's wife, who had been hoping her husband might return in time for the pair of them to finish their game, was collecting the scattered tennis balls from the court and looping up the net. Through the gathering dusk he saw her smile and shrug as she waved her Slazenger racket in a wry greeting.

In Roger's kitchen Alice assembled a tray of hot buttered toast and cups of milky Horlicks. He watched her as she entered the drawing room and set the tray on a low table beside his chair.

"Might help to eat something, your doctor said," she murmured as she sat down in the chair the doctor had used when he examined his patient. Roger's hands were hanging limply. She took one in both of hers.

"You're cold!" he said, looking at her with some concern. The drawing room fire, which Roger sometimes lit on the cooler summer evenings, was laid. He crossed the room to it, struck a match and stooped to hold it to the crumpled newspaper under the kindling. As the flames caught, Alice joined him and they knelt, side by side, watching the fire take hold, throwing its warmth and light towards them. She shuddered. "But you're still shivering, Alice!" he said, and he fetched a tartan rug from a fireside armchair, shook it out and draped it round her shoulders. Then he knelt in front of her, his eyes scanning her face.

"Ah," she said gently, "you can see me, now."

"What?" he asked, vaguely.

"Before . . . on the bridge. After the . . . accident. You couldn't."

"Couldn't? Couldn't what?"

"Couldn't see me. You were looking at me, Roger, but . . ." Alice paused. She was confused. The shock of Margery's death and then Roger's extreme reaction to it was, perhaps, beginning to affect her. "It was as though you were somewhere else. Somewhere so dreadful that you couldn't see or hear me. You seemed to be experiencing things that . . . sort of . . . dislocated you from what was happening. It was as though you were being attacked. And I wanted . . ." Her voice had thickened, her throat was closing on the words and tears began to roll down her face. "I wanted, so much, to help. To protect you, and I couldn't. Because you were . . . not there. Oh, my darling man . . . Where were you?"

Afterwards, when, either together or separately, they tried to remember the sequence of events that followed, each recalled them differently. She remembered feeling overwhelmed with the shock of what had happened to Margery and with its effect on Roger. She remembered him wrapping her in the warmth of the tartan rug and drawing her tentatively towards him. Then he had put his arms carefully around her, held her closely against him and rocked her as tenderly as he might have rocked a distressed child. She remembered his voice, almost a whisper, in her ear, but could never precisely recall the words he used.

He remembered seeing her white face and streaming eyes. Then he had eased her towards him, held her and become suffused by an overwhelming sensation of protective intimacy that was new to him. He had intended to apologise for frightening her and he wanted, somehow, to prevent her from becoming infected with the curious malaise of his own complex personality. Instead he was overtaken by a succession of emotions that he had never before experienced. Emotions that had not been part of his relationship with his first wife. Between him and her there had been affection, trust and restraint rather than the sense of passion that he felt lay at the root of his relationship with Alice Todd. Although he and Frances had lain together and conceived their son, there had been an inhibition on Roger's part, a deference to her delicate health, that had, he now began to understand, denied him the pleasures of unrestrained lovemaking.

Alice's concern for him was in sharp contrast to that of his parents when, long ago, they had assumed responsibility for him when he had got into difficulties, like a swimmer in a violent sea. They had meant well and had been, on his behalf, both defensive and secretive in their attempt to protect him from the consequences of a foolish and potentially tragic act on his part. But they had been determined that he should deal with the difficult situation not in his way but in theirs, and because he had been young and injured by what he had done, he had obeyed them. The consequences of this had been far-reaching and dangerous, colouring not only his relationship with Frances, the girl he probably should not have married, but, much later, his role as father to a son whom he had failed to unconditionally support at a time when the boy most needed to be accepted and nurtured. When Christopher had cracked, Roger had seen his breakdown as evidence of a flawed character and had reacted inappropriately, just as his own parents had reacted to him, applying the same damaging solution.

Alice Todd, unlike Roger's first wife, was neither insecure nor fragile. She had learnt, since the failure of her own marriage, to be independent. Although neither insensitive nor invulnerable, Alice had not needed Roger's protection or sought his indulgence. Yet now, because of him, she was shivering, shocked, and responding to him as he endeavoured to comfort and warm her. For each of them the status quo was subtly shifting.

They had gone up the stairs and into Roger's bedroom, reacting to an impulse neither of them questioned or resisted. The room, lit by a summer sky which was hesitating between twilight and early darkness, discreetly welcomed them.

Later, lying in the bed and watching her dress, Roger, adopting an ironic formality, said that he blamed her for what he called "this delightful indiscretion".

"Me? And how is it my fault?" she queried, smiling and slipping her arms into the sleeves of her cardigan. "You seduced me!"

"True. But it was always my intention to do things in the proper order."

"The proper order?"

"Yes. Declaration. Proposal. Nuptials. Bed. Twice I got perilously close to the proposal bit."

"Did you?"

"Yes! But you are always so damned busy, Alice!"

"Am I?"

"Yes! With your duties as warden, I mean. And to Edward John as a mother and . . . well . . . to yourself . . . if you understand what I mean. You don't give a fellow a fighting chance!" She looked at him in surprise and then, after a moment, smiled. He watched, overwhelmed with tenderness, as she faced the mirror on his dressing table and, using one of his pair of tortoiseshell brushes, attempted to tidy her hair, her eyes on his via the silvery looking glass.

As he took the car down through the lanes to the lower farm he felt almost overwhelmed by a sense of release that he could not at first identify. He felt able to be not only protective but joyously confident and possessive. His mind was uncluttered and focused. All of his five senses were acutely aware of Alice, beside him. His subconscious was responding to her. At some level he was astonished that he had come so far in his life before understanding how complex and yet how sublimely simple being overwhelmingly in love with someone could be.

"Are you all right?" he kept asking her. "I so much want to be certain you are all right!"

"Of course I am!" she laughed, happily infected by his mood. They had, she realised, with a feeling of relief, declared themselves. They had not only admitted but successfully demonstrated their feelings for one another.

"There is so much I have to tell you!" he said. "I need to explain to you why I couldn't . . . Why it seemed to be so important *not* to tell you, or anyone, certain things . . . Why I believed that the best line of defence against disaster is denial!"

"Denial?" Alice echoed, and then asked what disaster he was referring to, but he went on quickly, almost as though he was thinking aloud.

"I've been locked into that denial ever since. You have been pushing at it, of course."

"Pushing? Have I? Pushing at what?"

"You, and to a lesser degree, the Webster girl."

"Georgina?"

"Yes. She was the first to challenge me on the Christopher situation." The lane levelled and the dark shape of the lower farm lay just ahead of them. He brought the car quietly to a stop and they sat for a long moment without speaking.

"Roger," Alice said, a sudden note of urgency in her voice. "Do you have a key to the hostel door?"

It was, they both realised suddenly, almost midnight. The low building was in total darkness, the wind-up gramophone silent in the empty recreation room. Rose's cottage, too, stood, a familiar shape in the darkness.

In the light from his dashboard Roger searched through his bunch of keys for the one that fitted the Lower Post Stone lock and detached it from his keyring. He heard Alice sigh with relief. And then she was laughing, smothering the sound and, as Roger's shoulders, too, began to shake, begging him to be quiet. But the laughter, an accumulated effect of the night's extraordinary events, proved uncontrollable. If it had been free to sweep over them and run its noisy course, it would, eventually, have eased them. Instead they were forced to suppress it or run the risk of waking everyone within earshot.

"Oh Alice!" he spluttered, eventually. "You are in desperate trouble, my dear! What will Rose say? What will Gwennan think of this?" Alice, beyond speech and still struggling to stifle her own laughter, put her finger against his lips to silence him. This sobered him and suddenly they were still. He took her hand, turned it and kissed her palm. After a moment she reached for the key, took it from him, leant towards him and kissed him on the mouth.

"You will tell me everything," she whispered, "everything you want to. When you're ready to. But not tonight." He watched her until she had gone quietly through the farmhouse gate, along the cobbled path into the porch and had closed the heavy oak door behind her.

CHAPTER
SIX

"Mr Bayliss all right, is 'e?" Rose enquired next morning, entering the kitchen where the warden was going through the ritual of preparing breakfast.

"Oh, yes," Alice said, pushing a wooden spoon through the porridge. "Doctor Talbot said it was the shock. It takes people in different ways, doesn't it. And poor Gwennan. Awful for her. First on the scene and everything. Was she all right last night?"

"Bit quiet," Rose answered. "But not as bad as Mr Bayliss be all accounts. Vomiting, Gwennan said. Pale as a ghost and breathin' funny. You'd think he could cope with a bit of blood, what with the cattle and that."

"But this was Margery Brewster's blood, Rose! Someone he'd known for years!" The girls, by this time, were slouching sleepily into the kitchen and dropping into their chairs, depressed by last night's news and by the fact that it was Monday and the start of another gruelling week of labour. Alice, grateful for the fact that their arrival put an end to Rose's interrogation, turned her attention to Gwennan.

"Yes, I'm all right, thank you, Mrs Todd," she assured the warden, taking her place at the table and picking up her porridge spoon. "There'll be policemen,

153

I suppose?" she said. "Askin' questions about the accident?"

The inspector arrived after supper that evening, and Alice led him into her sitting room and sent Annie to fetch Gwennan who, after some time, arrived from the bathroom with a towel wrapped round her damp hair.

"I were havin' me bath," she announced, defensively. "There's only so much hot water here, see, so you 'as to take it when you can get it."

"From Wales are you, love?" the officer enquired, identifying Gwennan's lilting accent. "My wife comes from there. Dolgelly, she were born." Gwennan was unimpressed. "Right," he finished lamely. "Well, Miss . . ."

"Pringle. Gwennan Pringle."

"Miss Pringle . . . If you'd just tell me, in your own words, what happened?"

Gwennan appeared to Alice to have rehearsed her account of the accident, which she delivered concisely and without hesitation, describing it from the moment she and Annie had seen the registrar's car careering downhill to the point where Mrs Brewster's body had been driven away in the back of the ambulance.

"So, until Mr Bayliss arrived with Mrs Todd you were alone at the scene, right?"

"Yes. Like I said. Annie had run back to the higher farm for help. I would of gone on'y Annie can run faster than me."

"And you approached the victim?"

"Yes. Like I said," Gwennan sounded slightly impatient, "I went to see if I could help her."

154

"Did you touch her at all?"

"Yes, I touched her shoulder. Then I took one of her hands."

"Did you think the poor lady was dead?"

"Yes, I was certain she was, what with her not breathin' and all the blood."

"And then what happened?"

"I just told you!" Gwennan snapped, irritated by his apparent lack of attention to the precise account of the sequence of events on the bridge which she had already given him. "Mr Bayliss's car come down the hill from the direction of Ledburton, and he and Mrs Todd got out and took a look at Mrs Brewster but there wasn't nothing they could do for her, no more than what I could have. After a while the ambulance people came and they fetched her away, and that was when Mr Bayliss come over funny — because of the shock, the policeman thought — and Mrs Todd said I was to go up to the higher farm and tell Eileen to call Mr Bayliss's doctor. Then I was to come back here. Which I did," Gwennan concluded, staring soberly at the inspector, who thanked her for her account which matched both Alice's and Roger Bayliss's.

"Will that be all, then, Mrs Todd?" Gwennan asked, pointedly directing her question to the warden. The inspector closed his notebook, slid it into a pocket in his tunic, and glad to be relieved of the necessity of any further dealings with Gwennan, nodded to Alice.

"Yes, Gwennan. Thank you," Alice said. After bestowing a cool smile on the inspector, Gwennan withdrew from the room.

Alice showed the inspector out, but as the glow from his dimmed headlights moved away down the lane, she heard a voice behind her.

"Could I have a word, Mrs Todd?" Gwennan asked. "Somewhere private, if you don't mind."

Gwennan's expression, when she had seated herself in Alice's room, had changed from the one she had worn for the policeman. She now appeared concerned and ill at ease. Alice asked her what was wrong.

"It's about Mrs Brewster," she began. "I did something, see." Gwennan's breathing was audible in the quiet room, her face was pale and she kept clenching and then unclenching her fists. "It was on the spur of the moment and I'm not sure why I did it! It just came over me in a flash, and before I knew it, I'd done it!" Alice asked her what it was she had done. "It was the gin." Gwennan began.

"The broken bottle," Alice prompted, nodding.

"Yes. On'y it wasn't broke when I got there, see! It must have been caught up somehow, in Mrs Brewster's clothes, and when she rolled over it slid out onto the road." Alice waited for more information, a puzzled expression on her face.

"But the bottle *was* broken, Gwennan. It was shattered. There were fragments of glass all over the —"

"No!" Gwennan interrupted, her voice low and urgent. "Not when I got there it wasn't! Honest! I broke it, see? I smashed it!" Alice stared incredulously.

"But . . . Gwennan . . . Why?"

"'Cos when I leant over Mrs Brewster she was reekin', Mrs Todd! Reekin'! Of gin! You could smell it on her and some of it was runnin' out of her mouth! But the bottle wasn't broke! It was half empty and the top was on! Screwed on tight it was! Caught in her sleeve, I reckon. Like she'd had the bottle on her lap, where she could get at it to take the odd swig! If they'd found her like that . . ." Gwennan's eyes searched Alice's face. "With the bottle half empty and her smellin' like . . ."

"Like a distillery."

"Yes, like that, Mrs Todd! So I tipped the gin over her clothes and on her poor face and her hair! Then I smashed the bottle so it looked like it got broke in the accident! That was when you and Mr Bayliss come. I thought you might of seen what I done, but you didn't, did you?" Alice shook her head.

"But . . . Gwennan . . ." she said. Her concern was huge.

"I know, Mrs Todd! I know I prob'ly shouldn't of! But it flashed through me mind how awful it would have been — everyone knowing it was the drinking that killed her and laughing at her behind their hands the way folk do in these parts! And her poor husband! I could hear a car coming, so if I was going to do something I knew I had to do it quick! And before I could think any more I done it! And it worked, didn't it! Everyone thought she stank of gin because her clothes got soaked in it when the bottle broke. That's what you and Mr Bayliss thought, didn't you?" Alice admitted that it was. "And I never told no lies to the inspector, Mrs Todd! I answered his questions truthful! Like I'd been under oath!"

★   ★   ★

157

With the cause of death undisputed, no other vehicles involved and reliable witnesses to the whole tragic sequence of events, Mrs Brewster's body was released for burial, and a week later the Post Stone girls, impressive in their Land Army uniforms, formed a guard of honour along the path from the lychgate to the door of Ledburton church. They followed the coffin into the dim interior, took their places in the pews and soberly sang "He Who Would Valiant Be". Gwennan kept her eyes on the highly polished toes of her regulation shoes, glancing only briefly at the flower-covered coffin as it was carried slowly past her, the flower heads of the wreaths nodding in time with the footsteps of the pall-bearers, out into the sunny graveyard and on, under the shade of yew trees, towards the newly dug heap of earth beside the grave.

In her head Gwennan asked the dead woman, "D'you know what it was I done, Mrs Brewster?" Maybe Mrs Brewster did not know. Certainly her husband did not. Nor her daughters or the local newspapers, the gossips and the scandalmongers. Perhaps it was to be something between Gwennan herself and her maker. And Mrs Todd, of course. Mrs Todd knew. Alice had said that as Gwennan's action had no bearing on the accident itself, and that as the police had not enquired about the circumstances of the breaking of the gin bottle, she was not obliged to tell them. And it was possible, Gwennan told herself, whenever her conscience worried her, that the smell of gin on the registrar's person might, just possibly, have gone unnoticed. But in her heart she doubted this and was proud of what she had done. Perhaps, as Sergeant Kinski had told her, she was, after all, a kindly and well-meaning person?

On the day after the funeral Gwennan was, herself, involved in an accident. A laden cart, having been backed into a byre where its load of straw had been pitchforked into the loft, was being moved out into the yard when Prince, normally the most even-tempered of the carthorses, was startled by something and had shied, taking the cart a few yards with him, back into the byre. Gwennan, who had been behind the cart, found herself caught off balance and flung heavily against the solid granite of a drinking trough. Winded, she felt her ribs crack and a searing pain went through her chest. The skin on her sternum was grazed and blood began to seep through the dark-green Aertex of her shirt. Moments later she was sitting, white-faced and gasping, on the steps of the mounting block in the yard, shaking her head and refusing to be taken to hospital.

"But you have to go, Taff!" Annie said. "It's the law!" Unable to resist the hands that were easing her to her feet, she was carefully lowered into the passenger seat of Roger Bayliss's car. With Annie in the back seat he drove, as smoothly as he could, to the hospital in Exeter and then sat, waiting with Annie, while the doctors examined Gwennan's injuries.

"No!" she protested when a nurse and a young doctor approached her. "I'm all right! It's on'y bruises, see! Don't touch me! I don't want no one touching me." They fetched an older woman whom they referred to as "Matron". Whether it was the result of the pain or in response to the woman's authoritative manner, Gwennan allowed them to take her into a cubicle where they removed her shirt, exposing torn skin and a vivid discolouration across her chest and right shoulder. When it was obvious that no amount of protest on her part would prevent a thorough examination of her injuries, Gwennan became subdued, lying still, while they X-rayed her and moved their fingers carefully across her sternum, pressing against her chest, assessing the tenderness of each rib and exploring the tissue of her small, flat breasts. She lay, staring passively past them into space. Then they left her.

When the matron returned, together with the young doctor who carried in his hand a sheaf of X-ray photographs, she was smiling encouragingly at Gwennan.

"No bones broken in the shoulder, luckily," she announced, "but it will be very sore. You've cracked three ribs, which will hurt a lot to begin with and will take about six weeks to recover. So, no heavy work for two months and complete rest for a couple of days. After that you should do what you can to get moving. Your ribs won't let you do more than is good for you. So, let's get you dressed and we'll put a sling on that shoulder."

"What about the other, though?" Gwennan asked, dully.

"What other, dear?" the matron asked as she folded fabric for the sling.

"The other thing that's wrong with me." The matron was puzzled. She had seen no evidence of any other injury.

"What other thing?"

"The cancer."

"Cancer?"

"Yes. In me breast. You must of felt it when you touched it." The matron, who while assessing the damage to Gwennan's ribcage had thoroughly palpated her chest and felt nothing abnormal under her sensitive and experienced fingers, repeated her examination with the same result.

"Did you feel a lump?" she asked her patient.

"Yes. The size of a gooseberry it were. And me nipple looked sort of funny."

"Funny?" the matron asked, continuing to work her hand over Gwennan's breasts, first the right, then the left. "Well it isn't now. They both look exactly the same to me. And there are no lumps. None at all. When did you say you found one?"

"A bit more than a year ago," Gwennan told her. "It were just after my sister died of the cancer. Like my Auntie Rhiannan had. It runs in the family, see. I know what's going to happen to me. I seen it all before."

"You thought you had symptoms and you didn't see a doctor?"

"What was the point?" Gwennan said. Her mind had not yet fully absorbed what the matron's words suggested. "My sister Olwyn saw doctors. So did Aunt Rhiannan. They cuts bits out of them and sent 'em home. Didn't do them no good. They got ever so ill and then they died."

"Give me your hand," the matron said, and she took Gwennan's hand and moved the fingers over the contours of her flat breasts. First the right, then the left. "There," the matron said. "Nothing but perfectly normal tissue. Now. Sit up and look in that mirror over there." Gwennan looked. "See? Two identical nipples."

"They weren't like that when I looked before," Gwennan said. She was experiencing a strange sensation. A sort of excitement. A void, where something dark and threatening had been. "And there was a lump. There was. I felt it! I did!"

"And you did nothing about it?"

"No."

"So . . . for an entire year, you never felt for the lump again? Or examined the nipples?"

"No. No, I never did. Not once." The matron seemed almost affronted. It was as though she perceived Gwennan's reaction to her symptoms as an insult to the medical profession in general and to herself in particular. She sighed and went to the small handbasin in the corner of the cubicle, where she washed her hands as though ridding herself of contact with this strange young woman.

Gwennan had walked painfully out of the examination cubicle and back to the waiting room. After details of her injuries had been given to her employer, together with a certificate exempting her from work for ten days, and suggesting light duties for six weeks after that, he

162

and Annie led her out to the car. Watching them go, the matron and the young doctor exchanged glances.

"How could that happen?" the young man asked. The matron shrugged.

"Lumps come and go," she said. "Nipples can pucker for a variety of reasons. Probably the sister's death had something to do with it."

Some hours later, when Gwennan, wearing her sling, might have been preparing to exploit her invalid status, she had other concerns on her mind.

"Is it very painful?" Alice asked, glancing at Gwennan, who was sitting, frowning into the cup of tea Alice had put in front of her.

"Pardon?" the girl said, vaguely, adding that no, since she had taken the two aspirins the matron had suggested, it didn't hurt much as long as she kept still. "Mrs Todd?" she asked suddenly. "Do you believe in miracles?"

They drove across the Exe valley to a riverside pub which Alice recognised as the place where she had once been lunched by Oliver Maynard, a naval adjutant from a nearby Fleet Air Arm establishment, who had sought her company when she had first arrived at the farm.

"You've been here before?" Roger asked her, noticing her reaction to the terrace where half a dozen tables were set for lunch. When she told him how it was that she knew the place he smiled. "Ah, yes, the commander fellow. I remember him." He was recalling, Alice guessed, his own success in beating off a rival. "Wonder what became of him? Where shall we sit?" Alice chose a table, deliberately avoiding the one she and Oliver had shared and at which she had refused his suggestion that they should take their relationship a stage further towards the affair he obviously had in mind.

The lamb chops were succulent and the home-made raspberry ice cream so delicious that Alice and Roger both indulged in second helpings of it.

Roger became silent as they drank their coffee. Alice sat, the brim of her straw hat shielding her eyes from the sun, gazing across the valley and very aware that Roger was watching her. He leant forward and covered her hand with his. He was looking at her intently now and she met his eyes.

"You don't have to tell me anything you don't want to, Roger," she said, sensing that there were facts he wanted her to know but that he was unsure how to broach them.

"I need to explain these things that happen to me, Alice. And why I react as I seem to, to some situations . . . and people. I've been trying to work out why. And I certainly owe you an apology for — yes I do, Alice," he insisted, when she smiled and shook her head. "I am very fond of you. More than fond. You know that. You've told me a lot about yourself and what happened between you and your husband . . . Not, perhaps, in so many words, but I've seen what you went through as a result of his treatment of you and how you've coped with it all. And what have I done since we met? Nothing but burden you with my complicated afflictions and lumber you with my incomprehensible behaviour." She smiled but he obviously intended to be

164

taken seriously. "I haven't succeeded in asking you to marry me but you are too perceptive not to be aware of my feelings for you. So, why haven't I proposed marriage to you?" He paused, uncertain of her reaction. "You have obviously sensed that I have problems with my relationship with Christopher and that I react in an unhealthy way to . . . to . . . well . . . accidents, such as poor Margery's death. And yet I have failed to confide in you. Failed even to pay you the compliment of believing that you would have the intelligence and the . . ." he hesitated and then, very quietly continued, "the compassion to understand why it is that I have been stupid enough to allow something that happened so long ago that it feels as though it belongs to an altogether other life, to ruin the present and possibly contaminate the future too!" He called the waiter over to their table and asked for more coffee and a second brandy. Alice suggested they should take the drinks down to the riverbank, where a solitary table and chairs stood on the landing stage. They made their way down the sloping bank and settled themselves at the table. Roger watched the waiter unload the tray, Alice poured the coffee, slid Roger's cup over the surface of the table to him and sat, cupping her brandy glass while Roger lit a cigarette.

"I was at public school when the First World War started," he said at last. "My father had been head boy in his day and an older cousin was, when I arrived there, captain of the school cricket eleven." They watched as a heron flapped languorously across their field of vision and landed clumsily in the shallows on the far side of the river.

"I am listening," Alice said, swirling the brandy slowly round her glass.

"To begin with everyone thought the war was a bit of a lark," Roger said. "We believed it would all be over by Christmas, of course. Everyone did at that point. No one had the slightest idea about what really lay ahead. Some of our sixth-form boys, who were old enough, marched off to volunteer — and we all cheered. We younger ones were green with envy. We felt cheated. After a few months the headmaster began reading out names of old boys who'd been reported missing or killed in action. Some of them were the older brothers of my friends. You'd file into assembly, there would be prayers and a hymn. Then the head would read out the names — Howarth major, when you were standing next to Howarth minor. But we still cheered when the next group marched off, and there were white feathers for anyone who didn't volunteer and a wooden leg for our best rugby player when he came home on crutches and with his face scarred almost beyond recognition. There was, we began to understand, a darker side to this war. Some people tried to ignore it. Which would probably have been the best thing to do. Maybe that's what I should have done, and maybe, even then, I was guilty of having an unhealthy reaction to it all." Roger flicked his cigarette stub out into the river. "You would have been too young to remember much about it, Alice, but that war caught me at a time when I was, I suppose, at my most impressionable."

166

"And suggestible?" Alice asked.

"Possibly. But at the time, you don't know that you are suggestible, do you?" Alice shook her head. She had been a toddler when the war began. Having lost both her parents almost before she could remember them, she was being mothered by her Aunt Elizabeth. She vaguely recalled Armistice Day, or possibly only thought she did, having been told about it and subsequently seen newspaper photographs and newsreel footage of celebrations which always looked grainy and grey, suggesting to her that it was the images she remembered, rather than the actual events.

"My closest friend at school was Robert Thomas," Roger told her. "We called him Rob. His older brother, Leo, had been at Oxford when the war began and he'd enlisted, become an officer and survived most of the early scraps. Ypres, Mons and so on. He seemed to have a charmed life. I had met him once when I was staying with the Thomas family in the summer holidays of 1913. Rob and I became a bit obsessive about the war. We put together a scrapbook full of facts and newspaper cuttings about it. We had a sort of roll of honour, adding the names of boys from our school as they were reported dead or missing, week after week. We listed their rank and regiment, any decorations they had been awarded and the circumstances of their deaths — if these were known. More often than not, they were not known. They simply vanished along with thousands of others. Bodies never recovered. 'Known only to God' as they were afterwards described. Then, in 1915, Leo was wounded at the second Battle of

Ypres. He died, not cleanly but horribly, of gangrene, after they amputated first one and then the other of his legs." Alice didn't speak but slowly shook her head. "It had a curious effect on Rob and me."

"What effect?"

"It made us angry!"

"Understandably."

"Incredibly angry. And there was nothing we could do with the anger. We wanted to —"

"To put an end to the carnage. To see the war stopped."

"No! Not stopped, Alice! We wanted it won! We wanted the German army routed! Otherwise our people would have given their lives for nothing! And we felt an overwhelming sense of guilt! Those men were dying! They were going out into the trenches, facing what had to be faced and we, because we were too young, were not! You see, in our eyes we were men by then! At sixteen we were strong and fit! We asked, repeatedly, to be allowed to volunteer and were refused. But in the end we managed it."

"Managed to enlist? At sixteen?"

"Some friends of Leo's told us how to apply to the medical unit. We'd be used as stretcher-bearers. Bringing the wounded in from the lines and delivering them to the field hospitals." Alice was staring at him in astonishment. "I know, I know," he said. "We had no concept of what we were in for, and even now, even after all this time . . ." He fell silent and Alice watched as he swallowed his brandy and gathered himself. "We worked in pairs. One at each end of a stretcher on which we laid the injured and the dead. Often our load consisted of more than one man — or the body parts of more than one man. We slithered through the mud, Alice, pulling men and bits of men out of the gore and then struggled back to the bright lights of a tent that passed for a hospital, where we delivered our load. The casualties who didn't survive that initial journey were laid on the ground, side by side, outside the tent. The luckier ones were patched up and transported to a larger hospital, and if they made it that far, shipped home to die or recover." He spoke fluently and in a low voice, as though he was visiting territory no less painful for being familiar to him. "We worked together, Rob and I, through what became a disorienting nightmare. Nothing we had read, or seen or heard had prepared us for what we experienced. We were covered in blood. And not only blood, Alice. Other things. Guts. Brain. Bone fragments. Our clothes and our skin were sticky with it. The air we breathed tasted of warm blood! I remember looking at Rob and seeing his face, just recognisable under his tin hat. He stared at me and saw, I'm certain, his own feelings mirrored. Over and over again we delivered our dying and our dead and over and over again we were ordered back to the lines. Days and nights ran into each other. I don't know which of us cracked first. I remember that there was a group of riflemen behind us, moving forward to relieve a section of men in the trenches. We would have been silhouetted against the gunfire ahead of them and they must have seen us drop the stretcher and turn back. Which of us turned first I don't know. We ran together, clinging to each other, aimlessly, away from the lines. The riflemen claimed afterwards they thought we were Germans infiltrating Allied lines. Or deserters — no one had much time for them. Anyway, they fired. I sensed the impact when Rob was hit and felt him go down." Roger had finished his brandy. He sighed and looked at Alice almost as though he was glad to be back with her, here above the river on a quiet afternoon.

"And . . ." Alice hesitated. "He was dead?"

"I supposed so."

"And you?"

"That was when it all got very strange. I have absolutely no recollection of anything that happened to me from then on, for almost a whole year. I discovered, slowly, afterwards, that our headmaster used contacts he had in the War Office, and that because I was under age and more or less out of my mind, it was decided that I was not to be shot as a deserter but repatriated, in a straightjacket. My treatment must have been pretty radical. Whatever it was, I knew nothing about it because a lot of heavy sedation was involved. Even after I was released into the care of my parents I was out of things most of the time. They took charge of me. Their way of dealing with it — they saw the entire situation as a colossal failure on my part — was to deny it ever happened. They were deeply embarrassed about it, and everyone — friends, neighbours, even family — was told I had been extremely ill, having been infected by the blood of a diseased frog which I had been dissecting in a chemistry class at school!" His face broke, briefly, into a wry smile. "I was forbidden to mention my

170

escapade in France and was so damaged by the whole situation that for a while I almost believed my parents' story! I certainly didn't, to begin with, have the strength to resist them. When I asked what had happened to Rob they refused to tell me. Eventually I made my way to his parents' house. I had remembered that they lived in Weymouth and I rode there on my bicycle. It was a heck of a way and I could barely stand by the time I turned up on their doorstep! I suppose I must have known Rob was dead. I think I just needed to have it confirmed after my parents' evasiveness. Rob's father gave me the details. He was shot dead. Both of us, Rob posthumously, were charged with desertion and vilified for falsifying our ages on our application forms. Rob's mother reacted badly to my visit. She needed to believe I had instigated the whole wretched scheme. But I hadn't. We were equally determined, Rob and I. Equally committed. It must have been impossible for her. I mean, there I was, gaunt, sick and shaking. The last time she'd seen me I'd been a robust schoolboy, knocking tennis balls about the garden with her son."

"But you were alive, Roger, and her boy was not."

"Precisely. Pretty hard on Rob's father too. But he was very decent about it. Lashed my bike onto the back of his car and drove me home — I doubt if I'd have made it otherwise. Set me back a few months, that episode did. Back to the phenobarbitone, etcetera. It was about then that I started to accept the fact that if I was going to survive — you feel you have to, at that age, the will to live asserts itself despite everything — I had to do what my parents wanted. Handle it their way. So

I did. I went to agricultural college. Time passed and I had begun taking over a share of responsibility for the farm when my mother, who had been in poor health for some time, died, and father, to everyone's surprise, remarried and took off for Bournemouth where his second wife already lived in some style. So there I was, walking wounded by then, psychologically speaking, but coping, getting to grips with the running of the farms. That was when I met Frances. She was a . . ." he hesitated, uncertain how to describe the young woman he had married when they had both been barely out of their teens. "A fragile person," he continued. "With a dependent disposition. I think this did me good in a strange way. It encouraged me to take charge of things. She never did know what a mess I was, under my carapace! We were living 'happily ever after', Frances, Christopher and I, when we lost her — quite suddenly, as the result of a pregnancy that went wrong and revealed a more serious problem. Chris was only nine years old at the time. I didn't handle that very well. Didn't know how to help myself, or the boy. I think I was scared, Alice. I felt as though I'd fought my way through a lot but that I couldn't expose myself to any more . . . Any more loss, I suppose I meant. I just wasn't up to it. Then, when Chris joined the RAF, I was faced with two possibilities. One was that I might lose him altogether. And the other was that he might . . . might lose himself, in the way I had lost myself in my war. And then, when he did, when he cracked up . . . Well, you know how I reacted. I have no excuse, Alice. But there was a reason for it, and the reason was that I was incapable of anything else. Anything better. I love that boy, Alice. But I failed him. He has survived that failure and is, understandably, in the process of making a life for himself without my destructive input. I don't propose getting in the way of that."

Alice had leant across the table and taken his hands in both of hers. She was shocked by what he had told her. Mixed with that reaction was the knowledge that she had been right to suspect that some major experience had damaged him and was responsible for his reaction to Christopher's problem.

"You must tell him, Roger!" she said, gravely. "All of it."

"I have thought about it, Alice."

"And decided what?"

"To say nothing. What would be the point? All this goes back too far. It's history. Just as the horrendous events that triggered it all are history. I'm damaged goods, Alice. I've been experiencing these moments of disequilibrium more frequently lately. They had almost stopped and then, when that Italian fellow was injured, and again and more seriously when poor Margery died . . . Well, you saw what happened. When Chris cracked up I had some bad days. Kept them pretty much to myself but they happened just the same."

"It was probably Christopher's breakdown that sort of reactivated it all. But now that it's over . . . and when you talk to him about it . . . won't it —?"

"No, Alice," he interrupted. "I'm convinced that my relationship with Chris is beyond recovery. I don't want his pity. I have to let him go." Stunned, Alice let the seconds pass before she spoke.

"Without telling him why? Without giving him the chance to let you know he understands? Without him knowing how you feel about him? Without giving him your blessing?"

"Well, I daresay I'll manage that!" Roger said, almost amused. "I'll go and dance at their wedding, if that's what you mean. It's in three weeks time, by the way. I was summoned to dinner by the Webster parents. All very civilised. It's to be a quiet, family affair. You're on the guest list, I gather. They consider that you've been a good influence on Georgina. I don't think I would be so sanguine were I in their shoes and my daughter was off to the other side of the world."

"I think that's more your responsibility than mine!" Alice said, and he looked sharply at her, surprised by her tone.

"Driving him away, you mean?"

"In effect, yes. You are so stubborn, Roger! Can't you see it?"

"And now you're cross with me!" He was concealing his concern behind a show of innocent confusion.

"No! You fool!" she said. "I'm not cross! Just . . ." She struggled unsuccessfully for the right word and only managed, "Sorry!"

"Sorry?"

"Yes! And more than sorry, Roger! Desperate! For Chris. For you. And, heaven help me, for me!" She got up from the table, stumbled up the riverbank and wove her way between the tables on the terrace. Roger saw

174

her go through the open french doors at the rear of the pub and disappear into its shadowy interior. As he settled the bill he could see her through the lobby window, standing beside his car. The wind had risen and she was pulling her jacket more closely round her.

They drove for some miles without speaking.

"Try this," Alice began. "Try putting the past out of your mind. Try thinking about what happens now and what happens next. To you, to Christopher, to Georgina . . . to all of us, Roger. Don't think about how things got locked into this state. If you want to tell him about what happened to you and Rob, then tell him! If not, confine yourself to letting him know how much you value him. How you've always valued him. How it was the difficult events in *your* life that shocked, disappointed and depressed you, not him, or his life! And if you feel it's best to let him go to New Zealand, then let him! But don't let him leave believing you don't care!"

They had arrived at the farmhouse gate and as Alice reached to open the car door Roger put his hand on her arm to stop her.

"No," she said. The door was open and she was easing away from him. "Let me go, Roger. Please, my dear. I don't want to be involved in this . . . this unhappiness anymore. I'm sorry."

CHAPTER
SEVEN

Since she had opened what she called her "tea room", Rose's work in the hostel was officially reduced to three hours each morning, when she would help Alice with the clearing up of the kitchen after breakfast, clean the bathroom and spend what remained of her time with mop and broom wherever they were required. Most mornings she met the postman at the farmhouse gate and scanned the letters before propping them on the dresser where the girls would find them when they arrived back from work.

"'Nother letter from the sergeant for our Marion! I don't know what 'e finds to say to her!"

"It's love, Rose!"

"Is it, though? Or is 'e just stringin' 'er along?"

"I think it's pretty serious," Alice said, preparing to cross the yard to the barn where half a dozen hens had established themselves amongst the disused mangers, and where, with any luck, she might find enough eggs for a batter for the toad-in-the-hole she had planned for tonight's supper.

It had occurred to Alice to wonder how Marion and Winnie would resolve their ambition to be joint landladies of their own pub if "the little sergeant", as both the girls called Marvin Kinski, was to propose marriage to Marion, who seemed, from Alice's observations and the almost daily letters between the two of them, to be very attached to him. How would Winnie take it if her best friend and potential business partner was to become a GI bride, board a ship and vanish into the uncharted territory of the United States of America?

Kinski, originally from the Bronx, was a professional soldier and had consequently spent most of his adult life in army accommodation on a succession of military bases scattered across his vast country, without forming an allegiance to any particular part of it.

Aside from appearing to be slightly preoccupied, neither Marion or Winnie had sought Alice's advice on the subject and she, with other things on her mind, was content not to involve herself in it.

They sat facing each other in a café in Exeter with a steamy windowpane between them and the rainy street outside. Their hands were clasped on the stained tablecloth, their teacups were empty and there were only cake crumbs on their plates. A small box, its lid open, exposing a modest diamond set in gold, lay between them and Marion's eyes were anxiously searching the sergeant's face. This was the third time he had proposed marriage and each time a similar discussion had taken place.

"But what sort of a wife would I be, though, Marvin, if I was someone as broke their promises? Someone who didn't keep her word?"

"But what if it was the other way about?" he asked her. "What if it was Winnie who wanted out of this plan of yours? Suppose she was the one who'd found herself a fella? What would you have done? Hey?"

"I dunno!" Marion sighed. "But anyroad she 'asn't, 'as she!" Marvin was chewing gloomily on the damp stub of his cigar.

"Seems like it was a pretty weird arrangement for two lookers like you and Winnie to make! Most girls like you dream of meeting Mr Right and living happy ever after!"

"Like our mums did, you mean? With too many kids and no money? Workin' all the hours God sent? Livin' in cold, poky little 'ouses. Dad down the pub! Not much ''appy ever after' in our street, Marvin!" She looked at him and her expression softened. "Win and me weren't much good at our lessons in school but we wasn't stupid! We wanted summat better than what our mums 'ad!"

"It won't be like that with me, babe!" he said, stroking the back of her hand. "I promise you it won't be! We'd have decent married quarters right from the start; then, after a bit I'd buy us a house of our own."

"It's not that, lovey! I'd live in a tent if it meant bein' with you! It's Winnie I'm thinkin' of. Winnie and our plan we made!"

Marvin's cigar was beyond redemption and he abandoned it in his empty teacup.

"Reckon we should talk to her. She's your buddy, Marion. She won't want to stand between you and your happiness."

178

"'Course she won't, Marvin! She'd say I'm to wed you! She'd smile as she waved us goodbye! She's a good egg, is my Winnie! But I can't do it to her, Marvin, I just can't!"

For weeks the situation remained unchanged. Winnie insisting that Marion shouldn't let their arrangement regarding the pub influence her response to Marvin's proposal and Marion determined not to let down her oldest and best friend. Marvin continued to write affectionate letters and, whenever he could, visited his girl. The solution to the problem came from an unexpected quarter.

Dear Marion and Winifred, the letter began. It was from Marion's uncle Ted, whose advice the girls had sought, more than once, about the practicalities of realising their dream.

I have been giving some thought to this plan of yours re running a pub and I reckon it'd be tough for you two, with no track record in the liquor trade nor the hotel trade neither come to that, to cut the mustard with the breweries or the law when it came to licences and so on. I was thinking that perhaps by now you might have gone cold on the idea and in a way I daresay that would be for the best. But it so happens that the landlord of the Red Cow, a few yards down the road from me, has just this week gone to his maker and his widder, Dolly, don't want to stop there on her own. I've been doing his accounts for him these last couple of years to help him out like and although the place is a bit run down as it stands, I rate that pub as a good un. There's a steady bar trade and Dolly's been doing well letting out the bedrooms to commercial gentlemen. What I'm suggesting is that you two girls and me form a partnership. I'll manage the business side of things, the accounts and all, and you two can run the bars and the bed and breakfast side. I could put up some cash for the deposit if you are still a bit short and with my contacts in the town I reckon I wouldn't have no trouble getting a licence. Of course we would need to sort out the details money-wise so when you've had a chance to think about it drop me a line. I reckon you could get a few days leave couldn't you, to come and have a gander at the pub and so on? Hope you are both keeping well as I am.

Yours, Ted.

Another letter had arrived at the farmhouse that day and was lifted down from the dresser shelf and read by its recipient.

"You ought to be pleased," Gwennan told Evie. "Having your bloke come through the war without a scratch on 'im!" But Evie clearly was not happy with the news of the imminent demobilisation of her husband.

"'E wants me to leave 'ere and go back 'ome," she said, without any enthusiasm at all.

"Well of course 'e does!" Marion said, impatiently. "And it's just as well he can't see the look on your face, Evie! What's wrong with you?"

Evie got up from the table without finishing her pudding.

"Nothin'" she said. "I'm goin' for a bike ride before it gets dark." Avoiding the inquisitive looks and the raised eyebrows of the other girls, she left the kitchen.

"I reckon she's seein' someone!" Marion announced. "All this traipsin' about the countryside on her own and goin' for bike rides!"

"She likes the countryside, Marion, you know that," Alice murmured, stacking the pudding plates. "That's why she chose to join the Land Army."

"There's more to it than that," Winnie announced, carrying a stack of plates and following Alice out to the scullery. "What you don't know, Mrs Todd, is that when us girls gets a lift into Ledburton for a drink at the Maltster's, Evie often comes with us and then slopes off on her own. She turns up at the pub in time to come back 'ere with us lot. So where does she go to, eh? We reckon she's meeting up with some bloke!"

"While that poor husband of hers is fighting for king and country!" Gwennan, who was eavesdropping, declared. "Disgraceful, I call it!"

"And no business of ours!" Alice said, firmly.

"That would depend on who it is she's seein', wouldn't it, Mrs Todd?"

On the following Saturday night, when the few girls who had been into the village came home as usual together, in one noisy group, Evie, who had left the hostel when they had, was not with them.

"She came with us as far as the church," Annie told Alice, "and then she went off on her own. For a stroll, she said. We waited for her at closing time, so we could all walk home together, but when she didn't show up, we thought she might have started back on her own. But she hadn't, had she? And we don't know where she is."

With Edward John asleep, Alice sat reading in the light of her bedside lamp. By midnight she was nodding over her book when the click of the latch on the farmhouse gate brought her back to full attention. She was in the cross-passage by the time Evie had quietly pushed open the unlocked front door.

"Come into the kitchen," Alice said, and when they were sitting, facing one another across the table and tears were rolling down Evie's face, she asked her, quite gently, what the matter was.

"I bin seein' someone," Evie said. "I know I shouldn't of and I never meant to, even though things between me and my 'usband 'ave never been right."

"Never?" Alice asked. "Then why did you —?"

"Marry 'im?" Evie paused. "Lookin' back, I shouldn't of, 'cos I never really liked 'im much. Mum and I was on our own, see. My dad left us when I was little and we never knew where 'e was after that and there was no money. Mum took in Norman as a lodger. He was a lot older than me and Mum's a woman as needs a man to take charge of things. And that's what Norman did, see. He sort of took control of everything and pretty soon, when I turned sixteen, he decided we should get married and Mum agreed with 'im. I know I shouldn't of done it 'cos I weren't properly in love with 'im or nothing but 'e was kind to me then. He bought me clothes and took us to the seaside for our 'olidays and that. I got pregnant pretty well straight off 'cos that's what Norman wanted. But it turned out I couldn't carry the baby, and when I lost it, the hospital said I wouldn't be able to 'ave no more kids on account of my womb was messed up. After that Norman 'ad no time for me. 'E said I wasn't a proper woman no more and Mum always took 'is side. 'E sent me out to work and made me give 'im me wages. When 'e got called up I was glad and I thought p'raps 'e'd find some other girl and leave me. I know it's awful but I even hoped 'e might get killed like so many of 'em did. I wanted to get away from Mum an' all, so when I 'ad to do war work I come down 'ere to be a land girl. I wasn't lookin' for no trouble, Mrs Todd, honest! But then I met Giorgio."

"Giorgio?"

"Yes." She hesitated, knowing the effect her next words would have on the warden. "He's one of the Italian POWs . . . Oh, I know we're not s'posed to talk to 'em, Mrs Todd, and I never. Not for ages. But there was this day when 'e was workin' on 'is own. They trusted 'im, see, the guards did. 'E was fixing a drinkin' trough and I'd broke me 'oe and been sent up to the 'igher farm for Ferdie Vallance to mend it, and there was Giorgio and there was me and . . . And after that we managed to see each other quite often. It weren't easy, but since VE Day the guards 'aven't bin that fussy, and quite a few of the prisoners sneak out of an evening. I'm that fond of 'im, Mrs Todd, I really am!

I've never felt for anyone like I do for 'im! Not ever in me life! We made this plan, see, for when the war's properly over. 'E'd apply to stay 'ere in England — they can, see, if they're 'ard workers and their farmer wants 'em. Giorgio works for Mr Lucas and 'e thinks the world of 'im. I was gonna get work down 'ere and be with 'im. That's all we want, see. Just to be together. Only Norman gets out the army in two weeks and in 'is letter 'e says if I'm not home when 'e gets there 'e's comin' down 'ere to fetch me! What'll I do, Mrs Todd?"

Since Georgina had been released from the Air Transport Auxiliary and was dividing her time between her parents' home and Christopher's cottage it soon became necessary for her to arrange some form of transport other than her brother's motorbike.

"It's just not on, Georgie," Lionel complained. "You use the blessed thing more than I do!" The solution to the problem had been lying at the back of one of the Webster barns for the last twenty-odd years. The Brough Superior had once been the pride of the young John Webster. On it he and Isabel, during their courtship and the early years of their marriage, had ranged the valleys of the Exe, explored Dartmoor, and in the summers, visited favourite beaches on the South Devon coast. With the arrival of first Georgina and then Lionel the bike became redundant as a form of family transportation and had, because John had been unable to bring himself to part with it, stood ignored and almost indistinguishable from a clutter of disused farming equipment which had accumulated over the years. With the combined efforts of both his children, John set about restoring the basically sound machine and Georgina was soon roaring through the countryside, rejoicing in her independence.

During the weeks preceding her wedding and while officially living at her parents' home, she frequently stayed overnight with Christopher at the woodman's cottage.

"You reckon 'tis proper?" Rose enquired of Alice as the two women assembled the ingredients for a stew for the land girls' supper. "Them two, shacked up together and not yet wed? What be 'er folks thinkin' of, I ask myself!"

"It's only a matter of weeks until the wedding, Rose, and these days —"

"These days . . ." Rose interrupted, blustering with selfrighteousness, "all you get 'these days' is excuses for bad be'aviour if you ask me!" She clattered a saucepan or two to emphasise her disapproval. This seemed to relieve her and after a moment she asked Alice if she had been invited to the wedding.

The occasion was to be a quiet one which only immediate family members and a few neighbours would attend. Alice was included, but of the Post Stone girls only Annie, who had always been close to Georgina, together with Hector as her escort, had been invited. As Georgina had no young cousins, she asked Edward John to act as page boy.

"Page boy?" he asked, suspiciously. "What do I have to do?"

"Not a lot," Georgina told him. "You just walk down the aisle behind me and hold my flowers while I'm being married."

"Flowers?" he asked, doubtfully. "I have to hold flowers?"

"Only a very small bunch," Georgina reassured him, "and only for a minute or so."

"I don't have to wear a lace collar or anything, do I?"

"Goodness no! Your school uniform will be fine. Would a white carnation in your buttonhole be acceptable, d'you think?"

On the south side of the Websters' home, which was rather more than a farmhouse and slightly less than a manor house, someone had once constructed an orangery which, as the years turned, had become a conservatory. Four wide, glazed doors connected it to the dining room, and while it was hoped that fine weather would allow the reception to take place on the terrace outside the old orangery, its fragile glazing would, in the event of rain, provide shelter and easy access to the house. Isabel and John stood in the humid warmth of its quiet interior, diffused light filtering through overgrown palms and creepers. One or two ancient wicker chairs leant drunkenly, as though about to topple over and tip their flat and faded linen cushions onto the tiled floor.

"Bit of a clear out?" John suggested. "Couple of hours with the pruning shears? Get rid of those chairs and hose the spiders out . . .?"

"I suppose it is a very romantic place for a quiet wedding," Isabel sighed, having imagined something grander for her only daughter.

"Well, it's what she wants," her father said.

It had always been the Websters' intention to raise their children to value independence above all, but there were those who felt that this strategy had backfired on them when Georgina's emigration plans had first been made public. Isabel had winced when people pointed out to her how far away New Zealand was. "Christopher's contract is only for two years," she told them, as brightly as she could. "Then they'll be home on leave, and quite possibly for good!" But people shook their heads, sighed and gave anecdotal accounts of other young couples who had sailed off to the Antipodes and never returned.

"Fancy Georgie on'y askin' Annie to 'er weddin'," Mabel said with her mouth full. A group of the girls were eating their sandwiches in the cart shed one rainy midday. Mabel, who missed the camaraderie of the hostel, often joined the girls at lunchtime, sometimes alone, occasionally with one or the other of her twins on her knee.

"Well, she couldn't of asked all of us! There'd be too many," Gwennan said. "And they was always special friends, Annie and Georgie was." Gwennan, since her "miracle", had, Alice noticed, become considerably quieter and less irritable. Whether she was biting her habitually spiteful tongue or whether her three years among people who were consistently less aggressive and critical than she had finally exerted a benign influence on her previously unpleasant character, Alice did not know. But the change in her was undeniable. When the girls suggested making a collection for a wedding present for Georgina, it was Gwennan who pointed out that as the couple were about to sail for New Zealand the last thing they needed was more in the way of luggage, and it was she who solved the problem, arranging for a photographer from Exeter to take a picture of all the girls, the farmhands, including Rose, Mabel and Ferdie, plus the children Scarlet O'Hara, Winston and Arthur Vallance, and with Alice herself and Edward John at the centre of the group. The photographer posed them charmingly, some perched on the farmhouse gate, a few on the low wall, others ranged in front of it, the old building, with its undulating thatch protectively held between the two solid chimneys, forming a familiar background. The photograph was enlarged and elegantly mounted onto a presentation card on which all the girls inscribed their names, together with goodwill messages to the newly-weds. Everyone was pleased with Gwennan for thinking of something so practical and appropriate, and when Alice voiced their collective appreciation, Gwennan, out of habit, attempted to conceal the pleasure she felt in their obvious approval.

The wedding was to take place in the early afternoon. Hector had contrived to be in the area on official War Artists business and arrived, looking impressive in a suit. Annie was amazed by his elegance and even more delighted with him than usual.

"It was Pottie," he told her, laughing at her surprise, when she went to the gate to greet him and stood gazing and smiling as he extracted himself from the confines of his bull-nosed Morris. "She absolutely forbade me to go to a wedding as I was!"

"And how were you?" Annie giggled.

"Pretty much as usual, I suppose! Anyhow . . ." he shot his cuffs, "what d'you think?" His hair, which usually flopped over his forehead, was Brylcreemed and sleek. "The shoes are my own but the suit belongs to my brother Hugh and the tie is Father's!" She told him he looked wonderful.

His eyes moved over her. He wasn't sure what it was that made Annie so beautiful. It didn't occur to him to analyse her appeal. Was it the lustrous dark hair? The heavily lashed eyes? The perfect proportions of her face? The generous, smiling mouth? The full-skirted, tight-waisted, pale-linen frock? He didn't know. The sun glinted on the thick lenses of his spectacles and Annie could feel his smile bathing her in an irresistible warmth.

"And so do you!" he said. "Look wonderful, I mean. You look absolutely stunningly . . ." There were no words for what he felt. So he simply wrapped his arms tightly round her and they stood, conscious only of each other and unaware of the smiling faces watching through the small panes of the farmhouse windows.

The church in the village closest to the Webster farm, and hardly larger than a chapel, was festooned with hedgerow flowers, predominantly by towering foxgloves whose vivid purple was accentuated by the shocking pink of campions and punctuated by studs of brilliant yellow buttercups, all in a haze of Queen Anne's lace and meadowsweet.

Christopher, Edward John and Lionel, in his role as best man, turned to watch Georgina as she moved down the aisle towards them. The heavy, ivory silk of her pencil-slim, full-length skirt and long-sleeved, fitted jacket, which accentuated her narrow waist, had been recovered from the wedding dress which her mother had worn twenty-two years previously. The brim of her pale, wide-brimmed hat was pinned back with a single silk rose.

Alice, watching from the front pew of the groom's side of the aisle, with Roger Bayliss beside her, caught the expressions on the faces of the group watching Georgina's approach to the alter. The benign vicar was the most composed. Edward John was staring with undisguised amazement at this bride, the first he had encountered and the most beautiful, he was certain, in the entire world. Colour rushed into his cheeks when, precisely on cue, he stepped forward to take Georgina's small bouquet from her. Lionel, too, seemed lost in contemplation of the sight of his sister, almost as though she was a beautiful stranger, to whom he was, to his astonishment, related, while Christopher stood transfixed, his eyes on Georgina and his face illuminated by the soft light falling on him through a stained glass representation of the Archangel Gabriel. Then, spontaneously, he stepped forward and kissed her. A ripple of laughter went through the congregation and the vicar wagged a finger in mock disapproval.

"Not yet, young man," he said quietly. "Not quite yet, if you please!"

★ ★ ★

Although the upshot of Roger's revelation to Alice concerning his traumatic experience in the First World War trenches had convinced her that this was what lay at the root of his failed relationship with Christopher, he had refused to be persuaded to broach the subject with his son. Despite the fact that he had not sworn her to secrecy, either to Christopher himself or to Georgina, Alice knew that he was assuming her discretion and that to breach his confidence could have only negative results for all of them.

With the number of land girls at Lower Post Stone now reduced, it was possible for Alice to invite her friend Ruth to visit her at the farmhouse, where several of the small, spartan bedrooms were now unoccupied. Ruth, used to the sophistication of her London apartment, smiled patronisingly and bent her head under the low, oak lintel of the door. A cheap dressing table stood between the narrow twin beds and there was a small wardrobe which listed slightly on the uneven floorboards. Ruth stooped and peered out through the tiny window at the view over the farmyard towards the barns and then glanced nervously round the limited space which was to house her for the next two nights.

"No mice, I hope, Allie? Or creepy-crawlies?" she enquired.

"No. But don't expect to be able to use the bathroom in the morning until the girls have left for work!"

"Oh . . ." Ruth looked slightly put out. "And what time will that be?"

"About six-thirty," Alice told her.

191

"Good grief! I won't even be conscious at six-thirty!"

"I think you will be," Alice sighed, "with my lot thundering about the place!"

It was after supper on Ruth's first evening at Lower Post Stone that the conversation between the two women, as they strolled along a footpath which ran through the water meadow, centred on Alice's concern regarding Roger's history and the effect its secrecy was having on the newly-weds.

"I honestly don't think Christopher would have chosen to emigrate if his father hadn't made him feel such a failure."

"Well, you can't be sure of that, Allie. And one has to recognise the appeal of emigration to those two young things. Just imagine — sailing off together into the sunset! What a honeymoon! Crossing the world! 'Dipping through the Tropics by the palm-green shores'! Those P&O boats are the most tremendous fun!" Ruth paused, catching in Alice's face a concern which, she guessed, was related more to Roger Bayliss's loss of his son and heir than to the adventures of the newly married couple. "But I do see what you mean, Allie. It's a miserable business." They walked on in silence for a while, the long grasses flicking past their legs, the midges drifting above their heads. "So . . . when you tried to persuade Roger to tell Christopher about what happened in . . . when was it?"

"Nineteen sixteen," Alice murmured. "He wouldn't commit himself to telling Chris about it and he obviously hasn't."

"How do you know?"

"Because Georgina would have told me!"

"Yes . . . unless . . ."

"Unless the son is as secretive as the father, d'you mean? Oh! Heaven forfend, Ruth! No. I'm sure he hasn't spoken to Chris about it, and I have a horrible feeling he won't."

"So he didn't promise to?"

"No. He didn't promise to." There was another pause in their conversation in which, because the light was fading, Alice suggested that they began making their way back towards the farmhouse. Bats were flickering through the dusk and a three-quarter moon was becoming brighter by the minute as the sky darkened.

"The man must be insane!" Ruth sighed. She had listened carefully when Alice had given her an outline of the facts of Roger Bayliss's First World War disaster, and had then asked a succession of pertinent questions. They walked for a while in silence, then she said, "He's not only ruining his relationship with the boy, but with you, Allie! You are fond of him, aren't you? Come on, admit it."

"Yes. I am fond," Alice said, miserably, twisting a stem of meadowsweet in her fingers.

"Are you lovers?" Ruth enquired almost casually and without turning her head in Alice's direction.

"We have been lovers," Alice said. "Once."

"Only once? Wasn't it . . .?"

"Yes it was. Very," Alice said.

"Then why only once, for God's sake?"

"Because the whole thing has become so complicated! I couldn't tell Christopher about his father. I couldn't tell Georgina. And then, at the wedding, there I was, Ruth, sitting beside Roger in the pew watching Georgie and Chris make their vows, and at the reception, smiling and sipping hock. I have never felt so useless! I had begged Roger, practically on my knees, not to let Chris leave for New Zealand without telling him. What more could I do?" They walked in silence for a while and then Ruth brought up the subject of Alice's prospects as a consultant for Woodrow Bradshaws and Associates.

When Alice Todd had first arrived at the farmhouse the kitchen had been a shambles. With often as many as ten hungry mouths to feed, it was largely in the interests of self-preservation that she had persuaded Roger Bayliss to allow her to make alterations to it. She studied her requirements, drew up scaled plans, and with her employer's permission and on a tight budget, transformed the space and facilities available to her. The effect on her workload was huge and she soon regained the energy that had been draining from her. Rose became better tempered, the girls' evening meal was always on time, and Alice was even able to improve on a menu constrained by food rationing. It was when word got around the neighbourhood and Alice's design skills had been sought and implemented in the kitchens of several other hostels and small establishments in the area, that it occurred to her that her future, which since the collapse of her marriage had seemed, to say the least, precarious, might be less so than she had feared. An introduction to a London architectural conglomerate resulted in the distinct possibility of a career with them as a culinary design consultant, an idea which pleased and increasingly interested her.

"It's time to make the decision, Allie. Charles Maitland won't wait for ever for you to make up your mind. We were discussing it the other day and he needs you in London for at least a week, in which he will introduce you to his colleagues and the Woodrow Bradshaws clients and sort out the details of your contract. With the hostel running at half strength it should be possible for you to take some time off, shouldn't it? You'll stay with me, of course, and most importantly you'll be away from here and more able to get things into perspective with this wretched Roger!"

"He's not wretched!" Alice protested. "Well, I suppose he is a bit . . . But then so am I!"

Ruth returned to London but continued to mastermind what she saw as Alice's deliverance from the depths of Devonshire and the gloom of her relationship with Roger Bayliss. Her voice, slightly strident, on the telephone a few days later informed Alice that everything was arranged. She had simply to get herself to London on the following Monday and be prepared for a stay of approximately ten days. Rose arranged for Albertine Yeo to deputise for her at the tea room and it was suggested that Edward John could remain at his boarding school for the one weekend his mother would be in London.

"But why can't I come home as usual?" he protested, referring, as he always did now, to Lower Post Stone Farm as "home".

"Because you can't stay here with the girls, if I'm away," Alice explained.

"But Rose will be here," he argued, sulkily.

"No," Alice told him, "Rose will be across the yard in her cottage. You would be alone, here, with the girls and that would be . . ." she hesitated, "inappropriate." Her son stared uncomprehendingly at her but could see from her expression that she was not to be persuaded.

"Well, couldn't I stay with Mr Bayliss at Higher Post Stone, then? Jack always collects me from Ledburton on Friday evenings and Mr Bayliss often takes me to the bus on Sunday nights, and he's promised to show me how he keeps the farm records of the crop yields and the livestock and the milk gallonage and everything, so we could do that while you're away."

Alice approached Roger regarding the leave she needed. They had barely spoken since the wedding. The date of the departure of Georgina and Christopher was approaching but she saw no point in raising the subject of Christopher's continuing ignorance of facts which, Alice was certain, would radically change his view of his father.

"This trip to London is in connection with your consultancy career, I take it?" he asked her. She nodded.

"My work here is almost done, Roger. We both know that. I have to think of the future. Mine and Edward John's."

"Will he like London, do you think?" Roger asked. Alice, unwilling to debate that subject, did not reply and after a moment he continued, quietly, "As to the future, you have one here, if you want it, Alice. With me. As my wife. You know that. I am, perhaps, not quite the man you would like me to be but I am, I promise you, absolutely devoted to you and to a certain extent to Edward John. Not only because he is your son, which is an advantage, of course, both to him and to me, but because he is such an exceptionally nice child. Why are you smiling?"

"Because you are so adorable!"

"And yet you cannot accept me! I know why, of course. It is because you feel that a relationship that has failed so catastrophically as the one between me and my son bodes badly for one between me and you and your son. That's it, isn't it?"

Alice was too honest to deny it. She took his hand in hers and they sat in silence for a while.

"Let's not discuss it anymore now," she suggested at last. "I owe it to Ruth to explore my prospects in London. Chris and Georgie don't sail for another month or so. There's still time. I don't mean time to stop them going, I think it's too late for that now, but . . ." She paused. "You know what I mean, my dear." She patted his hand and then withdrew hers, which subtly changed the mood of their conversation. "And now," she said, "I have a request. Not my own, actually, but Edward John's."

"Oh?"

"He would very much like to spend the weekend I'm in London, with you. I promised I'd ask you but you mustn't feel in any way pressured or obliged . . ."

Roger's pleasure was obvious, and to Edward John's delight, arrangements were put in place, and on the following Friday, three days after his mother's departure on the London train, Jack, who had, as usual, met the Exeter bus in Ledburton, dropped the land girls off at Lower Post Stone before delivering Edward John to the higher farm, where Eileen produced her best chocolate pudding for his supper, saying that having a hungry boy in the house reminded her of the old days when Master Christopher had been a growing lad.

"I have something I need to deliver," Roger announced over breakfast on the Sunday morning. "D'you fancy a trip up into the forest?"

"In the truck?" Edward John asked. "Can I drive it?"

"No! You most certainly cannot!"

Edward John watched Roger carry a mahogany box out to the truck and stow it carefully in the cab. The box was approximately eighteen inches wide and a foot deep. The initials T.G.M.B. were engraved on a brass plate which was set into its lid.

"Who is T.G.M.B.?" Edward John wanted to know.

"My father," Roger told him. "Theophilus Glover Martin Bayliss."

"Wow! What's it got in it? Is it a wedding present for Christopher?" For a moment Roger seemed fazed by the question. Then his face relaxed into something close to a smile.

"Yes," he said, "I suppose, in a way, it is."

"Can I see?" Edward John tried and failed to lift the lid of the box.

"No," Roger said. "You can't. It's for Christopher."

"Is it a surprise?" Edward John wanted to know. Roger had forgotten how inquisitive children were. Then, as quickly as the boy's attention had been captured by the box and its contents, it turned to the more interesting prospects of the journey in the truck.

"Well, if I can't drive the truck, can I change gear?" he asked, climbing up into the cab, catching Roger's eye and smiling beguilingly.

Roger had already shown Edward John the basic principles of gear changing, and after they had turned off the lane and begun to climb the track that wound uphill through the trees, he reminded him of the various positions of the gear lever and, with his own hand poised to resume control should Edward John lose it, allowed the boy to grasp the knob. Biting his lip with concentration, he waited until Roger gave the word and then neatly moved the lever, grinning triumphantly as he felt the engine respond.

"Excellent!" Roger said. "Very well done indeed! Now we are in second gear. Up ahead, where the track levels off, we'll change up, into top. If you listen to the engine it will tell you when we need to do this, but don't do anything until we both agree that the time is right. OK?"

"OK," Edward John agreed.

Georgina and Christopher had heard the approach of the truck. They were sorting through Christopher's books, preparing to put them into the tea chests which stood ready to receive them, when Edward John came bounding into the cottage, followed more slowly by Roger, the mahogany box in his arms.

"It's a surprise!" Edward John announced to Christopher. "Can he open it, Pa?"

"Pa?" Georgina echoed in surprise. "Mr Bayliss isn't your Pa!"

"I know that!" Edward John laughed. "He's Christopher's Pa. Well? Can he open the box?"

"Not now," Roger said, dropping a key, which was attached to a brass chain, into Christopher's palm. "It is the sort of surprise that needs to be opened in private."

"A private surprise?" Edward John said, mystified.

"I've got some of Eileen's currant buns somewhere," Georgina announced, locating a cake tin and neatly diverting Edward John's attention. "D'you want one?"

Edward John helped himself to a bun and Roger heard Georgina asking him where his mother was and him telling her she was in London visiting his Aunt Ruth.

"Only she's not my aunt," he said with his mouth full. "She's my godmother. She won't be back 'til Friday. My mother, I mean, not Aunt Ruth. She wants my mother and me to go and live in London."

"And would you like that?" Christopher asked, conversationally, easing a pile of his books onto the table.

"No!" Edward John said. "I'd hate it! I want us to stay at Lower Post Stone for ever!" His words and the passion with which he delivered them created a silence in which the three adults watched him polish off his bun. "What?" he enquired, looking from one face to another. "What?" he repeated, puzzled by their reaction.

"I think I'll leave you to it," Georgina announced after Roger and Edward John had left for home. "Mama wants me to have lunch with her and some neighbours who were a bit miffed at not being asked to the wedding! Such a fuss! I'll be back by teatime. What about taking the bike over the moor this evening? To sort of say goodbye to it. Hmm?" Christopher took her in his arms and searched her face.

"Does that sound a bit . . . well . . . regretful, Georgie?"

"No! Not regretful at all!" she corrected herself quickly.

"What, then?"

"It's just that I love it up there when the light starts to go and I want to fix it in my mind's eye."

Christopher let the sound of the Brough's noisy engine dissolve into silence before sliding the key into the lock of the mahogany box.

Inside was a sheaf of documents, a large, buff envelope with the words "If undelivered return to H.M. Ministry of Defence, Whitehall, London," stamped across it. On top of this was a tightly rolled school photograph. Christopher unrolled it and weighted each end. He knew his father had been a pupil at St James's College, a minor public school in Dorset. The long narrow photograph was dated July 1915 and showed the two hundred and fifty-odd pupils and, centre front, the gowned staff, grouped round a venerable headmaster. Christopher searched in vain for his father but could not identify him among the rows of boys all wearing identical uniforms and with similar haircuts and respectful expressions. On the reverse of the photograph someone, whose handwriting he did not recognise, had written in pencil "Rob and Roger. Third row". Given this clue one face emerged. "Pa!" Christopher breathed, scanning the features that had become, suddenly, unmistakably familiar. He looked at the two boys, one on the left, the other on the right of his father, and wondered which of them was the "Rob" referred to. After a while he removed the weights and the photograph reverted to the tight cylindrical shape it had held since being placed in the box.

Under the envelope were dozens of newspaper clippings. They were yellowed and fragile. All bore dates of the early years of the First World War. Beneath these was a school exercise book in which, on page after page, were columns of names. "Beresford, James." Christopher read. "Johnson, Patrick, killed in action. Howard, Rupert, missing. Richardson, Norman (Prefect). Samuels, Ronald (Head of House), missing, presumed killed in action." Christopher realised that what he was looking at was a list of the boys at his father's school who had died or been reported missing, which, it transpired, amounted to the same thing, in the trenches of Mons, Ypres, Marne and Neuve Chapelle. Some of the clippings were of the faded images of incredibly young men, all wearing the uniforms of officers and

202

staring blankly, as though into their own particular infinity, at the lens of the camera.

The buff envelope was unsealed. Inside were approximately fifty letters, a sheaf of the reports of some sort of official military enquiry featuring the name of Medical Orderly Roger Glover Bayliss and an assortment of medical certificates and character references. On top of this was an envelope addressed, in Roger's hand, to Christopher.

Dear Chris,

Before you read all this and draw your own conclusions from it, I should explain, or try to explain, why this miserable story has been kept from you for so long. I think I believed, as my own parents, your grandparents did, that it was for the best if as few people as possible knew about it and that those who did know should be encouraged to put it out of their minds. They, and through them, I, was (and still to a great extent am), bitterly ashamed and guilt-ridden, particularly since I survived what happened and poor Rob did not.

The letter went on to describe the sequence of events which led to the two schoolboys, obsessed with the situation in France, enlisting, despite being under age, as medical orderlies and becoming so traumatised by the horrors they witnessed in the trenches that, exhausted and terrified, they deserted their posts and fled away from the lines where they had been sent to retrieve the injured and the dead. As they ran, Roger's account continued, his companion was shot dead, while he, court-martialled, convicted of desertion and about to face a firing squad, was discovered to be under age, pronounced of unsound mind and repatriated.

Your grandparents never admitted to anyone the truth of what had happened and I was forbidden to speak of it. I believe their intentions were good, and for a long time, even after they had both gone, I continued to maintain their method of dealing with it. In so doing I became a person who, as a father, was unable to respond when you yourself experienced your own setback. It may seem strange to you that it has taken my friendship with Mrs Todd to enable me to understand something that has for so long underpinned my life in what I now recognise as a dangerous and destructive way. I do not know how much my treatment of you has influenced your decision to emigrate but if I have made you feel that I do not recognise your heroic service in the RAF or comprehend and understand what you went through when your breakdown overtook you, I want you to know that, on both scores, I value and respect you and I deeply regret my treatment of you for which I have no excuses beyond the explanation above of how these things came about. I am happy that you have found such a delightful partner in Georgina and I trust that your work in New Zealand will prove rewarding. I will not try to persuade you not to go but I want you to know that if, at any point in the years to come, you should feel inclined to return to Post Stone valley, it is, my dear boy, yours.

"What's all this?" Georgina asked, arriving back to find Christopher sitting at the table on which was spread the contents of his father's box. "Chris?" she asked again, more seriously, catching his expression as he turned to face her.

He took her through the contents of the box to the point where the shell-shocked and traumatised boy was returned to his home and sworn, by his embarrassed parents, to secrecy.

"That's outrageous!" she breathed. "How could they do that?" Her reaction was, she realised, similar to what she had felt when Roger himself had responded so coldly to Christopher's breakdown two years previously. "Your poor father! To go through that . . . And then be told to shut up about it! And he must have felt so guilty! About his friend, I mean! My God, Chris! No wonder he . . ." She paused, staring at the blurred, monochrome photographs of the young officers whose names were undoubtedly listed in the wavering columns in Roger's exercise book. "Alice was right!" she announced. "She was always sure there had to be a reason for your father's treatment of you when you cracked up! And this is it! It explains everything! We must tell Alice!"

"She's still in London."

"Then we must tell her the minute she gets back!" Georgina grew suddenly thoughtful. "But I wonder . . . I just wonder . . . whether she knew!"

"How could she know?"

Georgina considered this question for a moment and then shrugged. "She has been a bit . . . I don't know . . . guarded . . . lately. Perhaps . . ." she hesitated. "Perhaps he told her."

"But if he had, she would have told you, wouldn't she?"

"Not if he asked her not to. Or even if she just felt he wouldn't want her to." They sat for some time considering the ramifications of the evidence in front of them, their minds exploring its implications. Georgina was the first to speak.

"Well . . ." she breathed, eventually, "you'd better go and see him, hadn't you?"

"Why?" he said.

"Why? What d'you mean 'why'?" Her eyes scanned his face and she shook her head uncomprehendingly.

"OK . . ." he said hesitantly, sensing her urgency. "But not straight away, Georgie. I mean . . . I don't want to embarrass him! What would I say? How would I . . . ?"

"Oh, my God, darling!" She stepped away from him. "You're as bad as he is! You don't have to say anything! Everything is *said!*" She laid her hands, palms down, on the papers on the table. "Just go to him! Tell him . . ."

"Tell him what?"

"Anything, Chris! That you're glad you know all this! That you understand! That you love him!"

"Love him? Love Pa?"

"Yes! You fool!" She was close to laughing at him.

"But I don't . . . Do I?"

"Of course you do! Why d'you think it upset you when he was so peculiar about your crack-up? And because we all love our pas!"

"Do we?"

"Yes, we do! Idiot! However impossible they are!"

"Can't I sleep on it?" he begged her.

"Not with me, you can't!" They were both laughing. She went to him, found his mouth with hers and kissed him.

CHAPTER
EIGHT

As her train cleared the outskirts of Reading, Alice became acutely conscious of the greens and golds of the summer countryside. She had enjoyed her days in London. Her prospective employers had been enthusiastic and welcoming. Their accountants had taken her through the contract they were anxious for her to sign and she had managed to conceal from them her astonishment at the generosity of the fees they were offering. She and Ruth had been to a matinee one afternoon and to a concert at the Wigmore Hall on the following evening, during which she had managed to put out of her mind her concerns about Roger Bayliss and about Edward John's probably negative reaction to the prospect of a move to London. Now, with the Berkshire countryside sliding past, she felt herself responding to the soft shapes of the distant hills, the acres of waving barley and ripening wheat, the cattle, hock-deep in shallow streams, all under a serene sky in which a scatter of small clouds seemed, because of the motion of the train, to hang suspended.

The envelope which reached her by post on the following morning was from her solicitor. It contained details of her divorce settlement. The modest assets accumulated over the twelve years of her marriage to James Todd had been divided into two approximately equal shares. To enable James to adequately support his new family, his brother Richard, a financially successful bachelor, had undertaken the cost of Edward John's schooling. Relieved of this expense, Alice could, if she chose, afford to replace the home of which the bombing of London and her failed marriage had deprived her.

With only five land girls still in residence, although more would soon arrive as temporary help during the harvest, Alice's workload was reduced. Rose, potentially fully occupied by her tea room, now spent very little time at Lower Post Stone, leaving Alice, after her visit to London and her glimpse into her possible future, alone with her deliberations while she cooked and cleaned for her reduced household.

Across the yard Dave Crocker stood, that morning, with a group of men who were wearing jodhpurs and carrying clipboards. Roger Bayliss had agreed to sublet one of the Lower Post Stone barns to a local riding school who needed extra stabling. Some alterations to the layout of the stalls were to be made at the tenant's expense and it was this arrangement which was, that day, under discussion, Dave Crocker representing his employer. When the men had gone he dropped in on Alice, half a dozen warm brown eggs in his huge, weather-beaten hands. He accepted her offer of a cup of tea and sat at the kitchen table, sipping, his heavy forearms resting on its worn pine surface, his eyes moving round the familiar space.

"How are things with you, Dave?" Alice asked him. "Are you glad to be back home or do you miss your colleagues? The army must have been quite an adventure, after being brought up here."

"Well . . . it were different, Mrs Todd, that's for sure," he said, and sat in silence while the clock ticked the passing seconds away.

"Is there any news of Hester?" Alice asked gently, hoping he wouldn't feel she was intruding into a sensitive area. "I mean . . . is she still with her parents? Or has she gone to —?"

"To America?" he interrupted. "No. She be with 'er folks, still." He grinned briefly and drained his cup. "I 'asn't seen nothin' of 'er in a long while but she knows where I be and she knows 'ow I feels about 'er!" He sighed and continued to let his eyes roam the familiar kitchen. "Nice to see this ol' place in good shape again."

"I wonder what'll happen to it when the hostel is closed," Alice mused. "I suppose it will be left to go to rack and ruin again . . ."

"No't won't," Dave said. "Mr Bayliss wants it kep up. 'E was on about un on'y t'other day. E says as it's to be maintained, like. An 'e's put me in charge of keepin' it in good order. I'm to take a look round, inside and out, every week 'e says, and keep a fire in, when the weather be cold or damp."

"But why?" Alice wondered aloud, remembering the near derelict state of the old building which had been unoccupied for a decade before being utilised, three years previously, as a hostel.

210

"I asked meself the same question," Dave said, "and I reckon 'tis 'cos 'e 'opes as young Christopher an' 'is misses 'll come and live 'ere when they gets back from that New Zealand they're off to!"

Alice had a second visitor that day.

"The most amazing thing!" Georgina announced, having tracked down Alice, who was in one of the hostel bedrooms where she had captured a spider in her duster and was releasing it out of the tiny window. "Christopher's father brought him a box filled with documents about something that happened to him in the First World War! I know! I know!" she said emphatically. "You're going to say 'but he was too young'! That was the trouble — well, part of it! He almost got shot as a deserter, Alice." Georgina glanced at the warden and then continued, "But the worst thing was that his parents were ashamed of him. Ashamed! Can you imagine? And when he was brought home — just think what a state he would have been in — they hushed the whole thing up. Pretended it had never happened. He was forbidden to talk about it to them or anyone. Can you believe it?" Alice could and did. "No wonder he was so weird to Chris when *he* cracked up! He's never told a soul, all his life! Until now, that is. We think that's because he wanted to explain to Chris why he treated him so oddly when *his* breakdown was happening. In the box he brought, on top of all the documents, there was a letter from him to Chris. It said he felt Chris might have got the wrong impression and he didn't want him to go overseas as the result of a misunderstanding. At the end of the letter he says he

211

doesn't want to dissuade us from going, but I think, maybe, he hopes that one day . . ."

"You'll come back?"

"He doesn't say that in so many words, but . . ."

"How do you feel, *really* feel, about going, Georgie?"

"I do rather hate the thought of not being here. Both of us do. I mean . . . this is home. For Chris and me. For my folks it's not so bad. We've got Lionel, and presumably he'll take over from my father one day. But the Baylisses have owned and farmed Post Stone valley since parish records began." Georgina sat in silence for a while. Then she said, "What would you do, Alice? If you were Chris and me?" Alice laughed and shook her head.

"At this moment, Georgie, I'm having enough trouble trying to sort out my own complicated life! You have to deal with yours, my dear. You and Christopher." She paused, watching Georgina accept her words. "And I try never to give advice," she added, smiling. "You know that."

"No. You never do. But you're very good at pointing out the things that need consideration. So couldn't you just do that? Please?"

"I don't think I need to," Alice said, sliding her duster across the narrow window sill. "But I am glad that Roger has told Chris about what happened to him. Very glad indeed." She was conscious of Georgina's scrutiny as she shook the duster out into the quiet afternoon air, pulled the window to and fastened it. They sat down, facing one another, each on one of the two narrow single beds.

Alice's lack of curiosity regarding the details of Roger's experience gave credence to Georgina's suspicion that Alice possessed more of the facts of it than she was admitting.

"I think you knew, Alice," Georgina said thoughtfully. "I think you knew about it and you couldn't tell me or Chris because Roger had made you promise not to!"

"On my honour, Georgie," Alice answered, truthfully, "I never promised him anything and he never asked me to."

Georgina was tempted to pursue this. It would have been easy to suggest that it was only because Roger trusted Alice not to abuse his confidence that he had sensed that it was unnecessary for him to ask her not to breach it. Whether it was her respect for Alice, her affection for her, or simply a measure of her own developing maturity that made Georgina hold her tongue, she did not know, but she smiled and after a moment altered the focus of the conversation by complimenting Alice on her powers of perception.

"You always said there had to be a reason for the way Mr Bayliss treated Christopher and you were right! Perhaps . . ." she hesitated, anxious not to offend Alice by prying into her feelings. "Perhaps knowing about that and understanding him better will . . . make things easier between you two? I mean . . . you do like him, don't you." As often happened with Georgina, this was a statement, not a question, and Alice smiled at her as she continued to speak, asking, ingenuously, "Do you think you are on the rebound, Alice? From your marriage, I mean? Is that why . . .?" Georgina let the question die and there was a pause before Alice responded to it.

"Well, I suppose I am — not exactly on the rebound but certainly still reacting to losing James," she said. "I never imagined, when we were first married, and then when Edward John was born, that things could just . . . fall apart like that. I suppose no one ever does believe that their marriage will fail. I don't suppose you think yours will, Georgie, do you?" Georgina looked slightly taken aback and then shook her head.

"And yours probably wouldn't have, if it hadn't been for the war," she said. "People behave very oddly when there's a war on, don't you think?" Alice agreed and then sat for a while in silence before continuing.

"The thing I'm left with, Georgie, is a reluctance to put myself in that position ever again," she said. "I don't want to be dependent. I don't want to be waiting to be come home to. To being told what is going to happen without having any say in things. To having my decisions made for me. I consider myself very lucky that I have discovered that I'm rather good at something."

"At designing kitchens and things," Georgina said. "And earning lots of money!"

"Well . . ." Alice said, modestly, "enough to provide for myself and Edward John and set us up with a new home and —"

"Brilliant!" Georgina said, punching the air as though applauding Alice's achievement. "Off you go, then! Your future beckons, Alice! What are you waiting for?"

"There are complications," Alice admitted in a low voice.

"What complications?"

"Edward John for one. He's very happy at his school and to move him now would unsettle him."

"But it's only prep school, Alice. He'll be off to public school next year anyway, and until then he could stay where he is as a full-time boarder, surely?"

"Yes. But he adores living on the farm, Georgie!" Georgina rolled her eyes in frustration.

"And you adore Roger!" she said. "Yes you do, Alice! You do! You're simply going to have to choose between pleasing Roger and keeping Edward John happy or going to London and becoming a career woman — like your awful friend!"

"Ruth . . .? How can you call her awful? You've only met her once!"

"Because she's trying to whisk you off to London while I want you to stay here and make my father-in-law happy! But like you, Alice," she said, brightly, getting to her feet, "I don't give advice! And now I'm going home to my husband . . ."

"Who is taking you off to the other side of the world when you would much rather stay here!"

"No I wouldn't, Alice! I can't wait for this adventure . . . but I must confess it's the voyage I'm after! It's Port Said and the Suez Canal and Colombo and . . . flying fish and whales and yes . . . I know . . . one day the ship will dock in Wellington and reality will be

waiting for us . . . But they say it's very beautiful there
. . . I'm sure we shall love it. No. Don't say anything,
Alice." So Alice did not say anything. What could she
say when she herself was so confused by her own
feelings?

The Bridesdale Civic Museum in the North Riding of
Yorkshire had a charming history. When, in 1876,
Henry Ormshaw inherited his father's manufacturing
business, he built rapidly on its success and became a
seriously rich man. He indulged his wife, Edith, by
commissioning a mansion a few miles outside the grimy
heart of the industrial town where his clattering factory
loomed, polluting and darkening the northern skies
with fetid smoke, and where the family fortune
continued to accumulate. Edith, daughter of a
haberdasher in Leeds, craved Gothic towers, oriel
windows, stained glass, balustraded terraces, an Italian
garden, velvets, damasks, Aubusson carpets, a ton or
two of elaborate mahogany furniture, gilt-framed
mirrors and a suit of armour — and she got them.

Three sons reached manhood, prospered and made
excellent marriages. A daughter, Eloise, was less
fortunate. From infancy her health was poor. Unsuited
to the harsh North Yorkshire climate she spent her
childhood indoors, seldom venturing further than into
the vast and overheated conservatory where, like the
exotic blooms it contained, she blossomed delicately.
Eloise learnt to play the pianoforte and to sing in a
small but tuneful voice. She embroidered in silk and
painted in watercolour, became intensely interested in

216

art and, as the years passed, indulged her hobby by putting together an increasingly significant collection of the work of respected local painters and sculptors. She was particularly interested in work depicting the industrial north and, long before his matchstick figures had become well known, had acquired paintings by the young and as yet undiscovered Laurence Stephen Lowry. When the weather was mild, Eloise drove in the brougham with her ageing mother to deliver soup, soap and cast-off clothing to the families of her father's employees who had fallen on hard times. She lived longer than expected but it was on one such visit that she contracted, at the age of thirty-eight, the typhoid fever which killed her. Her ageing parents and her fond and prosperous brothers, wishing to commemorate her life, were persuaded to donate the family pile to the town of Bridesdale and to fund, within its solidly ornate walls, the establishment of a civic museum where, as well as housing local artefacts, Eloise's collection could be permanently displayed, and over the years and with the benefit of carefully invested family money, it increased in size, scope and importance. In June of 1945 the trustees found themselves seeking a new curator. Hector Conway, seeing the potential for a museum featuring the art of working-class Yorkshire, applied for the position, was interviewed and found suitable. Part of his remuneration consisted of a modest grace and favour apartment.

"Hector's asked me to marry him!" Annie announced to Alice and proudly gave her the details of Hector's appointment, his salary, his responsibilities and the accommodation that came with them. With Annie's permission Alice announced this news to the land girls at supper time that night.

"What's a curator, then?" Winnie asked, spooning up stewed plums and custard.

"Sounds like it's someone as works in a bacon factory," Marion giggled. "When you getting wed, then, duck?" Annie wasn't exactly sure.

"Some time before the end of September," she smiled. "That's when Hector has to take up his appointment."

"Ooh! 'Take up his appointment', indeed! There's posh!" Gwennan said, her clipped Welsh voice cutting across the background murmur of approval. Even now that her personality had mellowed, Gwennan was still unable to resist a sneer when an opportunity arose.

A small package had arrived for Annie that day and was waiting, on the dresser, for her to claim it.

"It's from Hector!" she announced happily, recognising his handwriting and stripping off the brown paper wrapping.

"It don't look like it's a ring, though," Winnie said. "Not in a box that shape, it don't. Could I have a drop more of that custard, Mrs Todd? Ta."

"No, it won't be a ring, cos we're not having a ring," Annie said, and then exclaimed at the sight of a slim, leather-bound book, "Robert Browning's poems! It's not a first edition, obviously, but it's a very early one! Oh, it's lovely!" She ran her fingers over the worn leather and turned a radiant face to Alice. "Look, Mrs Todd!"

218

"A book?" Marion exclaimed in disbelief. "You get engaged to 'im an' 'e gives you a bloomin' book!"

"It's a very special book," Alice said. "An early edition of the love poems of a great man! It's a wonderful present, Annie, and a very romantic one!" Gwennan was unimpressed.

"Well!" she said, her chair scraping noisily back from the table, "there's no accountin' for taste! But if a fiancé of mine was to give me a second-hand book instead of a ring I'd tell him where to put it! I'm goin' to 'ave me bath now, before you lot runs off all the 'ot water!"

With the hostel's complement of land girls now reduced, there were hours in Alice's days — and once supper was over, her evenings too — which were her own and in which she and Roger resumed what was, in fact, although they might not have admitted it to themselves or to each other, a courtship. With the relationship between Roger and Christopher no longer shackled by a long-standing secrecy, Alice watched for signs of a relaxation of tension between the father and the son. She did not expect that the habits of half of Roger's lifetime and two thirds of Christopher's would melt like frost in sunlight, so she took care, when the subject was broached, not to enquire too closely or pry too eagerly into the state of the fragile contact which, she hoped, was being slowly established between the two of them.

There were hours each day when, within the routine of the running of both hostel and farm, the lovers could be alone. In the evenings, after Eileen had fulfilled her housekeeping duties, the farmhouse at Higher Post Stone would be their undisturbed territory and they would withdraw to the quiet intimacy of Roger's bedroom and the soft, double bed in which he so much wanted her to lie as his wife. Sometimes, as the light faded, they rode, she on his mare and he on Talisman — the hunter that had been Christopher's twenty-first birthday present — up over the higher grazing land and onto The Tops where Dartmoor rolled to the west, wearing the sunset of those summer evenings like a warlock's cloak, while, to the east, below them, stretches of the Teign estuary reflected the same bewitching colours.

While each of them was as certain as the other where the depth and intensity of their feelings was concerned, both of them had drawn with them, into this relationship, the complex experiences of their lives; the inevitable legacies which they did not want and had not chosen but which nevertheless existed and could not be ignored.

"It would be so easy," Alice sighed, "for me to stay here, with you, for ever."

"And it would be so easy for me to let you." This was what they said. This, for weeks, in different ways and using different words, was all they said. But every day, whether together or briefly apart, they were growing closer. More focused on one another. And so they would remain, until their other considerations had found their places in order of precedence and, in consequence, the future became slowly clearer to them.

With her mind fully occupied by her own affairs, Alice had not, over the last weeks of July, been paying very much attention to Marion and Winnie, whose own circumstances, she knew, had been complicated by the return of Sergeant Marvin Kinski, by his renewed pursuit of Marion and her obvious affection for him. The question was not so much should she or shouldn't she accept his proposal, but how she could square this with her commitment to Winnie and their long-term ambition to run a pub together, something which both girls had dreamt of and planned for since they were school friends.

The air of despondency, that had, for weeks, hung between these girls, seemed to Alice to have lifted slightly following a letter Marion had received from her Uncle Ted. The girls had requested a few days of leave in which to visit their homes, and once it had been established that their absence would not leave him short-handed at the beginning of the harvesting, Roger Bayliss had agreed to it. The girls arrived back at the farm bursting with news which needed, without delay, to be communicated to the warden.

"Oh, Mrs Todd!" Marion began. "You wouldn't believe 'ow well it's all worked out! I couldn't 'ave gone off and left Winnie in the lurch after all our plans, but now —"

"I didn't want the money, Mrs Todd!" Winnie butted in, confusing Alice by running ahead of the sequence of decisions that had transformed the girls' situation from the impossible into a workable, logical arrangement which, while it would separate them geographically, would leave them united in their affection for one another. "But she made me agree to take it, otherwise she wouldn't go and that was that!" she concluded, expecting Alice to have followed the plot.

"Sit down," she ordered them, indicating the chairs around the kitchen table. "Sit down, and starting at the beginning, tell me what all this is about."

The arrangement was a simple one. Uncle Ted was to take the lease of a pub called the Red Cow and invest some of his own savings in the deposit, the bulk of which would come from the funds that Marion and Winnie had jointly accumulated in their post office savings account. Ted would undertake the bookkeeping and Winnie would be the landlady, running the bars and the bed and breakfast accommodation for "commercial travellers", a lucrative arrangement which added considerably to the income earned in the public bar and the "snug". The viability of this plan depended on Winnie's acceptance of Marion's share of the money the girls had jointly saved. If Winnie would not agree to this Marion would reject Marvin's repeated and insistent proposals.

"I would of turned 'im down flat, Mrs Todd, no mistake, and for a while I thought I'd 'ave to, Winnie was that obstinate! But in the end she agreed to take it on, all of it! The pub and the money! Time was when there was no way she could of 'andled it all on 'er own, could you, Win?" Winnie smiled and shook her head.

"No, I couldn't of!" she agreed. "When we first joined the Land Army and come down "ere I was that under me parents" thumb I'd never thought for meself!

222

Even bein' a land girl was Marion's idea!" She glanced at her friend. "Yeah, it was, love!" she said, wagging a finger at Marion to prevent an interruption. "I just tagged along! But I reckon I've grown up a bit, since I bin 'ere, and seen the other girls takin' charge of their lives and that."

"But you always wanted the pub, though, Win!" Marion said.

"Yeah," Winnie agreed, thoughtfully. "I did . . . but it was you as first thought of it."

"Was it?"

"Oh, yeah. It was always you as first thought of things, Marion!"

"And you just tagged along, did you?"

"Yeah. To start with."

"You mean you wasn't so keen on runnin' a pub as what I was?"

"Not right at the start, I wasn't. Not as mad keen as what I am now, anyroad! I could no more of thought of doin' it on me own then than I could give up on it now! And I'll 'ave Uncle Ted to 'old me 'and, remember. I've got plans, I 'ave!" She turned to Alice, her face sharp with determination. "When I'm rich, Mrs Todd, I'll 'ire a manageress and I'll go to America and visit Marion and Marvin, I will! You'll see! I'm not sayin' as I won't break me 'eart when she goes! 'Cos I will! I'll be in floods! But I reckon I'll soon be that busy with me pub I'll be glad to see the back of the bossy cow!"

Winnie's acceptance of her changed prospects was not quite as wholehearted as she implied. A few days after the two girls had broken their good news to Alice she discovered Winnie one evening, alone in the bedroom she shared with Marion, who had just left the hostel for a night out with Marvin.

"It's nothin', Mrs Todd," Winnie protested, when Alice, seeing the tears and the red eyes, asked her what the matter was. "But I 'as to keep smilin' when Marion's around, see, so, tonight, while she's out, I've took the opportunity for a good blub. Don't tell 'er, Mrs Todd, or she'll start on about not goin' to America and I couldn't go through all that again!" They sat in silence for a while, one on each of the two narrow beds.

"You are a good friend, Winnie," Alice told her. "A really good friend."

"She'd of done the same for me, Mrs Todd."

"Yes. I think she would. And what's more, I believe she might even have rejected Marvin if you'd let her. But I think you would have regretted it — both of you — if you had."

"That's what I reckon, Mrs Todd! But it's still touch and go, sometimes. That's why I got to get me miseries over and done with when she's out! If she caught me at it . . ." Her throat closed on the words. Alice leant forward and patted Winnie's arm.

"Good thinking," she said, getting to her feet, and absent-mindedly straightened the counterpane she had been sitting on. She suggested that Winnie should join her in the kitchen for a mug of cocoa.

"Yeah, I'd like that, Mrs Todd. I'll be down in a mo." Winnie glanced at her pink nose and swollen eyes, reflected in the dressing table mirror. "When I seen to me face!" she added. "What a sight, eh!"

224

★ ★ ★

Gordon Brewster had, as Roger Bayliss's solicitor, drawn up the agreement between him and Rose, concerning her use of the old bakery, and more recently, the contract between him and the proprietor of the riding school which proposed to stable some of its ponies in an unused barn at the lower farm. Roger had ridden down, partly to see Alice and partly to check on the alterations to his barn, when the conversation turned to the subject of the solicitor's recent bereavement.

"How is he?" Alice had enquired. She had last seen Gordon Brewster at his wife's funeral when, flanked by his grown-up daughters, he had appeared dignified and even resigned to his grief.

"Doing pretty well, I would say," Roger told her. "Difficult time for him, obviously. Thought I might give him dinner one evening. The Rougemont, perhaps." He was adjusting his mare's girth and Alice, who had noticed a burr caught in the animal's mane, was picking it delicately out with the tips of her fingers. "Wondered if you'd care to join us," Roger added, enjoying the sight of her and the way the sunshine lit her hair. Alice considered and then refused, suggesting that in the circumstances of Gordon's loss, a man-to-man occasion might be more appropriate.

"How was your evening?" she quizzed Roger, some days afterwards.

"He talked about Margery a lot. Only to be expected, I suppose. Turns out he was becoming quite concerned about her."

"In what way concerned?" Alice asked.

"It seems she'd come to depend very heavily on her Land Army work. Apparently it meant a great deal to her and she was worried about what she was going to do with herself when it all came to an end — as it inevitably would have done." It was late afternoon and they were standing at the gate of a barley field, watching the old binder trundling round, the girls lifting the loosely bound stooks and propping them in rows across the stubble. "Then, out of the blue," Roger went on, "he started talking about her drinking."

"Drinking?" Alice queried, hoping she had misheard him.

"You yourself mentioned it to me once."

"Did I?"

"Yes. Must have been around Christmas time. After a party, I daresay. You said you thought she was hitting the bottle a bit!"

"I'm sure I never put it as crudely as that!"

"Maybe not. But, as I remember it, you were a little concerned. No?"

"Well she certainly enjoyed a 'snifter' as she called it, and she always wheedled a sherry or two out of me when she came to 'inspect' the hostel, but . . ."

"Seems it went a bit further than that. After the funeral, when her daughters were sorting out her clothes, they found a stash of gin in her wardrobe. Eight empty Booth's bottles and two full ones, in fact!"

"My God!" Alice was genuinely shocked. She had regarded Margery's drinking with little more than a passing concern and was unaware of the depth of the problem.

226

"And it seems that the car accident that killed her was not the first," Roger continued. "There had been several bumps and dents recently, one involving another vehicle on the Exeter road and which poor old Gordon didn't know about until his insurers contacted him." Roger caught Alice's look of concern and patted the hand with which she was gripping the top rail of the gate. "So you were right, my love, to have identified a bit of a situation there."

Alice was uncertain whether Roger, reacting as he had done to the scene of Margery Brewster's fatal accident, had been aware of the smell of alcohol which had, at the time, been attributed by the policeman, and indeed by Alice herself, to gin from the smashed bottle. Had he been, Gwennan's attempt to protect the Brewster family from embarrassment had clearly succeeded. But perhaps, his own reaction to the accident having been so extreme, Roger was, and now remained, unaware of the details of the scene which he and Alice came upon at the bridge that day.

While Alice's conscience would have been eased by a confession of all she knew, part of her mind explored the effect such a disclosure would have. Would Roger feel compelled to reveal the facts not only to the police but to the Brewster family? And if he did, what would happen to Gwennan? Would she be accused of withholding evidence? Would the police constable, who had taken that evidence, be reprimanded for his inefficiency? And how, Alice wondered, would Roger have regarded her own part in the conspiracy? At the time it had possibly been his own condition that had obscured from him the complexity of the accident. How would the situation be improved, for any of those people who were directly or indirectly involved in it, by the disclosure of facts which would inevitably damage them?

The binder had begun to make an odd rattling sound. Jack slowed the horse that was pulling it and climbed down to investigate.

"Sounds like that wretched pulley belt again," Roger muttered, leaving Alice and making his way into the field. She watched him go, striding across the stubble and then leaning over the machine while Jack pointed out to him where the fault lay. She would have to decide what to do about Margery's drinking problem. Whether to ease her own conscience by confessing what she knew or continue to deceive the person for whom, apart from her son, she cared most in the world. But she had already deceived Roger for nearly two months, although it was true that she had not, before today, appreciated how serious Margery's addiction had been. But the fact remained that no one had been injured other than the dead woman herself, and she would have wanted her secret kept and been mortified if Alice had eased her own conscience by revealing it. "No," Alice murmured aloud to herself. "I must never tell anyone. It's not as if I've lied; I have simply . . . not told the truth!" She was smiling, guiltily, at this less than spotless logic when Roger rejoined her. He was holding a piece of metal which had sheared in two.

"I'll have to get this brazed," he said. "Means a trip to the blacksmith's. We shan't get any more binding done today, so I've given the girls an early mark. Shall I drop you off at Lower Post Stone or . . .?"

"No, no," Alice said, easily. "You get off to the blacksmith's and I'll hitch a ride in the lorry with the girls."

As they lurched downhill, Alice wedged between Evie and Annie, whose bare arms were warm and moist with sweat to which dust from the binder clung, giving their skin a soft, velvety bloom, she realised she had made her decision. "If people would just stop confessing things," she thought to herself, "it would all be so much easier. But everyone will insist on unburdening themselves to me! Gwennan. Georgie. Evie. Winnie and Marion. Hester. Even Roger . . . So I have all their various transgressions to consider as well as my own!" Without realising it she spoke her next words aloud. "Thus conscience doth make cowards of us all," she said.

"That's Shakespeare," Annie announced. "Hamlet says that. I did it at school. Hector and I are going to the Old Vic when John Gielgud's in it. You can get tickets in the gods — that's high up at the back — for two and sixpence, Hector says! Why did you suddenly think of that, Mrs Todd?"

During the week which preceded the fire, the alterations to the smaller of the Lower Post Stone barns, converting it to its future use as stabling for horses and ponies from the riding school, had been completed. By Friday the first consignment — two horses, a mare and four ponies — had arrived and been settled into their stalls and loose boxes. The loft above the stabling, which had once housed Andreis Van der Loos and in which he had painted his depiction of the persecution of his race by the Nazis, was now cleared of the truckle bed on which he had slept and the table and chair where he had eaten the meals he cooked on a small, cast iron stove. His mural, thanks to the intervention of Georgina, Annie and subsequently Hector Conway, had long since been removed to safety by the War Artists Scheme.

The weather, that Friday, was foul. "More like March," Rose said, scornfully, as the rain fell, driven by a chill wind that had everyone reaching for sweaters, waterproofs and even scarves. Edward John, collected as usual from the Exeter bus and already put out by the cancellation of a school cricket match, reacted sulkily when his mother forbade him to cross the yard to see the ponies.

"No, Edward John," she had insisted. "You'll get soaked. There are no lights out there and supper is on the table. You can go and see the ponies in the morning."

The workmen, one carpenter and two young apprentices, had, that day, lit the stove in the loft and enjoyed its warmth while they used it to dispose of some rotten laths and various offcuts from the timber they were using. By the time five o'clock came, the lad who was sent to check reckoned the fire was out, but foolishly left it piled with unburnt wood and with its iron doors open. As the weather worsened and the wind rose to gale force, the wood inside the stove rekindled, blazing in the semi-darkness of the loft. Burning embers fell from it and ignited a pile of wood shavings. Soon, fanned by strong air currents in the draughty loft, the tinder-dry floorboards and rafters of the roof were well alight, and smoke, pouring from the rear of the barn, was being drawn away from the farmhouse and driven downwind of it. Consequently it was Roger Bayliss, from a window at the higher farm, who first became aware of the blaze and immediately telephoned the fire brigade, while at Lower Post Stone it was Gwennan and Edward John who smelt the smoke and saw the glow of the flames. He, wearing pyjamas and rubber boots, was already leading one of the ponies out of the smoke-filled barn when Roger Bayliss arrived in the farm truck together with Ferdie Vallance and Mr Jack. They were soon joined by the fire brigade and a hose was trained onto the rear of the barn. Both horses, the mare and one of the remaining ponies had been led out and released in the yard, but the remaining three ponies were in a loose box at the far end of the barn. When Edward John, his pyjamas soaked, his face and hands smudged with soot, had emerged with the first of the ponies, Alice had seized hold of him to prevent him re-entering the barn.

"No, Edward John! You're not to go in again! Ferdie and Jack will —" She was about to say "fetch the other ponies" when both men, empty-handed and gasping, staggered out of the barn, driven back by choking smoke.

"Can't get through to 'em!" Ferdie wheezed, eyes streaming and throat closing as he struggled to breathe.

"Them poor beasts!" he croaked, coughing and bending double in an attempt to clear his lungs. It was at that moment that Edward John twisted suddenly from his mother's grasp and headed into the barn. Rose caught Alice by the arm and prevented her from following him. It was Roger Bayliss who did so, vanishing instantly into the dense interior.

The scene was horrendous. Wreathed in belching smoke which the wind took and twisted, flinging it, choking and blinding, into the lungs and eyes of the onlookers, the interior of the barn was weirdly lit by the inferno which raged at the far end of it. In the yard, illuminated by the headlights of the fire engine, the land girls herded the terrified horses into the cider orchard and then, desperate to do something to halt the progress of the fire, began filling buckets with water from the pump and passing them from hand to hand towards the blaze. Rose, now joined by Annie, held onto Alice who continued to fight them, struggling to follow her son into the blaze.

"No, Alice! No!" Rose was yelling. She had pulled Alice round so that her back was to the fire and was shouting into her face. "Mr Bayliss'll fetch 'im out! Just you 'old still a minute! 'Old tight like a brave girl!" But the seconds passed, and when no one emerged and the crump of collapsing timber and masonry was adding to the uproar of the flames, it seemed impossible that anything other than disaster could follow. Then, through the smoke, three ponies solidified and hurtled out of the barn, followed, to a relieved cheer from the watchers, by Roger Bayliss, staggering slightly but with

Edward John across his shoulders, the boy's sooty arms tightly round his neck.

Later, with the flames extinguished, the fire engine gone, leaving one man on stand-by in case any burning embers should reignite, everyone had made their way back into the farmhouse.

Edward John, apart from being hoarse from coughing, soaked by the rain, blackened by soot and reeking of smoke, seemed none the worse for his experience. His mother ran him a bath, and leaving him with a towel, a bottle of shampoo, clean pyjamas, his dressing gown and his slippers, left him and joined Roger Bayliss who was waiting for her in her bed-sitting room. He turned as she entered. He had a glass in his hand.

"I'm doing a Margery Brewster," he smiled. "Raiding your sherry decanter. Thought I deserved one. You?"

"Please!" she said, huskily. He took her glass to her.

"You're shaking," he said gently, and sitting her in one of the small armchairs, put the glass into her hands. "Don't talk," he said. "Just drink." She took a large sip which seemed to steady her.

"That was incredibly brave of you," she said. "To go into that inferno. Incredibly brave. Especially . . ." she hesitated.

"Especially with my history of . . . how shall we describe it, Alice? Of overreacting to . . . emergencies?" He was relaxed and smiling. "D'you know, I was so concerned about your young man and what you'd think of me if I didn't fetch him out in one piece that any other sort of disaster paled into insignificance! Drink up!" he urged her, seeing the tears welling in her eyes, draining his own glass and reaching for the decanter. "And don't cry, my darling. Don't cry. All's well."

The land girls had gathered in the recreation room, and when Edward John entered it, on his way through it to the room he shared with his mother, they cheered him, their voices reaching Roger and Alice.

"Well done that boy!" Marion and Winnie bellowed.

"Bravo! You're a good lad, Edward John!" The voice was Annie's.

"Reckon you deserve a medal for what you done, boyo!"

"Indeed to goodness, Taff!" Evie teased in a poor imitation of Gwennan's strong Welsh accent. "Indeed to goodness, he do!"

"Shut it! Evelyn," Gwennan snapped. "I'm not so rude as to make fun of your stupid Brummie accent, am I? And believe me, you sound every bit as daft to me as what I does to you!" Leaving the banter behind him, Edward John entered his mother's room, closed the door behind and stood solemnly regarding Roger Bayliss.

"I don't think I would have got out if you hadn't come to help me," he said, his voice deepened and roughened by smoke inhalation. "Thank you, Mr Bayliss."

"Pleasure," Roger said, raising his glass. "Strictly speaking, though, you shouldn't have gone back in, you know. The odds were very much against you and you have your mother to consider." He watched the boy react to this, saw a trace of resentment and guessed

234

that Edward John considered it inappropriate for him to be quite so protective of Alice's position. "I know," Roger went on quietly. "It was the ponies. It was a hard call. You took a brave decision and you succeeded. Some you win and some you lose. That time you won. Good lad. But always consider the effect your actions have on other people." He smiled at Alice whose colour and composure were obviously returning. "Feeling all right now?" he asked the boy.

"Yes, thanks," Edward John said. "'Cept my throat's still sore from the smoke — but it's not as bad as it was." Roger emptied his glass.

"I'm going to leave you two to have a well-earned sleep," he said. Alice went to him and tried to brush a mark off his sleeve.

"That won't come off," he said. "It's burnt. Look." He poked his finger through the singed Harris tweed. "Clean through to the lining. Goodnight, my dear," he said. Then he stooped and kissed her lightly on the mouth. "Night, Edward John," he called, from the doorway. "Sleep tight!"

"Are you all right, darling?" Alice asked her son and he nodded, watching her as she removed the cushions that were scattered across the divan that doubled as his bed. He climbed in and let her settle the blankets and eiderdown around him. "He kissed you," Edward John said, looking up at her from his pillow.

"Yes," Alice answered. She sat down on the edge of the bed and waited for his questions.

"Does he love you?" Edward John wanted to know.

"Yes. I think he probably does."

"Oh. And do you love him?"

"Yes." There was a pause. He lay looking at her for a moment or two and then put his thumb between his lips, a habit she thought he had outgrown years ago. She took his hand and gently eased his thumb out of his mouth. He sighed and smiled at her.

"Well . . ." he said. "That's all right, then . . ."

CHAPTER
NINE

With the lease of the Red Cow signed and licensed to Edward Grice, and with Winnie nominated as manageress and having agreed to accept the girls' joint savings, Marion formally accepted Sergeant Kinski's latest proposal of marriage.

"Be that the eighth time of askin' or the ninth?" Rose wanted to know.

"Dunno, do I!" Marion said, tossing her head and allowing herself a glance at the cluster of diamonds which had, at last, found its place on the third finger of her left hand. "I 'aven't bin keepin' count."

"Not much, you 'aven't!" Gwennan said. "You've'ad the poor fellow danglin' for weeks and you still 'aven't named the day, 'ave you!"

Marvin Kinski's military career was under discussion as they spoke. His skill as an instructor had been noted during the run-up to the Normandy landings a year previously and he had recently presented himself well to a selection board, after which he had been informed that he was to be promoted to lieutenant and would shortly be posted to a US marine training academy in West Virginia. When he mentioned his forthcoming marriage he was advised to make the appropriate arrangements without delay.

"You could be shipped out any time now, Lieutenant," his commanding officer told him. The war with Japan was dragging on, but as soon as it was concluded the US army would be put on a peacetime footing and Kinski would be required to take up his new assignment without delay. "So if the future Mrs Kinski has it in mind to get spliced in Blighty, you need to get your skates on, soldier!"

"He's gonna be a lieutenant," Marion announced, pronouncing the word as he had.

"A loo-tenant? What's a loo-tenant, Marion?" Winnie asked, proud of her joke and the response it got from the other girls.

The need for haste in the wedding arrangements produced its own problems regarding where and when it should take place, but with Kinski based only a few miles from the hostel, and Marion firmly entrenched in her Land Army life, it was decided to celebrate the wedding at the higher farm and to do so on the lines of a more modest version of the VE Day festivities, which were still fresh in everyone's minds. Marion was only slightly put out when her parents, on receiving this news, declined her invitation to the wedding on the grounds that it was too far for them to travel. Her main concern then became the frock she would be married in.

"If I spends all me coupons on me weddin' dress," she wailed to Marvin, "I won't have none left for me trousseau! And I'll turn up in America lookin' like a freak!" Kinski, however, saved the day. He arrived one evening in a borrowed jeep bearing a bale of Chantilly lace. He burst into the recreation room, unfurled half a dozen astonishingly beautiful yards of it, sending it frothing across the slate floor at Marion's feet.

"Marvin! Wherever did you . . . ? You never nicked it, did you?" she queried, torn between delight and concern. He grinned and shook his head.

"Nah! It got 'liberated', baby!" he announced, delighted by her approval, his jaw chomping on peppermint-flavoured gum. "By a Corporal Abe Gwilt, US Marines. Seems he and his platoon came across a textile factory just south of Nîmes which had copped a bomb from your RAF guys. There was a coupla snipers in there, see, but once the boys had sorted them out they saw these rolls of the stuff lying around! Seemed a shame to let 'em burn! So they grabbed a few! What d'you reckon?"

The lace was exquisite, more so even than the girls appreciated. To them it was simply the prettiest they had ever seen, the softest they had ever touched. To an expert it was the finest quality in the lacemakers' range and had been, until the intervention of the war, destined for the wedding dresses of princesses, the ball gowns of duchesses and for creations designed for celebrations attended by the richest, most privileged and beautiful women in Europe.

"Streuth!" Marion exclaimed. "It's gorgeous, Marvin! You are a one! And there's loads of it, look!" She scooped up an armful of the delicate fabric, draped it around herself and posed provocatively.

"Enid could make it up for you," Rose announced. "She'm good with fancy silks and such. Used to make for Lady Fellowes and her daughters over to Bovey Tracey, she did. No one could touch our Enid!" Rose's sister Enid had been a seamstress for a leading Exeter dressmaker until the premises was razed to the ground when the city was blitzed. "'Er stitches was 'invisible to the naked eye' 'er ladyship used to tell 'er! And she never needed no patterns, Enid didn't. She could copy any dress you could show 'er, just by lookin' at a picture of it!"

The girls thumbed through fashion magazines and scoured Enid's pattern books. After interminable discussion a design was chosen which not only enchanted Marion but, in Enid's opinion, would make the best possible use of the challenging fabric. Using some of the parachute silk the girls had once salvaged from an RAF training exercise, Enid created a narrow sheath over which she layered eight yards of the lace so that it formed a full-length, bouffant skirt, flattened in front and springing from Marion's small waist to explode, at the back, into shimmering, floating folds which ended in a short, romantic train. The neckline was modest and the sleeves long, with cuffs tapered to a point, like lilies. The remaining lace would be used to make a bridesmaid's dress for Winnie.

While the war with Japan dragged on, plans for the wedding reception, which was to take place on a Saturday afternoon in mid-September, were progressing steadily. A cake would be baked by the cook at Marvin's barracks, Roger Bayliss would donate a barrel of cider, and his housekeeper, Eileen, would prepare an enormous bowl of trifle. There would be cups of tea for those that chose it, and beer would be supplied by the US military.

Then, on the sixth of August the US air force dropped an atomic bomb on Hiroshima.

"It was inevitable," Roger told Alice when they discussed it, scanning newspaper pictures of the smouldering wasteland that was all that was left of that vast city and its thousands of inhabitants, and solemnly reading the reporter's description of an event of such appalling scale that the other horrors of the war seemed almost diminished by it.

The carnage of Japan's final, desperate days before its inevitable surrender had become obscene. Fanatical havoc was wrought by kamikaze pilots who, hurling themselves into the paths of planes and onto the decks of aircraft carriers, died in a futile blaze of glory at the cost of not only their own lives, but those of countless Allied naval personnel and aircrew.

"Japan's war is over," Roger sighed, reading the gruesome newspaper accounts. "Prolonging the death throes is intolerable and had to be stopped. That bomb will stop them. They'll surrender now." But Japan did not surrender. It took another bomb, this time pulverising Nagasaki, to bring about the final capitulation.

"The Japs 'as surrendered," Gwennan announced to the girls, on the fifteenth of August, as they arrived back at the higher farm, sweating and exhausted by a day spent loading straw onto the ricks.

September the second was to be VJ Day, the official celebration of the end of World War Two, and with Marion's wedding planned for later that month, the land girls were in high spirits, which the horrors of the atomic bombs and the hideous revelations at Auschwitz, Ravensbrück, Buchenwald and the other notorious Nazi concentration camps failed to diminish. Georgina, visiting the farmhouse, first attempted to inject some sense of awareness of these horrors into their buoyant mood and, having failed to do so, complained to the warden.

"They don't seem to realise what's happened," she said. "I can't make them understand! All they can talk about is Marion's wedding dress! It's incredible!"

Alice, too, had noticed that the girls' attention was focused, more or less exclusively, on the good news and that they seemed disinclined to dwell on the chilling facts which were emerging as the Allied armies entered the concentration camps of Europe and the Americans used their ultimate force to blast Japan into submission.

"But it's all over now, i'n't it, Mrs Todd?" Winnie said, cheerfully, when Alice attempted to draw her attention to the terrible suffering and massive destruction wrought by the war. "It's peacetime now! The war's finished and done with! Blue birds over the white cliffs of Dover and everything, eh?"

"All the same, a bit of gratitude wouldn't go amiss, young lady, for the sacrifices 'as folks 'as made!" Rose admonished her. "And poor Mr Churchill! Got us through the war, 'e did, and before you can blink they've voted 'im out of 'is job and now we've got that

242

Attlee for prime minister! 'E'll be no good, you mark my words! You on'y 'as to look at 'im!"

"But 'e's promised to do ever such a lot for the workin' man, Mrs Crocker."

"That's as maybe, Winnie," Rose sniped back at her, "but if it weren't for Winston, your workin' man'd be Heil Hitlerin' Adolf be now! And you girls'd be forced to lie with Nazi soldiers and bear sons as would grow up into stormtroopers! 'Ow would you like that, eh?" Winnie considered this briefly. But she had more important things on her mind, such as whether or not she had enough clothing coupons left to buy new shoes to wear with her bridesmaid's dress on Marion's wedding day.

A week after the Japanese surrender, Marvin Kinski arrived at the farm.

"Sit down, babe," he instructed Marion, "and take deep breaths!"

"Why?" she cried in alarm. "What's up? You're never gonna jilt me, Marvin, are you?"

"It's worse than that!" he said, taking her hands to steady her. "They're shipping the regiment out on September fifth! I know!" he said, watching her face fall.

"It's the sort of thing that happens when you marry a soldier, Marion," Gwennan announced without much sympathy and an obvious enjoyment of the drama.

"You would 'ave to say that, Taff, wouldn't you!" Annie breathed.

"But it's true, though!" Gwennan insisted.

"And you always 'as to 'ave the last word, specially if it's a nasty one, don'cha?" Evie added.

It was decided, in the circumstances and having checked that, at a pinch, Rose's sister Enid could have Marion's wedding dress ready in time, to bring the wedding forward and celebrate it together with VJ Day on the second of September.

On the afternoon of the Saturday before Marion's marriage, Annie came downstairs wearing a blue dress with a pattern of small daisies on it. In her hand was a wide-brimmed white hat, decorated with a blue velvet ribbon.

"Ooh! Like that frock!" Winnie said, encountering Annie in the cross-passage. "New, is it? You suit blue! And that's the hat you wore at Georgie's wedding! What's the big occasion?"

"Hector's taking me shopping in Exeter." Annie's answer was deliberately vague and she had coloured slightly as she spoke. "He'll be here in a minute to fetch me." Winnie was instantly curious.

"Since when d'you wear a posh 'at for goin' shoppin' in bloomin' Exeter?" she wanted to know. "And what you got in that bag?" she added, eyeing the larger than usual handbag that Annie was carrying. She was saved from further interrogation by the arrival at the farmhouse gate of Hector's car, and she moved quickly past Winnie, out through the porch and down the path to join him.

When, later that evening, Annie had not returned to the hostel, Winnie wanted to know why. Alice, contriving to look more innocent than she felt, told the

244

girls that Annie had asked for and received permission to have an overnight pass.

"But she's with Hector! Where've they gone to?" the girls wanted to know.

"They may be visiting friends," Alice told them.

"Annie 'asn't got no friends round 'ere!" Gwennan declared, her sharp eyes fixed on Alice's face.

"Well, perhaps Hector has," Alice said coolly. "You can ask her tomorrow, Gwennan, when she gets back."

It was supper time on the Sunday when the girls heard the familiar sound of the bull-nosed Morris engine and a few moments later, as it drove away, Annie joined them in the kitchen. Almost instantly Marion spotted the gold band on the third finger of her left hand.

"Annie Sorokova!" she said, her face colouring with indignation. "You've on'y gone and got married! You 'ave, 'aven' cha? Well I'll be . . . You done it to beat me and my Marvin to it! You rotten little cow!" There where howls of laughter and Annie had to be hugged by everyone and then scolded for keeping her intentions from them.

"You knew, di'n'cha, Mrs Todd!" Evie announced, her usually grave face, for once, wreathed in smiles. "You knew all along and you kep' it to yourself!"

"What could I do?" Alice laughed. "I was sworn to secrecy!"

"But why, Annie? Why di'n'cha tell us?" the girls demanded. Annie smiled, sat down at the table and explained to them that there were several reasons for her silence.

"First off, Hector and I are not religious, so we didn't want to get married in church. And then Hector was only told a couple of days ago that they want him to start his new job on the fifteenth, so . . ."

"But what about your 'oneymoon?" Marion wanted to know. "Aren't you 'avin' no 'oneymoon? No engagement ring and no 'oneymoon! I dunno what things is comin' to!"

"Well, there was last night!" Annie happily confessed. "And we're going to Amsterdam. That'll be a sort of honeymoon but it's mostly because of Andreis's mural. There's a museum being opened, see, to do with the German persecution of the Jews, and Andreis's mural is to be on permanent display. They wanted Georgie to come too, 'cos she was the one who helped me keep the painting safe in the loft 'til the War Artists people could come and fetch it — but she's too busy getting ready for New Zealand she says. So it'll be just Hector and me!"

"Ooh!" Evie's voice was tinged with envy. "You are lucky, Annie! Just Hector and you! In Amsterdam . . . Oh, Annie!"

"There's romantic!" Gwennan added, impressed and even benevolent.

"It's getting like 'Ten Green Bottles' this place," Rose announced the next day. "First off we lost poor Chrissie. Then Georgina joined the ATA. Then that girl who left to join the ENSA, never can remember 'er name . . . and young Nora, goin' back to 'er posh folks. Then Hester, poor lamb . . . Marion'll be on a boat to

246

America before you can blink and Winnie'll be off to run 'er pub! Then there's Annie, over to that Dutch place and then up north! 'Twon't be long afore the boss closes this place down. Tell the truth, I'm surprised he 'asn't done it afore now!" Rose paused, finally having reached the point where the question which interested her most could logically be asked. "And what about you, Alice? There'll be no one 'ere but you and Edward John! Then I s'pose you'll be packin' up and movin' to London for to do your designing work, eh?"

Rose's curiosity brought Alice's dilemma into sharper focus than she welcomed. The time was approaching when she could no longer avoid the difficult decision she was being forced to address. She had no doubts now about Roger. On every level their relationship was strengthening. Their intimacy was intensely satisfying, their trust absolute. She shared many of his opinions, and where she did not, enjoyed the way he debated, putting forward his own views and evaluating hers. She loved him. There was no doubt of that. She adored him. But she had adored James. She had fallen in love with him and married him. For years they had been happy. Or was it merely happy enough? Had she, in those early years of her marriage, felt as confident and as easy and as valued with James as she now felt with Roger? Hadn't there always been something in her relationship with James that produced a small, cool area of uncertainty? And didn't that uncertainty have something to do with James always being so much in charge of everything? Always controlling. Always making the decisions and managing their lives, hers, his and Edward John's? When, in 1937, their son was four years old and she wanted another child, James had vetoed the idea on the grounds that with a war looming it would not be prudent. In 1943, when their house was bombed, Alice had been overruled when she wanted to rent somewhere safer but still close enough for James to reach his work at the Air Ministry and where the family could remain together. But James had moved his wife and nine-year-old son to Devonshire where he had virtually abandoned them in favour of the young woman who eventually became his second wife.

This damage to Alice's self-esteem was huge and her initial reaction had been to protect herself — by becoming independent — from ever again being exposed to a similar experience. She had achieved this, and for more than two years now had provided for herself and her son. She had discovered and developed a skill which was about to provide her with a healthy income. She already made her own decisions. She could soon have her own home and the same self-determination that many educated, intelligent, modern women wanted and were increasingly achieving. She would, in fact, be like her friend Ruth. Ruth. Smart, successful and alone. But did she want to be like Ruth? Did she want, for instance, to put her own ambitions before the happiness of her son, who dreaded the prospect of life in London? Did she want to see Roger's face when she told him she was withdrawing from his life? That she was rejecting him and everything he was offering to share with her? Did she want to continue to be alone? If only something would happen to show her which decision was the right one. Although she was not a religious woman she went, one quiet afternoon, and knelt in Ledburton church for half an hour, asking for guidance. But she had received no sign. No shaft of light illuminating an appropriate text or drawing attention to one or another of the saints. What was she expecting? A challenging glance from the Archangel Gabriel? A knowing smile from Lucifer? A look of mild reproach from the Virgin Mother?

She returned to the hostel where, before long, Rose's voice demanded her attention and focused her thoughts.

"Think you'll enjoy life in London, do you, Alice? Wouldn't catch me movin' there! All them 'ouses an' folk pushin' and shovin'! Ferdie Vallance couldn't get back quick enough that time 'e went up there for to fetch 'is Mabel 'ome! What a to-do that were! Still, it's what you'm used to, I daresay. You'm used to London town and we be used to Post Stone valley!"

"I've become quite used to Post Stone valley myself, Rose. And Edward John loves it here." For a while Rose looked at her in silence. Then she sighed.

"Well, I daresay you could stay here if you 'as a mind to. You knows what I means, Alice, dear . . . but I'll not pry no further into something as bain't my business . . ." She got to her feet and began to move towards the kitchen door. "And it's time I was thinkin' about getting my Dave's dinner started. Such an appetite that boy's got, you wouldn't believe. Even though he be still pinin' for 'is Hester."

Alice sat for a while, staring out through the open door into the familiar yard. At the still, afternoon light and the soft shadows of late July. But she had to choose. She must make this huge decision. For Roger. For Edward John. And for herself.

Since Hester had been released from the Land Army and returned, widowed and pregnant, to the Tucker smallholding on the north side of the moor, the state of the run-down property had, like her father's health, continued to deteriorate. While he lay, stripped of mobility, his useless limbs wasting, his wife's time and energy consumed by nursing him, Hester contrived to sell enough produce to feed them all. Each week, while her mother minded the eight-month-old Thurza, Hester would fill punnets with the fruit from the overgrown patch of strawberries, raspberry canes and blackcurrant bushes, hitch a ride into Bideford, and return with the few groceries that the money from the fruit had bought.

The Tuckers lived on eggs from their underfed hens, the milk of two ageing nanny goats, and stews made from the rabbits Hester trapped and simmered with stringy turnips, carrots and parsnips which had self-seeded in the neglected and stony soil. There was no chopped wood for the copper or the bath tub, so their bedlinen and their clothes were rarely laundered and their bodies seldom washed.

While Hester struggled to keep Thurza safe, clean and fed, her mind drifted over the events that had brought her to this situation. Although she mourned Reuben and was aware that, should she choose to, she could make the journey to his parents' home in Bismarck, North Dakota, and raise his daughter there, something restrained her, preventing her from seeing this as an obvious and perhaps even happy solution. She was unable to banish from her mind her father's harsh denunciation of her disobedience to him when he had forbidden her marriage to Reuben and cursed her with eternal damnation for flouting the rules of his own, fanatical convictions, convincing her that tragedy and pestilence would, in consequence, strike her and all those close to her. Reuben's subsequent death, Dave Crocker's injury and the onset of her father's sickness had persuaded Hester to believe in this curse.

Although the US military authorities delivered to her post office savings account the widow's pension to which she was entitled, she had left the money untouched, regarding it as the ill-gotten evidence — in her father's eyes — of her fall from grace.

Running parallel with this conviction, Hester also had a subconscious and unexplored sense of guilt involving Dave Crocker. There had been, she now sensed, something in her relationship with Dave that was inappropriate to a young girl engaged to marry someone else. Dave had been, she had persuaded herself at the time, more like a brother to her than a potential suitor. Yes, he had danced with her, taken her tobogganing, even admired the engagement ring Reuben had put onto her finger on the night of the Christmas party, but that had been innocent fun, hadn't it? Or was it something more? Something which, despite enjoying it and even being curiously excited by it, she had chosen to ignore? And was it, perhaps, this sensation of possible guilt, rather than her father's curse, that had made her unable to accept Dave when, last summer, in the cider orchard, he had proposed marriage to her, possibly too soon after Reuben's death? She had rejected him then, not because she found him unattractive or did not believe he would prove a good father to the child she was carrying, but because of a sense of betrayal where her dead husband was concerned. Even six months later, with Reuben's baby safely born, when Dave had sent the child a dolly for Christmas and Hester a letter, repeating his commitment to the two of them, she could not bring herself to answer him. Now the months were passing and time, for Hester, was nothing more nor less than a succession of days spent in an unremitting and exhausting sequence of work, her only reward the smiles of the little girl who so closely resembled her.

Then, one day, not long after the war in Europe ended, a lorry hesitated at the Tuckers' gate and someone climbed down from its cab, waved his thanks to the driver and approached the cottage.

Hester, from the distance of the strawberry patch, did not at first recognise him. He was taller and more robust than she remembered. The army greatcoat, discarded by a demobbed soldier he had met on the train from Cardiff and a size too large for him, added to the impression of grown manliness.

"Zeke!" she exclaimed, and Thurza, from her pram, waved her arms and shouted her own greeting to this interesting stranger.

He approached the two of them, kissed his sister, bent down to acquaint himself with the smiling baby and enquired, although he knew, "Who be this, then?"

"'Tis Thurza," Hester told him. "Me daughter!"

"That's easy to see!" he laughed. "With that 'air and those eyes she couldn't but be yorn, Hes!"

They went into the cottage and Hester was pouring boiling water into the teapot when their mother came down the stairs from their father's bedside. Zeke stood to kiss her cold cheek.

"Father bain't no better, then?" he asked her.

"No," she told him, glancing briefly at her daughter, "nor likely to be." She looked Zeke up and down. "Army finished with you, then, 'ave they?"

"Yes, Ma. 'Tweren't the army proper, though. Just coal minin'. Bevin Boys they calls us. Got demobbed early, 'cos of Father bein' sick." He paused, glancing at her bleak face, before continuing. "So's I could come 'ome to see what I can do to 'elp out 'ere."

Hester looked carefully at her brother. At the familiar, bony head with eyes slightly too closely set, nose too sharp and lips too thin for him to be considered handsome. But there was something different about him now, a confidence which Hester saw her mother register and perceive as a potential threat.

"Drink your tea, Ezekiel," his mother told him. "Then you'd best come upstairs and see your father. 'E'll want to know about the money."

"What money, Ma?"

"What you've earned, son. And the gratuity the army gives out to soldiers when they'm discharged. He'll be needin' that, your father. For 'is church." She eyed her son firmly, poured tea into a chipped cup, added milk and, moving carefully, went to the stairs and up them.

Zeke sipped his tea. Hester felt the scrutiny of his narrowed eyes and became conscious of her soiled dress, scuffed shoes, broken fingernails and unwashed hair.

"You'm lettin' yourself go a bit, Hes, aren't you?" he asked her, not unkindly. "I never seen you like this afore, and when you was down with them land girls, you —"

"Cut me 'air and wore coloured frocks! Yeah, I did, Zeke! An' you come pokin' your nose in and then went runnin' off 'ome, tittle-tattlin' to our father. Tellin' 'im I'd gone to the devil!" He dropped his eyes.

"Yes, I did do that, Hes, and I'm truly sorry for it! In them days I did as Father said without question. But you was braver than I was. You stood up to 'im and Ma and you wed your fella." He searched her face and saw the shadows under her eyes and the pale skin, drawn thin over the delicate bones. He saw how much older and more careworn she had become since he had last seen her. "So what's goin' on, Hes?" he asked her. "Why don't you go to America, to your in-laws there? I thought that's what you was gonna do. Or what about that Dave Crocker down to Post Stone as fancied you? Or don't 'e care for ee no more?"

"'Ow could I leave 'ere, Zeke?" she rounded on him sharply, avoiding his question. "With Father that poorly he can't so much as stand no more? And Ma worn out with carin' for 'im? It's all I can do to keep us fed, without doin' washin' and ironin', brushin' me 'air and worryin' 'bout what I looks like!"

As Hester spoke she felt a curious sensation of relief. Her brother had come home. There were two of them now. And he, who seemed to be no longer simply their father's censorious acolyte, was regarding her with something close to affection showing in his sharp, sensitive face. Their mother was calling to them from the top of the steep stairwell.

"Your father says as you'm to come upstairs, Ezekiel. Now this minute, he says! And you're to bring your sister."

Zeke had not seen his father since the first symptoms of his illness had been revealing themselves. Then, he had been stumbling, misjudging steps, dropping tools, lurching into walls. Tests were carried out. Doctors gave him a name for his disease and told him that nothing could be done to cure it. Since Zeke's last visit Jonas's body had given up its useless struggle to resist the relentless progress of the paralysis that had overwhelmed it, and now he lay in his bed more a carcass than a man. Both his nightshirt and his bed sheets were stained where gruel had dripped from the spoon with which his wife fed him. His hair was lank and his beard straggled from the sharp bones of his jaw. His huge, useless hands lay occasionally plucking at the soiled sheet. His skin had an odd sheen to it. An unhealthy iridescence, as though he was made of melting wax. He was, Zeke realised, almost unrecognisable. Except for his eyes. They were as terrible now as they had always been. They had scared Zeke as an infant, threatened him as a growing lad and bullied him through his adolescence. During those years Zeke had accepted this. Both Jonas's children had been reared to fear their father and had seen their mother constantly defer to him. They had experienced no other relationship between a father and a son, a father and a daughter or a husband and a wife. They had watched their father rant. Not only when he preached to his intimidated congregation but at the flinching subordinates who acted as officers within the hierarchy of his church. Neither Zeke nor Hester had ever witnessed any resistance to Jonas's will. They were unaware that other fathers did not make their children cower or that the penalty, in most families, for failure to instantly obey did not result in a torrent of uncontrolled verbal and physical abuse, until submission was absolute.

As Zeke reached the foot of his father's bed and stood, regarding the wreckage of this once powerful man and met the eyes that were locking onto his, he experienced a familiar sense of weakness which began to sap his energy. His father's eyes, blazing in the sallow mask of his face, were once more overwhelming him. All the potency of the sick man seemed to have sited itself in these two glowering orbs, turning them into one unassailable source of energy from which Jonas would continue to dominate and terrorise. Zeke felt his mind being penetrated, dissolving under the familiar and irresistible dominance which was being exerted over him by all that remained of the man who lay, otherwise helpless, in a bed odorous with the stench of his sickness.

"I do not see you pray," Jonas mumbled, his voice slurred, and when Zeke hesitated, the paralysed man repeated the single word "pray".

Zeke went down on his knees at the foot of the bed, closed his eyes, lowered his head and was surprised how easily the words came back to him, reaching him from his earliest memory of an overshadowed childhood. Raising his head enough to look into his father's eyes he began to mouth the familiar phrases.

"Oh, Lord God, forgive me my transgressions. Show me the evil of my ways so that I may resist the temptations of the flesh. Make me repent each sin and know that if I fail to make amends, your wrath will descend upon me and deliver me to Lucifer and the everlasting flames of hell. Amen."

"Amen," their mother echoed.

Thurza, growing restless in Hester's arms, began to protest. This distraction took Zeke's attention and had the significant effect of breaking the eye contact between him and his father.

Later, walking beside his sister as she pushed her little girl along the lane in her pram, Zeke understood that it had been Thurza's sharp cry that had released him from his father's attempt to reimpose his will. He had refused, after that moment, to re-engage his father's eyes, focusing his own, guardedly, on his mother and, more easily, on his sister or his niece. When his mother attempted to raise the subject of the money his father wanted for his church, Zeke forestalled her.

"The money I've brought 'ome bain't going to the church, Ma," he said. "If we're to make enough to live on 'ere, us'll need to put that money into this place. We need more livestock for a start and proper feed for 'em. First off I must buy a van for to get the produce into market on a regular basis." As his mother drew breath to protest Zeke silenced her. "No, don't you argue with me, Mother! I've thought this through, careful like, and if I'm not to 'ave a free'and 'ere I'll be off, and now I've seen the state of things, I'll take Hester and the little 'un with me, 'cos there be no future for 'em 'ere! It'll be touch and go for a bit, as 'tis, but 'tis worth a try and I'll give it all I got, for Hester's sake and for 'er baby."

Although, during his absence, Zeke had not been fully aware of the sharp decline in his father's health, or the effect this had on the running of the family smallholding, the experience of being free of Jonas's dominance, and in a situation where he had had to learn quickly how to survive within a group of feisty young conscripts, had allowed Zeke's underlying character to emerge. Although he retained a sense of responsibility where his parents were concerned — and for his sister's welfare, should she need him — Zeke had begun, during his months in the south Welsh coal mines, to perceive the width and breadth of the world and become aware of the day-to-day things which his upbringing had obscured from him. He had even begun to grow ambitious. Once his duty to his parents was discharged he would address his own life and make something worthwhile of it. His obligation to return to the smallholding and do what had to be done in terms of labour, to revive it and, if possible, make it prosper, would be on his terms. So, having delivered his ultimatum and while continuing to avoid the father's eyes, the son had got to his feet and gone noisily down the stairs, followed by his sister.

Zeke acted swiftly and before long there were half a dozen point-of-lay pullets in the yard, a new cockerel had seen to it that two hens were brooding large clutches of eggs, a plough was borrowed and the overgrown acres made ready for seeding. The last of the soft fruit was picked and delivered to Bideford in a small, rusted van. Wood for the copper was chopped, and with the fuel stove back in commission there was hot water for baths. Every day the washing line sagged under sheets, blankets and assorted garments. Hester bathed herself and Thurza and washed their matching, auburn hair.

Jonas, his body sponged, his hair cut, his beard trimmed, lay in a clean nightshirt between laundered sheets, his head on a freshly ironed pillow. To begin with, his eyes retained their poison but, as the weeks passed, and although initially no one noticed, they began to lose their dangerous intensity. His wife was the first to become aware of this.

"I do believe your father may be feeling better," she said to her daughter one day as she heaved a blanket out of the copper and put her weight to the handle of the mangle. "'E seems easier in'iself and 'is eyes bain't so angry-lookin' no more."

"You gotta think about your future, Hester," Zeke said one day as the two of them hoed their way along a row of spinach. "Ma says as there's money comin' to you every week, from the US military. You should be spendin' it, Hester. Thurza be growin' too big for 'er clothes and yours is in tatters! I'll take you in to Bideford next market day and you can kit yourself out, right?"

"But that be Reuben's money, Zeke," she told him. "I can't take that!"

"You 'as to, Hes! 'Tis yorn! 'Tis meant for you and Thurza! You're Reuben's widder! Thurza's 'is baby! I reckon 'e'd turn in 'is grave if 'e knew you two was goin' short!"

She watched her brother labouring from dawn till dusk. It would be months, if ever, before the smallholding would begin to adequately provide for the four of them. But if she gave some of Reuben's money to Zeke, he could spend it on tools and equipment, seed and fertiliser. He could repair the pigsty, fox-proof the chicken house, buy in more livestock. And Zeke was right. Thurza had outgrown her baby clothes, and her own cotton frocks and winter skirts were threadbare and faded. The elbows were out of her winter jumpers. So she went to the post office in Bideford and withdrew some of Reuben's money, bought clothes for Thurza and replaced some of her own worn garments. She folded a handful of the notes and passed them to her brother in one of the rare moments when their mother's sharp eyes were not on them.

"I can't take this, Hester, 'tis yorn!"

"You can spend it on this place, if you choose," she told him. "There's lots needs doing, you knows that. Reuben would say it was the right thing, I'm certain. So take it, Zeke." So Zeke took the money and used it to repair the henhouse and the pigsty. He bought four young porkers for fattening and two more goats and a pair of geese, intending to breed from them. Hester and her mother cleaned the cottage, gradually restoring it to the spartan, cheerless order which had prevailed throughout the years when the siblings had been raised there. And as she cleaned and cooked, minded her baby and helped her brother with the livestock, Hester considered the possibilities that were open to her. She thought of America, she thought of Thurza's future if she were to remain on the smallholding. A lonely child, reared without the company of other children, making the long, solitary walk each day to and from the village school. And she thought of Dave Crocker and how he'd said she could go to Lower Post Stone any time she liked and be his wife. How he had told her he wanted her and her alone and that no one else would do for him, then or ever. And she remembered how she had felt, the day they had spent together on the snowy hills of the Post Stone valley.

"But, Alice, you don't have to choose!" Georgina was visiting Lower Post Stone and together she and Alice had crossed the yard to collect eggs for the custard tart the warden was proposing to make for the land girls' pudding.

"Why don't I?" Alice asked.

"Because," Georgina told her, "if ever there was a case of having a cake and eating it, this is it!" Alice glanced at Georgina with a mix of incredulity and impatience.

"Everything always seems so simple to other people," she sighed. "You have absolutely no conception of how complicated it all is and how many people have to be considered!"

"That's only because you're not concentrating on the most important factors. Chris says the rest of it will simply fall into place when you sort out the key issues."

"Oh, does he. And what are these 'key issues'?" Alice enquired stiffly, wondering what she would say if she was asked to answer that question and feeling relieved that she had not been.

"That there are two things that you very much want to do. Right?"

"Two?" Alice queried, hoping that Georgina would not challenge her to name them. There seemed to her to be as many things as there had always been and a lot more than two. She wanted Roger. She wanted the independence which a career in London would give her and for that career to be successful. She also wanted a home of her own and for Edward John to be able to stay where he could pursue his interest in farming. And she wanted Roger to be happy. That seemed to her to amount to five, if not six issues and there were, she feared, others which should be added to the list.

They had crossed the yard and re-entered the cool interior of the farmhouse. Alice put the eggs carefully into a bowl and sat down at the kitchen table.

"Your consultancy work wouldn't impose a nine-to-five routine on you, would it?" Georgina asked, taking the chair opposite the warden.

"No," Alice told her. "Each commission would involve a few weeks of consultation and site visiting, followed by the drawing up of plans . . ."

"Which could be done anywhere, couldn't it? I mean, you wouldn't be obliged to be in London while you were doing the designs, would you?" Alice had already considered this.

"No," she said. "Not until the project reached the stage where the selection of equipment was under discussion. Why?"

"Because you could do all that part of the job at Higher Post Stone, couldn't you?" Before Alice could interrupt her, Georgina went enthusiastically on. "You could have a small studio at the farm and a glamorous little pied-à-terre in London! Edward John could stay on at his prep school in Exeter until he goes to Wellington, and you'd be home at the weekends and for the best part of his holidays. Roger would be the happiest man in the world and most probably see more of you than he does now — and the magic of your romance would stay alive for ever!" Georgina concluded, triumphantly. Alice laughed.

"You make it sound so easy!"

"That's because it *is* easy, Alice!" The warden sat in silence for a while, trying, as she had been for some time, to identify the downside to what seemed, on the face of it, to be a perfect solution and one which had already occurred to her. She had, however, been convinced of the necessity of making a choice. Surely she had to choose? Having everything one wanted was so seldom possible, how could it now be possible for her? But perhaps that was the problem? Perhaps she was so preoccupied with the responsibility of having to make the right decision that she was overlooking the possibility that she did not, after all, need to make one.

"I wonder what Roger would have to say to that?" She spoke almost to herself and was taken aback when Georgina immediately answered the question she had barely asked.

"We'll soon know," Georgina announced.

"What makes you so sure of that?" Alice was looking keenly at her now.

"Because my beloved husband is, even as we speak, putting the idea to him!"

"How dare you two poke your noses into this!" Despite herself, Alice was laughing.

"Because you are both so hopeless! Chris and I couldn't sail off into the blue with you two still shilly-shallying! Go to dinner tonight at that pub on the river."

"Which pub?"

"Oh, you know, Alice! The one where you have your major scenes and —"

"Major scenes? Me?"

"Yes! You! You and that naval man for a start."

"Oliver?"

"Yes, Oliver, when he tried to seduce you . . ."

"And failed!"

"And you and my father-in-law, when the pair of you fell out over Christopher!"

"How did you know about all that?" Alice asked. Georgina shrugged.

"Not sure," she answered, truthfully. "From Rose, probably. Local intelligence is pretty good in these parts! Oh, don't be cross, Alice! It's only because we love you!"

It was not summery enough, that evening, for Alice and Roger to eat outside. The water meadows which the pub overlooked were shrouded in a chill, luminous mist. The publican had lit a fire in the inglenook and on his recommendation they chose to eat his wife's excellent fish pie.

Earlier, while Alice had listened to Georgina's plans for her future with Roger Bayliss, he, at the higher farm, had listened to Christopher's, for him, with her.

"Gross impertinence!" Roger said, enjoying his meal and amused by the young couple's two-pronged intrusion into what he considered to be a private matter. "I thought it was parents who meddled with their offsprings' intentions, not the other way around! And, of course, they'll never believe that I had already thought of that solution and was about to put it to you, without any help from those two upstarts!"

"Were you?" Alice was astonished. "Oh, Roger, were you? Really?" The two of them sat for a moment while each realised that both of them had arrived at an identical solution to what had seemed to be a collection of insurmountable obstacles to their happiness together.

"But are you certain you wouldn't mind me being away a lot of the time?" she asked him after they had unravelled the plan.

"My darling, I shall simply relish your company even more thoroughly when you are with me! What I could not have tolerated would have been for you to feel you had to choose between me and something you very much wanted to do! That you would, on my account, have felt obliged to withdraw from an experience you needed to enjoy. And you don't have to deny yourself anything — you really don't have to — provided you are happy with a semi-itinerant lifestyle." He was laughing at her.

"It's called commuting, Roger. I shall commute!"

They decided on an absolutely private wedding at the registrar's office in Exeter. This, they agreed, would take place just before Christopher and Georgina, who would act as their witnesses, embarked for New Zealand. The hostel would, by then, be empty, the two retained land girls, Gwennan and Evie, being billeted at the village pub. Alice and Edward John would move into Higher Post Stone where Roger proposed to give what he described to Alice as "a small celebration to establish your changed status". To this, Rose and Dave Crocker, Mabel and Ferdie Vallance, Mr and Mrs Jack, Mr and Mrs Fred, Evie and Gwennan would all be invited. In the meantime, in view of the excitement over the VJ Day celebrations and Marion's wedding, Alice and Roger would keep their plans to themselves.

If the perceptive Rose or the inquisitive Georgina noticed that Alice seemed increasingly relaxed and happy over the following days, they attributed this to the easing of her responsibilities as warden and to the general mood of euphoria which pervaded the hostel and its inhabitants.

Edward John, Alice knew, was becoming concerned about his own future. Like any normal twelve-year-old he was living from day to day through the weeks of freedom that the long summer holiday allowed him, occupying himself happily in Post Stone valley, while Roger Bayliss recognised and relished the boy's sound instincts where farming was concerned. He was observant, identifying problems almost before Roger himself. His keen eyes had, on more than one occasion, forestalled complications in an ailing animal. It was he who spotted the breach in a hedge through which the sheep could have entered a field of brassicas, where they would have gorged themselves until they became dangerously bloated. On another occasion, when a calf had torn its shoulder on barbed wire, Edward John had applied pressure to the wound and maintained it while Mr Jack fetched the vet to cauterise it. Then, with the bleeding stopped and the danger of infection avoided, Edward John, before Roger Bayliss himself was even aware of the incident, had led the calf carefully back to the byre and released it into the safety of a loose box.

"But what will you do when the hostel closes?" he asked his mother. "Am I to go back to school in Exeter for my last year in prep school, or what?"

"Things are working out nicely, darling," Alice told him, changing the subject so that he was prevented from asking for details. "I'm sure you'll be pleased. Yes, you'll be staying at Exeter for another year. Let's just get Marion's wedding and this VJ Day thing over and done with and then you and I will have a long talk about the details. Right?"

"OK. As long as we aren't going to have to live in London or anything foul like that," he said, trying to engage her eyes. "We aren't, are we? Mother?"

"Talk later," she said, retreating. "Promised Marion I'd go upstairs and help her sort out her veil! Time you were in bed, sweetheart. Chop-chop!" and she was gone. He would not, he vowed to himself, go to London. If necessary he would leave home and work as a farmhand. Or he'd stow away on a ship and go to New Zealand where Christopher Bayliss would give him a job as a lumberjack. Or he'd go to Australia and be a jackeroo.

Marion, waiting for her wedding dress to be finished, spent her evenings in front of her dressing table mirror, fretting over which hairstyle would be best suited to her headdress.

Annie sent a postcard from Amsterdam.

Dear everyone. It is wonderful here and Andreis's mural is now on display in a museum. There was a ceremony with speeches and the curator thanked Georgie and me for taking care of it until the War Artists' people fetched it from Lower Post Stone. Then Hector took a bow as it had been his project, and a little Dutch girl dressed in the national costume gave me a bunch of tulips. There is an art gallery here full of Van Gogh's work and Hector and I spent a whole afternoon there. You would not believe how beautiful his paintings are but no one bought any when he was alive which is so sad. See you at the wedding. Lots of love. Annie Conway XXX.

"Fancy!" Mabel exclaimed when the girls took the postcard up to the higher farm to show her. "Just fancy our Annie being Mrs Hector Conway!"

"No more special than you bein' Mrs Ferdie Vallance, be it?" her husband wanted to know. "And anyhow, who wants to spend their 'oneymoon lookin' at bloomin' pictures?" But Mabel had the last word, pointing out that a honeymoon spent looking at pictures was better than no honeymoon at all — which was what she'd had.

"Considerin' the state you was in," Gwennan's strident Welsh voice intruded sharply through the chatter, "you was lucky to 'ave a weddin' at all, madam! Let alone an 'oneymoon!"

CHAPTER
TEN

Dave, having redecorated his mother's café, now, and rather to her surprise, turned his attention to the cottage which had recently passed from her tenancy into his.

"'E's fixin' it up lovely!" she told Alice, proudly. "Proper distemper, 'e be usin'! None of your old whitewash!" For several weeks Dave was to be seen, in the evenings and on Sundays, wearing paint-spattered overalls, washing his buckets and brushes at the yard pump. Rose had asked him, late one evening in the kitchen that smelt unpleasantly of drying paint, if he was still hoping that Hester would come to him. Dave had shrugged his shoulders and avoided his mother's eyes.

"Will I pop over to the Tuckers' place for to see 'ow she be?" Rose offered, as casually as she could, putting a mug of Horlicks in front of him.

"Leave off, Mother," he mumbled. "Like I told you, 'tis up to 'er now. She knows where I be to and 'ow I feels about 'er. I don't reckon it'd be proper for me — or you, come to that — to go pokin' round up there."

"But maybe she thinks things 'ave changed, son! And you doesn't want 'er no more! Thought of that, 'ave you?" Dave had thought of that, and although he declined to discuss it with his mother, this, together with several other disturbing possibilities, haunted him. Someone new might, even now, be courting Hester. Her demon father might have forced her into a vow of celibacy or she might, after all, have decided to sail to America and live out her life in Bismarck, North Dakota, with Reuben's family who were, after all, her family now — and Thurza's. Despite the fact that these and other unattractive scenarios disturbed Dave's sleep on a regular basis, something in his logical, practical, proud, Devonian soul kept his resolve intact. He had told Hester, not once but several times, how much he loved her, and if that meant nothing to her or she did not believe it and know, without doubt, that it would always be true, then she was not the girl he thought she was. Not, perhaps, the girl he loved and wanted. And so he waited. Not hopefully, but with a resignation and determination that would continue until the day he died. His mother, aware of this, feared for him.

The value, in terms of good public relations, between the departing American troops and a British civilian population which had welcomed, befriended, entertained and, in cases such as Marion's, even gone so far as to marry them, had not escaped the US authorities, who identified and began to actively draw attention to the forthcoming marriage between a Miss Marion Grice, a British land girl, and one of their own soldiers, the recently promoted Lieutenant Marvin Kinski. Interest from local and national press offices and news agencies, both here and across the United States, was encouraged. News cameramen arrived at the farm, together with official US military photographers, and took pictures of Marion and Winnie at work. For this occasion both girls dressed themselves, not in their usual, workaday dungarees, but in a curiously glamorised version of their official Land Army uniforms. They curled their hair, applied their makeup, and with their hats perched ridiculously on the backs of their heads, went smilingly through the motions of milking cows, heaving forkloads of straw onto wagons, biting into rosy apples and driving livestock through the most picturesque of the farm's gateways.

Before long this project had escalated astonishingly. The romance and subsequent wedding of an attractive land girl to a serving GI Joe, who had fought on the beaches of Normandy and later in Okinawa, was perceived as the perfect human interest story to splash across the cinema screens of the globe, and it was decided that the Pathé News corporation would shoot the event and screen it as part of their worldwide coverage of the VJ Day celebrations.

The filmed sequence was to be brief and would be shot, following the wedding ceremony, outside the entrance to the chapel of the military establishment where the groom was based. In it, the newly married couple, the uniformed lieutenant and his bride, who would be clad in priceless imported lace, the provenance of which would not be questioned, and attended by her equally extravagantly attired bridesmaid, would be seen to emerge into a storm of confetti

272

thrown by a couple of uniformed land girls and a buxom matron, a Mrs Rose Crocker, and a family of farm labourers, including their infant twins, the name of their daughter — Scarlet O'Hara — having been particularly well received by the American film crew. The bride and groom would then process between a guard of honour, and after this brief but glorious moment of celebrity, be returned to Higher Post Stone farm for a private and more modest celebration of their union.

Marion's reaction to the unveiling of this plan built from modest excitement to a state of euphoria which, had she not been blessed with a strong constitution, may well have killed her. Here was she, Marion Grice, born and raised in the back streets of Leeds, neither clever nor even slightly beautiful, whose behaviour, as she grew from scrawny kid to feisty young woman, had been less than impeccable; who had sat, chewing her fingernails, watching her heroines, the stars of the 1930s cinema, as they simpered and shimmied across the crackling, silver screen of the local fleapit. Here she had succumbed to most of the common childhood ailments, been repeatedly infested with headlice and contaminated with impetigo. She had scuttled home through the freezing Yorkshire rain to a tiny, cold, overcrowded house, attended a school where very little had been properly taught and even less properly learnt, and had accepted all of this as her lot. It had been something of a miracle when, as a result of the war, she had escaped the rigours of her childhood, even if only to exchange them for the rigours of labouring on the

273

land. Another miracle, in the form of a Christmas snowstorm, had brought Marvin Kinski into her life, and despite the hazards of the war they had been both lucky enough to survive it, and smart enough to recognise how important that first encounter had been to their future happiness. And now, by another miracle, she was, however briefly, to be a film star! Millions of faces across the world would be raised towards the screens of a thousand cinemas. A trillion eyes would see her, Marion Grice, radiant and glamorous! She would be on Marvin's arm, wearing a dress of priceless lace, with a veil and a bouquet! She would be a married lady. Marvin's married lady! She could barely breathe. She would, she thought, as the amazing occasion grew closer, most probably die of sheer happiness. But not, she decided, before the wedding and the filming and the reception and the voyage to America and Marvin, there on the dock at Hoboken to meet her and then to live happily ever after with her. Definitely not before all of that.

"But I thought you was going to Canada to live with your cousin there?" Evie queried, with her mouth full, during supper one night. The number of land girls gathered round the familiar table had, by now, dwindled to four and conversation turned, more often than not, to the future.

"Yes, I was thinking of that," Gwennan said, vaguely. "Before . . ."

"Before what?" Winnie wanted to know but Gwennan declined to answer. No one knew or would

274

ever know about the terrible fear she had felt when she discovered a lump in her breast shortly after her sister died and how, only days after she had performed an uncharacteristic act of kindness in concealing the real circumstances of Margery Brewster's fatal accident, she herself had been assured that she was not, as she had feared, about to die of cancer. It had seemed to her that the two events were in some way connected. That her reprieve was a reward for the single charitable act in her mean-spirited life. She had, at the time, surprised the warden by asking her whether or not she believed in miracles.

"Before my uncle asked me to become a partner in his business," she said, tartly and with some pride, in answer to Evie's question.

Alice, Marion and Winnie recalled that on the night when the original intake of land girls sat down to their first meal together, they had taken it in turn, moving clockwise round the table, to introduce themselves to each other. When her turn came, Gwennan had primly informed them, her pronounced Welsh accent unfamiliar to them, that she had been brought up by her uncle who was an undertaker in Builth Wells. The girls, particularly Marion and Winnie, had, for some reason, found this amusing. Gwennan had been insulted by this reaction and the angrier she became the more the girls had laughed at her. It had been the first of many incidents which had established, and over the years maintained, the cool and frequently waspish relationship between Gwennan and the rest of the Post Stone land girls.

"And what's 'is line of business, then?" Evie, who had not been present on the earlier occasion, enquired conversationally as she helped herself to more carrots.

"He is a funeral director," Gwennan announced, relishing the upmarket phrase which was, in fact, fairly new to her. "His partner is to retire and I am to become his assistant."

"Oooh!" Marion exclaimed, unable, even in her current magnanimous state of mind, to resist an opportunity to tease Gwennan. "So, what d'you 'ave to do, then, Taff? Walk be'ind the 'earse wearin' a top 'at?" Winnie, responding as Marion intended, giggled into her teacup.

"Don't be stupid," Gwennan snapped, dismissively. "My duties will consist of the running of the funeral parlour, booking the chapel of rest and making the appointments at the crematorium. I shall liaise with the gravediggers and —"

"Liaise with the gravediggers!" Winnie echoed.

"Streuth, Taff! That sounds like a barrel o' laughs!" While Gwennan told the girls that they had no proper respect for anyone, dead or alive, and should be thoroughly ashamed of themselves, Alice looked at Gwennan's hard, humourless face and visualised her, soberly dressed, discussing with the recently bereaved, and possibly in Welsh, the choice of coffin handles and the composition of wreaths.

One evening, as the girls were sitting over cups of tea after their evening meal, someone knocked loudly on the open door to the cross-passage.

276

"Anyone expectin' a visitor?" Gwennan wanted to know. Heads, except for Evie's, were shaken. She, Alice noticed, looked suddenly stricken, the colour draining from her face, and when a voice called loudly, demanding to know if anyone was at home, she got to her feet.

"It's Norman," she said in a low voice. "Me 'usband."

The kitchen was hushed as Alice and the remaining girls tried to make sense of the muted conversation which was taking place in the porch. Minutes passed. The words were inaudible. First his, then hers. Then his again, and after a moment's silence, hers. Then Evie was standing in the kitchen doorway, her eyes on Alice's, the girls staring.

"I'm to go with 'im, Mrs Todd," she said, and when Alice failed to react, repeated the words, adding, "Now, 'e says. I'm to fetch me things and go with 'im, this instant."

"But you can't," Alice told her, calmly. "I am responsible for you and you can't leave here without permission from the Ministry of Agriculture or from Mr Bayliss. It's against the law." Alice was moving towards the door. "You sit down, Evie, and I'll go and explain things to your husband." But Evie was shaking her head.

"It won't do no good, Mrs Todd. Norman's bin to see Mr Bayliss. 'E's shown 'im the papers — the wedding certificate and everything — and Mr Bayliss said I'm to go!"

Winnie, peering through the kitchen window, saw the man who was Evie's husband leaning against the stone pillar of the farmhouse gate. He was heavily built with thinning, Brylcreemed hair and a thick, flushed neck. As he shook a Woodbine out of a crumpled packet and was searching his pockets for matches, Roger Bayliss's Riley came quietly to a halt in the lane.

"Ooh! Mr Bayliss 'as come!" Winnie reported to Alice and the girls in the kitchen.

"What d'you make of this?" Roger asked Alice when they had withdrawn into the privacy of her room. "This husband of hers seems a pretty unpleasant sort of fellow, so despite the proof that he and Evelyn are married, I thought I'd come down to see what you think about it. What do you reckon?" he asked, correctly sensing a complication.

"Sit down," Alice suggested and she gave him the details of Evie's unhappy marriage and her relationship with Giorgio. Roger sighed when he understood that the "local bloke" that Evie's husband had suspected was "paying attention" to his wife was one of the Italian prisoners of war who worked on his neighbour's farm.

"Oh Lord," he said. "I thought we'd avoided that particular scenario!"

"I thought so too," Alice told him. "I have discussed it with the girls from time to time and warned about the complications of getting involved with the POWs but . . . poor Evie . . . She's terribly in love, Roger . . ." They sat in silence for a while and then Roger delivered his verdict.

278

"The facts are, Alice, that I can't prevent her husband taking her home. What she does with her life after that is her own affair, but I have to say that I have some sympathy for the fellow. He has, after all, been fighting for his country, and while he's been away his wife misbehaves with what, only a few months ago, was an enemy soldier!"

"There's more to it than that, Roger. Much more."

"If you say so, my dear. I'm sorry for the girl and I hope things turn out happily for her, but based on my obligations and Land Army protocol . . ."

Evie packed up her belongings.

"No point in takin' me Land Army gear," she sighed, piling her uniform onto a chair. Then she sat down on the bed in which she would not sleep again, and dropping her head onto her knees, gave way to huge, silent sobs. Alice sat beside her and put her arm round the heaving shoulders.

"Giorgio won't know where I've gone, Mrs Todd!" Evie moaned. "I can't even say goodbye to 'im!"

Roger put Evie and Norman into the back seat of the Riley, closed the boot on her small pieces of luggage, and without a word being spoken, drove them to Ledburton Halt and left them on the platform, standing side by side, staring soberly, as though into the bitter and unhappy lives which lay ahead of both of them.

Two days later, just as the light was going, Marion knocked on Alice's door, apologised for disturbing her and told her that she and Winnie had noticed a man lurking in the lane.

"Only it don't look like no one we knows, Mrs Todd, 'cept it could be Evie's Eyetie fella, p'raps. Lookin' for 'er."

He was walking aimlessly, head bent, back and forth in the lane. He wore a khaki dust coat over the fatigues which, in a better light, would have identified him as a POW. He pulled at his cigarette, exhaled the smoke in a long sigh, and was staring at the face of the farmhouse when Alice emerged from the porch and made her way down the path towards him. Seeing her, he dropped the cigarette stub onto the ground at his feet, trod it out and turned, uncertainly, to face her.

"Are you Giorgio?" Alice asked. He nodded vigorously.

"*Si, signora*. Am Giorgio."

"Are you here to see Evie?" His face was lean and the brown eyes were deeply set under a high forehead crowned by a tangle of dark curls. He was, Alice guessed, in his late thirties.

"She all right?" he asked. "Only she no come when she say she come. I not here for trouble, *signora*, but I worry she sick?"

"No," Alice said. "She's not sick." She hesitated, wondering how best to break it to him that Evie was no longer at the hostel. But he seemed to have guessed what had happened. He stared at Alice. He shook his head hopelessly and turned away.

"Her husband come for her, I think," he said flatly, his face expressing the desolation he clearly felt. "She was feared he would do that. He come for her and he took her, no?"

"Two days ago," Alice told him. "She was very upset that she couldn't say goodbye to you."

"No!" Giorgio said emphatically. "No goodbye for Evie and Giorgio! She come to Napoli for be *mia sposa*!"

"Your wife? But Evie is married, Giorgio. And you? Surely a man of your —?"

"I not now married!" he interrupted her. "*Mia sposa* die when Napoli is bombed!"

"But Evie has a husband, Giorgio! He has been serving in the British army!"

"But they no love, *signora*! She tell me all how he treat her! She tell you too, I see in your face!" He moved close to Alice, placing his palms together in a gesture of supplication, struggling to put his words into her language. "Please . . . you tell me where she go, *signora*!" he asked desperately. "I write . . . letter! Tell me the . . . the . . . *l'indirizzo* . . . the address, *signora* . . . the place she live! *Per favore, signora! Per favore!!*"

"I don't know her address!" Alice told him, truthfully. "They will have it in the office at the higher farm — or the Land Army will know . . . But I don't. I'm sorry, but I don't. And I'm afraid, in the circumstances, the people who do know may not agree to tell you." Alice was uncertain whether or not Giorgio had understood her. He turned away and sat down heavily on the low wall. Alice told him again how sorry she was that she couldn't help him. He ignored her and after a moment she left him, went into the hostel and through to her room, where she tried to concentrate on the book she was reading. From time to time she glanced out of her low window and saw him, a blurred shape, still sitting motionless on the wall as the evening grew darker. Then she heard a rush of footsteps in the cross-passage and someone ran out through the porch and down the pathway to the farmhouse gate, approached Giorgio, thrust something into his hand, and moving fast, re-entered the hostel. Footsteps had been thudding up the stairs before Alice reached the cross-passage.

"Who was that?" she called from the bottom of the two narrow flights of stairs that led up to the girls' bedrooms. No one answered. Whoever it was had left the front door open. It was almost ten o'clock. None of the girls had gone out that night, so Alice closed the door and slid the bolt into place, noticing as she did so that Giorgio was gone.

"I think one of our girls gave Giorgio Evie's address," she told Roger. "I don't know which one and I haven't asked, but somebody ran out to him, gave him something and shot back upstairs before I could see who it was."

"And you didn't pursue it?" he asked, in surprise.

"D'you think, in the circumstances, I should have done?" Roger considered this for some moments.

"Maybe not," he conceded. "But I can't see a happy ending for them, can you? If he goes after her he'll get arrested for breaching the terms of his status as a POW, which could mean gaol, whereas if he keeps his head down he'll be repatriated pretty soon anyway."

282

"Not all of them want to go, though, do they?" Alice said. "I heard that some of them, whose employers value them as farm labourers, are going to be allowed to stay here indefinitely." Roger smiled at her.

"You're such a romantic, my darling!" he said. "You'd like to see this Giorgio chap track young Evie down, scoop her up and carry her off into the sunset, wouldn't you? When in fact, by the look of that husband of hers, poor Giorgio would end up spattered all over Coventry or wherever it is the wretched couple live!"

"It's not funny, Roger. It's actually very sad. For all of them."

"Yes it is," he agreed. "But I'm glad I was able to avoid involvement and it's probably just as well you were not instrumental in passing on that address."

"I wonder if we'll ever know what happens to them," Alice mused.

"Probably not. He'll get shipped home and given a hero's welcome in Naples — they're always a bit short on heroes, the Italians. Then he'll find himself a nice new wife and live happily ever after."

"Yes," Alice said. "He might. And that'd be fine for him. But what about poor Evie?"

September the second, the day of Marion's wedding and the celebration of VJ Day, began at the lower farm with a delightful sense of broken routine. Apart from the milking which, overseen as usual by Mabel, fell that morning to Mr Jack, the work schedule for both the higher and the lower farms had been suspended. One by one the remaining residents at the hostel woke, yawned, stretched, rolled out of their beds and relished the fact that today was going to be different and special.

The marriage ceremony would take place at the military chapel, and at the request of the Pathé film crew, apart from the bride and groom, only Rose, the Vallance family and Alice were to attend it. Everyone else would assemble at Higher Post Stone and be waiting to welcome the wedding party there. Here, Marion and Marvin would receive their guests, and after speeches from Roger Bayliss, Marvin's commanding officer and a young, ginger-haired marine named Casey Murch who was Marvin's best man, the cake would be cut and toasts would be drunk to the bride and groom and to the bridesmaid. A bugler from the camp would play "God Bless America", after which, in an adjoining barn and to the sound of the wind-up gramophone borrowed from the hostel recreation room, there would be dancing.

In the Crocker cottage Rose was carefully pressing her best frock. The silk print was, in fact, a hand-me-down from one of the lady clients for whom Rose's sister Enid sewed. On the previous day, with a neat pillbox hat, which pre-dated the outbreak of war by several years, on her greying head, and a pair of new white gloves on her hard-worked hands, Rose had inspected her reflection in her looking glass and been satisfied with what she saw.

Her son, that morning, his hair tousled from sleep and wearing only the bottom half of his pyjamas, sat at the kitchen table, spooning up the porridge his mother had made for him.

In the heat of the harvest fields Dave was in the habit of stripping off his shirt and exposing his well-muscled torso to the summer sun. Rose had seen the way the village girls looked at him. He could take his pick of any one of them. The eligible ones as well as those who, already married, were inclined to stray. The land girls, always aware of Dave's unresolved relationship with Hester, regarded him as spoken for and therefore out of bounds, more like a brother or a member of the extended farm family.

Leaving his empty porridge bowl on the table Dave slouched into the scullery which also served as a wash house. Rose could hear the running tap as he sluiced the cold water over his head and shoulders.

"Put your 'jamas in the copper while you'm there, Dave," she called to him. "And which shirt will I iron for you to wear for the weddin'?" He came back into the kitchen. He had pulled on the old overalls he wore for his redecoration work. They were a faded blue, spattered now with white distemper. He stood, fastening the buttons. There was a tear across one knee.

"I bain't goin' to no weddin', Ma," he told his mother. "Marion's no special friend o' mine and I don't reckon I knows 'er bloke from Adam."

"But 'tis VJ Day, son! That's why Mr Bayliss be givin' you a day off in the first place!" She looked at his sulky face. "Well, then, if you don't fancy a slice of the weddin' cake at least come up after, for a drink of cider!" He didn't respond, fetched a can of distemper from the porch and was carrying it towards the staircase when his mother noticed the colour on its label. The other cans, most of which were now empty, had been labelled white. This one was pink. A soft pink. The colour of the palest apple blossom.

"Pink?" Rose exclaimed. "You're usin' pink?"

The only room Dave had not yet redecorated was the tiny space, hardly more than a box room, under the eaves at the back of the cottage. He stood, looking at his mother, the can of pink distemper in his huge, capable hands. He was bashful. Half-smiling. Almost embarrassed. He shrugged his shoulders, knowing his mother had guessed where the pink paint was to be used and why.

"Oh, my dear boy!" Rose sighed, her flat iron going cool in her hand. "What am I goin' to do with you? Whatever am I going to do?"

In the hostel, everything that could go wrong that morning did. The boiler went out and Marion, who had promised herself a long, solitary bath, enriched with an expensively aromatic oil "liberated" by the then Sergeant Kinski when he was relieving Paris, had to wait over an hour for the water to heat up, and even then it wasn't warm enough for the extended soak that Marion had in mind and she was forced to climb out after only ten minutes, shivering and with her skin puckered with goosebumps. Then Winnie, practising walking in her bridesmaid shoes, caught a heel in the cobbles of the porch, sprawled full length and chipped a front tooth on the doorstep.

"It don't show, honest, Win," Marion tried to console her, while Gwennan insisted, less comfortingly, that no one would be looking at Winnie anyhow, because all eyes would be on the bride.

In view of the volume and delicacy of Marion's lacy dress it was decided that rather than risk snagging it on the rough timber of either of the two, steep staircases that led down from the girls' sleeping quarters, Marion should be helped into it in the comparative safety of Alice's room, from which she could move, through the recreation room, along the cross-passage and out to a waiting staff car, supplied by the US military, which would convey her to the camp where, in place of her absent father and properly attired, Roger Bayliss would be waiting to escort her to the altar.

Roger's involvement in the ceremony had been the result of Alice's persuasion. He had reluctantly agreed to give Marion away, but the question of how he should be dressed for the occasion had proved to be a more formidable problem and one which his son had been instrumental in solving.

On an evening when the newly married couple were having dinner at Higher Post Stone, Alice, who had also been invited, had raised the subject.

"Top hat and a morning coat with tails, Pa," Christopher had announced, firmly. "Nothing less will do for Pathé or, indeed, for our Miss Grice, if this dress of hers is as grand as it sounds!"

"Well, as I possess neither top hat nor tails you'd better think again," Roger laughed, pouring Châteauneuf-du-Pape into Alice's glass.

Eileen, who was in the dining room clearing their dinner plates, hesitated and then spoke.

"Not meaning to intrude," she said. "but I couldn't help hearing what you said . . ." The faces round the dining table all turned in her direction. Encouraged by this attention, Eileen continued. "When Mrs Jack and I was in the attic getting bits and pieces together for Mabel Vallance's twins, we come across a trunk of Mister Bayliss senior's clothes and there was these pinstriped trousers and a jacket with tails. Morning ones, they call 'em, not the evening sort. And there was a white silk shirt and a cravat thing. All folded, they was, neat as ninepence, between sheets of tissue paper that was as white as snow still. Bit of a smell of mothballs but that's only to be expected. There was a top hat an' all! And a pair of shammy leather gloves — light as feathers they was . . ."

"No!" Roger said firmly. But as he looked from Alice to his son and then to his daughter-in-law he knew that to protest would be useless.

"Don't sulk, my darling!" Alice teased him while Georgina and Christopher, led by Eileen, clattered upstairs to the attic to retrieve the morning suit, the top hat and the gloves.

"I'm not sulking! It's just too ridiculous! Anyway, I am more heavily built than my father was, so even if the thing's not full of moth holes it won't fit me, thank God!" But it did fit. The jacket sat easily on Roger's broad shoulders, and although the waist was what Eileen called "a bit on the snug side", the length of the

288

trousers and the sleeves of the jacket were perfect. "Could of bin made for you!" she sighed, approvingly.

"It would only be for half an hour!" Alice pleaded, taken with Roger's elegant appearance. "Just for the Pathé cameras! You could change out of it for the reception at Higher Post Stone . . . Oh, please, Roger! It would mean such a lot to Marion and you do look so incredibly handsome!"

A compromise was reached. Roger would wear the outfit only briefly, changing into and out of it at the camp, appearing in it only before the cameras and carrying the top hat, which was, admittedly, too small for him, rather than wearing it. The whole exercise would, Alice assured him, be over in minutes.

Eileen was astonished. Having finished her work at the higher farm she bicycled back to the village, bursting with the news.

"All the years I've known that man I would never of guessed 'e'd do such a thing!" she told her neighbours. "'E's always bin a bit of what they call a stuffed shirt, 'as Mr Roger. Like 'is dad was afore 'im! It's that Mrs Todd!" she continued. "Brought 'im out somethin' amazin', she 'as. Reckon he'd do anythin' for her, 'e would!"

"'Cept marry her!" someone said.

"I wouldn't be too sure about that, neither!" Eileen concluded, watching the widening of the eyes around her.

After the departure of the wedding party from Lower Post Stone — which had created a chaotic scene caused by the simultaneous arrival of Roger Bayliss's Riley and two US military staff cars, all of which had to load their various passengers before confronting the difficulty of reversing in the narrow lane in order to move off in an organised convoy — a silence descended on the lower farm. The geese and ducks on the pond, who had watched, fascinated, the antics of the humans, now resumed the waddling, feeding and preening which normally occupied them at this time of day.

Dave, having applied a first coat of the pale-pink distemper to the walls of the tiny room at the rear of the Crocker cottage, and with that colour appearing now on his overalls, along with the splashes of white which had accumulated as he had painted the rest of the cottage, decided, while it dried, to eat the sandwiches his mother had prepared for his lunch.

He clattered down the staircase, noticing how much lighter and brighter it seemed with white distemper where the yellowish brown of the old paint had been for as long as he could remember. He peered between the thick slices of bread at the filling in his two sandwiches. Cheese and his mother's home-made pickle in one. Sliced beetroot in the other. He chewed as he moved about the kitchen, spooning tea into the pot and fetching the can of milk from the cool of the larder. He didn't pay much attention to the sound of a vehicle pulling up and standing, its idling motor rattling, at the farmhouse gate. After a moment or two he heard the sound dwindling as whatever it was moved off, down the lane. Then, just as he was about to fill his cup with the freshly brewed tea, a shadow fell across the step of the open door.

The scene outside the military chapel was bathed in arc lights. Marion and Marvin stood, posed and smiling, while a make-up girl tweaked Marion's hair and adjusted her dress to maximise the effect of its glorious lacy froth. The bride's smile was stunning. Not because they had told her to say "cheese" but because she was so happy that not to smile would have been an impossibility. Marvin stood to attention beside her, her arm through his, his face tight with pride. Grouped precisely around them were Roger Bayliss, immaculate, if slightly self-conscious, in his coat-tails, standing to attention, the top hat in his hand, Alice, laughing, Winnie, resplendent in her own dress of snow-white lace. Then, posed artfully round them, were Rose Crocker, Mabel — in her Land Army uniform, next to Ferdie Vallance who was clad in a shepherd's smock which had hung, unworn, from a hook in the byre for the last twenty years and was now topped by his favourite floppy-brimmed felt hat. Scarlet O'Hara was tucked under one of his arms and Winston under the other. Bulbs flashed and cameras rolled and then — after small adjustments were made when someone or other was either too visible or not visible enough, and "would the gentleman in the morning suit please smile?" and "could you pull down the baby girl's dress, Mr Vallance, because we're getting rather a lot of diaper?" — the bulbs flashed again and the cameras rolled until someone shouted "cut!" and it was all over.

Later, at the higher farm, Roger — the morning suit, the silk shirt and cravat, the top hat and the chamois gloves all abandoned in favour of a lounge suit — was seated with Alice at the far end of the two trestle tables which, end to end, ran down the centre of the yard. At the top of the table Marion and Marvin were on their feet and about to break the white icing of the wedding cake by inserting into it the tip of Marvin's regimental sword, when both of them became aware that they were losing the attention of their guests. Silence fell as heads turned, not in the direction of the bride and groom but away from them to where, below the yard, on the meadow that dropped down towards the lower farm, two figures could be seen approaching.

One figure appeared to be much taller than the other, but as the wedding guests squinted into the light of the lowering sun they realised that the shorter figure was a young woman and the tall one, a man, carrying a baby on his shoulders. The laughing child rode with one plump leg on either side of the man's neck. He had a hand round each chubby ankle while she, in order to steady herself, was clutching handfuls of his thick, dark hair in her small fists.

"Dave?" Rose's voice was shrill with disbelief.

"Hester?" Annie breathed, getting to her feet from her seat next to her husband and standing, astonished, a slow smile spreading over her face. And then everyone, including the bride and groom, was exclaiming and cheering and moving forward to hug Hester, slap Dave on the back, touch Thurza's soft skin and offer their fingers to her tiny hands.

"Just look at you!" Rose exclaimed, hiding her emotions behind a familiar, scolding tone. "You might of put on a clean shirt, son! Comin' up yer all covered in paint! Whatever was you thinkin' of?"

Dave, confronted by Hester, fully and deliciously aware of all the implications of her arrival at his door and eager to communicate and share his good fortune with his mother and the community to which he had belonged all his life, had been eager, once Hester's belongings had been carried into the cottage, to make the journey up the hill to the higher farm and join in the festivities there, now that, at last, he had so much to celebrate. He and his family had taken the short cut, following the steep footpath across the fields that lay between the two properties. The fact that he was wearing overalls that were torn and spattered with white distemper, to which had been added, that very day, splashes of pink, seemed to Dave to be an irrelevance.

Very little had needed to be said in the Crocker cottage when Hester had appeared in the doorway with Thurza in her arms. She didn't ask Dave if he still wanted her because she knew he did, and he didn't ask her what her intentions were because he knew, as certainly as he had ever, in all his life, known anything, what they were.

As he had unloaded his sister's possessions — her carpet bags and a small suitcase, together with Thurza's pram and folded cot — from his van, Zeke had found it unnecessary to instruct her to let him know if she ever needed his help. Instead he promised to visit her from time to time and to send her news of their father and mother. Then he had kissed her cheek, patted Thurza's curls and driven away.

Zeke had his own plans now. He would do the right thing by his parents. Before long, if he worked hard, the smallholding would yield enough to comfortably support the three of them. There was a girl he saw in Bideford whenever he drove into the town to sell his produce there. Polly had brown eyes and dark hair. Whenever he caught her eye she smiled and blushed in a way that made his heart lurch. He had taken her to tea at the café next door to her father's hardware store. He had bought her an ice cream and they had shared a plate of fairy cakes. One day he would bring her home to meet his folks and then, in the distant, rosy future of his imagination, he would ask her to be his wife.

The sun was setting by the time the bride, still in her wedding dress, climbed into Marvin's jeep and, with her veil flying in the slipstream and the yard echoing with cheers, was driven off towards Exeter and the crowning luxury of one night of conjugal bliss in the bridal suite at the Rougemont Hotel. Within a week Marvin's regiment was to be assembled in Portsmouth, ready to embark on its voyage back, across the Atlantic, to the United States. A handful of GI brides, Marion amongst them and with a brass band playing on the quayside, would wave them goodbye.

"See you stateside, babe!"

"Take it easy, now!"

"Love ya, honey!"

"Byeeee!" But tonight it was a swift and romantic ride through the breezy dusk, along the familiar lanes, through the village, where people stopped in their tracks to stare and wave.

"'Tis one of they land girls over to Post Stone!"

"Married, she was, this afternoon, in the chapel at the base!"

"A GI bride, she be!"

"Marion Grice 'er name was!"

"A flighty young madam she were, too, when 'er first come down 'ere!"

"Two of 'em, there was, billeted at the pub! Right goings-on!"

"Look at 'er now!"

"Butter wouldn't melt!"

"Fifteen yards of lace was in the skirt of 'er dress, Rose Crocker says!"

"Didn't get that on her clothing coupons, I'll warrant!"

"Black market most like!" And they shook their heads, rolled their eyes and clicked their tongues in indulgent disapproval.

Christopher and Georgina, on their way back to the woodman's cottage, would drop Dave, Hester and Thurza at the lower farm. Rose, who had already been slowly preparing the accommodation above the tea room for her own eventual occupation, was, now that Hester had arrived, to take up residence there that night.

"But you're not properly moved in yet, are you, Rose?" Alice asked her.

"I got all I need," Rose firmly assured her. "I'll fetch the rest tomorrow. I bain't goin' back to the cottage tonight! Not with them two lovebirds in residence, I'm not! Proper gooseberry I'd be!"

Dave, with Thurza on his lap, was sitting half-turned towards Hester, gazing into her smiling face. Rose's pleasure at her son's happiness was palpable.

"Just look," Alice murmured to Roger, drawing his attention to the now complete Crocker family. "Isn't that a lovely sight?"

"Another wedding, I suppose?" he smiled. "It's becoming an epidemic!"

"First Mabel and Ferdie," Alice laughed.

"Then Georgina and Christopher," Roger said. "Then Annie and Hector!"

"Now Marion and Marvin."

"And finally, you and me! Yes?"

"Yes," Alice said and she leant towards him and laid her forefinger against his mouth. "But no announcements today. You promised." He took her hand, raised it to his lips and kissed it. Discreet as he had been, both Winnie and Gwennan, from the far side of the yard, saw him.

"Cor!" Winnie breathed. "See that, Taff?"

"Certainly did!" Gwennan said, colour flooding into her sallow face. Winnie was about to move off towards a group of the girls when Gwennan put a restraining hand on her arm. "No, Win!" she said. "Don't say nothing, right? You can see they want it kept secret.

They'll tell us when they want to! When they're good and ready. 'Til then you hold your tongue, right?"

At Lower Post Stone Christopher had brought the truck to a halt. Thurza, having enjoyed the short, jolting journey down the hill from the higher farm, smiled at Dave and held out her arms to be lifted down.

"She's really taken to you, Dave," Georgina said.

"She better 'ad!" Dave replied, concealing his pleasure with a clumsy attempt at nonchalance.

"Seeing as 'e's 'er dad now!" Hester added.

"If that's all right with you, young madam?" Dave asked, settling the little girl on his hip. She smiled, exposing two newly acquired teeth.

Georgina and Christopher watched as Dave, with his new family, crossed the yard and entered the Crocker cottage.

"Ah!" Christopher said, catching Georgina's expression and teasing her. "Happy ever after, eh? How sweet! Want to borrow my hanky?" Georgina shook off her mood, laid her closed fist against his arm and warned him not to be such a miserable old cynic.

"I was just thinking what a rough ride it's been for Hester," she said. "You didn't see her when she first arrived here. She was unhealthily timid. Browbeaten by both her religious maniac father and her brother Zeke, who turned up here one day and threatened her with eternal damnation just because she'd had her hair cut and borrowed one of Annie's frocks! Then, after a few months of happiness with Reuben, he got killed and there was poor Hester, pregnant and with her father breathing the wrath of God at her! You wouldn't believe the things he said to her!"

"Well . . . she's survived, Georgie," Christopher said. "She came through it, as we all have, as though the war was a horrendous nightmare . . . And now we're all awake again."

"More than just awake," Georgina said, her mind travelling back across the years since she had left home, initially to join the Land Army — a time which, although she did not know it then, would remain, vividly remembered, all her life.

"More?" Christopher asked. "Yep. You're right I suppose. There is more to it than that. We are different people, aren't we? It has changed us all, one way or another." After a moment he laughed and added, "You, for instance, were quite impossible when we first met!"

"So were you!" She was sitting on the low wall between the farmhouse garden and the lane, facing the building and idly following the fight of a pair of house martins who were feeding a late brood of young. "And some of us are dead," she added, thoughtfully. "Chrissie died. And Andreis. Margery Brewster. And the pilot of the plane that crash-landed behind the barns. He could very easily have hit the hostel and killed everyone in it."

"But he didn't."

"No. He didn't."

In a week the hostel would be closed. The few remaining land girls would be billeted, as they had been before it was opened, in rooms above the bar at the Maltster's Arms. There was an air of impending desertion about the old building as the evening light played on the faded pink of the colourwashed walls and the low sun glinted off the small panes of its windows.

"We could live here, you know," Christopher said suddenly, and they both felt his words spread, like ripples in a pond, around them. "If we decided not to settle in New Zealand, that is." For a while Georgina considered this in silence.

"There are rather a lot of bedrooms," she said eventually, half-mocking him. "You wouldn't by any chance be proposing to fill them all, would you?"

"Certainly not," he smiled. "I was thinking more along the lines of removing the hideous partitions Pa had put in to accomodate you land girls. Come on. I'll show you."

They entered the quiet building, moving through the porch, along the cross-passage and up the narrow, curved staircases, he on one side, she on the other, emerging, laughing, on the landing above. Christopher showed her which were the original dividing walls of the upper floor and which had been hammered into position three years previously to convert the four large bedrooms into six smaller ones.

They returned to the cross-passage and entered what had become known as the recreation room. The three large sofas, warped by heavy use, their cushions faded and flattened, stood round the wide fireplace where the land girls had used them. The piano, its keys yellowing, was as Annie had left it on the previous evening, with sheet music propped open on its stand. Glen Miller, George Gershwin, Cole Porter. The low ceiling was heavily beamed. The windows at one end gave onto the farmyard, and at the other onto the overgrown front garden with its tangle of unpruned roses and clumps of marguerite daisies. Each had wide, oak window seats. The large Persian carpet had once been beautiful. Now it was threadbare, its vibrant colours faded almost completely to a uniform mottle of dull greens, pastel blues, pinks and golds. Georgina and Christopher stood, visualising what the room might look like as a family sitting room.

Through the open door to Alice's room, her possessions were visible. Her books. The small writing desk which had been her mother's — the only item of furniture she had brought with her to the farm — together with two large, paisley shawls which were thrown across the divans on which she and Edward John slept, he at one end of the room and she at the other. There was a model aeroplane on his bed and a scatter of comics. Alice's was tidy, with its row of cushions arranged neatly against the wall.

Georgina and Christopher did not intrude into the room but stood in the doorway, looking into it.

"Dear Alice," Georgina murmured. "Whatever we do to this house, this room should always be known as Alice's, don't you think?"

"I do," he agreed. "Nice idea."

They left the farmhouse, conscious of the fact that, although Alice, Edward John, Gwennan and Winnie would return to it that night when the celebrations at the higher farm were over, it was only a matter of days before it would be deserted.

"What an adventure it's been for the old place," Georgina said, pensively. "Will it miss us, d'you think?"

"Probably be glad to see the back of you all. Ten great girls lumbering about, clattering up and down the stairs . . ."

"Fighting over the bathroom!" Georgina said. "Quarrelling over the hot water! Wolfing our food in the kitchen. Caterwauling round the piano!"

"Listen!" Christopher said. They stood, quite still, while the silence settled round them and the half-light thickened. Then they began to hear the small sounds of the country evening. Sounds which for so long had often been drowned by the clatter and hum of the overpopulated hostel, by the rise and fall of the girls' voices, the comings and goings of the farm trucks and the GIs' jeeps, the rumble of the carts, the thud of the shire horses' hooves and the rattle of the oily tractor. Now they heard only the occasional distant bleating of sheep, grazing the short, wiry grass on the high ground above the valley. Jackdaws and house martins fidgeted drowsily round the chimneys and from somewhere, way down the valley, a pheasant's alarm call briefly reached them. Christopher took Georgina's hand and kissed it.

"It'll still be here," he said. "I promise you."

"Yes," she said. "I know. I know it will be."

Also available in ISIS Large Print:

On Wings of Song

Roberta Grieve

Rebellious society girl Arabella Raynsford is leading a double life as a music hall singer but to escape a possible scandal, she flees to Constantinople to join Florence Nightingale.

Arabella's ambitious mother wants her to marry wealthy Irish landowner Oswald Delaney but she has fallen in love with humble engineer Nat Sloane, a man her parents will never accept as a suitable husband. Besides, marriage will mean having to give up singing.

Will she be able to find her path to happiness?

ISBN 978-0-7531-8660-2 (hb)
ISBN 978-0-7531-8661-9 (pb)

Mrs Tim of the Regiment

D. E. Stevenson

Vivacious, young Hester Christie tries to run her home like clockwork, as would befit the wife of British Army officer, Tim Christie. However hard Mrs Tim strives for seamless living, she is always moving flat out to remember groceries, rule lively children, side-step village gossip and placate her husband with bacon, eggs, toast and marmalade. Left alone for months at a time whilst her husband is with his regiment, Mrs Tim resolves to keep a diary of family life.

When a move to a new regiment in Scotland uproots the Christie family, Mrs Tim is hurled into a whole new drama of dilemmas. Against the wild landscape of surging rivers, sheer rocks and rolling mists, who should stride into Mrs Tim's life one day but the dashing Major Morley. Hester will soon find that life holds unexpected crossroads . . .

ISBN 978-0-7531-8608-4 (hb)
ISBN 978-0-7531-8609-1 (pb)

The Secrets We Keep

Colette Caddle

It's four years since Erin Joyce left Dublin and bought a guesthouse in the remote, beautiful village of Dunbarra. The Gatehouse attracts a strange clutch of guests who, once ensconced, never want to leave. There's Hazel, a shy artist, and her sweet, silent daughter Gracie. Sandra, a brash American, wants to know everything about everyone. Then there's wise old easy-going PJ, who's seemingly part of the furniture.

But Erin's fragile happiness is thrown off-balance by the arrival of A-list Hollywood actor Sebastian Gray. Erin finds herself drawn to this handsome enigmatic man, who used to walk with a swagger but now prowls the country lanes with haunted eyes.

Sebastian isn't the only one in the Gatehouse with a secret. As Erin finds herself embroiled in her guests' secrets she starts to ask herself: will she be ready to reveal her own?

ISBN 978-0-7531-8566-7 (hb)
ISBN 978-0-7531-8567-4 (pb)

The Girl at the Farmhouse Gate

Julia Stoneham

An evocative story of love, loss and the tragedy of war

It is early spring in 1944 and Allied troops will soon invade northern France. Alice Todd is beginning her second year as warden of a Land Army hostel located in the wilds of Devonshire. Here she has won the affection and confidence of the girls in her charge and found herself caught up in lives which are complex, humorous and sometimes tragic.

ISBN 978-0-7531-8616-9 (hb)
ISBN 978-0-7531-8617-6 (pb)